SO-BZP-903

3 1613 00396 9568

Criminal Tendencies

Great Stories from Great Crime Writers

CALUMET CITY PUBLIC LIBRARY

CREME DE LA CRIME

Crème de la Crime is a publishing company that cares. From its inception it has worked with talented new writers who have faced rejection from more mainstream publishers. It is not surprising that it has taken this step and produced a book in support of the National Hereditary Breast Cancer Helpline and the Genesis Appeal, a charity specialising in research into breast cancer prevention.

It gives me great pleasure to urge you to buy this book, both to enjoy and to help save the lives of victims of this cruel disease.

– Lesley Horton, chairman of the Crime Writers' Association 2008–9

... it is good to see a publisher investing in fresh work that... falls four-square within the genre's traditions.

- Martin Edwards, author of the highly acclaimed Harry Devlin Mysteries

Crème de la Crime... so far have not put a foot wrong.

- Reviewing the Evidence

First published in 2009
by Crème de la Crime
P O Box 523, Chesterfield, S40 9AT

This collection copyright © 2009 Crème de la Crime
Stories copyright © the authors 2009 or dates as listed
Foreword copyright © Mark Billingham 2009

The moral right of each individual author has been asserted in
accordance with the Copyright, Designs and Patents Act, 1988.

All rights reserved. No part of this publication may be reproduced or
transmitted in any form by any means, electronic or mechanical,
including photocopying, recording or any information storage
and retrieval system, without prior permission in writing from
the publisher nor be otherwise circulated in any form of binding
or cover other than that in which it is published.

All the characters in this collection of stories are fictitious and any
resemblance to actual persons, living or dead, is purely coincidental.

Typesetting by Yvette Warren
Cover design by Yvette Warren
Front cover image by Lee Roberts and Yvette Warren

ISBN 978-0-9557078-5-8
A CIP catalogue reference for this book is available
from the British Library

Printed and bound in Great Britain by
CPI Cox & Wyman, Reading RG1 8EX.

www.cremedelacrime.com

Out of her Mind © Carla Banks 2006. First published in the CWA anthology *ID: Crimes of Identity*, published by Comma Press; also appeared in the Camellia Journal in 2008.

Games forWinter © Ann Cleeves 2004. First published in *Green for Danger*, the CWA anthology edited by Martin Edwards.

Push! © Lesley Cookman 1996. First published in *that's life!* May 1996.

Neutral Territory © Natasha Cooper 2007. First published in the *Daily Express*.

Mindstalker © Martin Edwards 2003. First published in *The Mammoth Book of Future Cops* edited by Maxim Jakubowski and M Christian.

The Octopus Nest © Sophie Hannah 2008. First published in her collection *The Fantastic Book of Everybody's Secrets*, in 2008, having won the 2004 Daphne Du Maurier Short Story Prize.

John Brown's Body © Reginald Hill 2001. First published in *Sightlines*, a Vintage Original.

12 Bolinbroke Avenue © Peter James/Really Scary Books Ltd 2007. Originally appeared in *Woman's Day* in Australia and New Zealand in January 2007.

The Pomeranian Poisoning © Peter Lovesey 1987. First published in *Winter's Crimes 19* (Macmillan)

Sneeze for Danger © Val McDermid 2005. First appeared in *Stranded* , her collection of short stories published by Flambard Press in the UK, and Bloody Brits Press in the USA.

Poor Old Frankie © Barbara Nadel 2008. First published in *Ellery Queen Magazine*.

The Masquerade © Sarah Rayne 2008. First published in *Crime Scenes* by Wordsworth Editions.

Waiting for Mr Right © Andrew Taylor 2002. First published in *Crime In The City* by Do-Not Press.

All other stories © the authors 2009.

About the authors:

Mark Billingham is the creator of the award-winning Tom Thorne series of crime novels and the standalone thriller *In The Dark*. His next novel, *Blood Line*, will be published in August 2009 by Little, Brown.

Carla Banks writes gripping psychological suspense novels under her own name and as **Danuta Reah**. The most recent is *Strangers*, published by HarperCollins.

A journalist by trade and breeder of pedigree goats by choice, **Stephen Booth** is now a full-time crime writer. *The Kill Call*, published by HarperCollins, is the ninth in his Ben Cooper/Diane Fry series set in Derbyshire's Peak District.

Simon Brett was a producer and writer for radio and television before turning to crime. His tenth Fethering mystery, *The Poisoning in the Pub*, is published by Macmillan. He lives in an Agatha Christie-style village on the South Downs.

Former BBC journalist **Maureen Carter**'s series starring mouthy maverick Birmingham detective Bev Morriss is published by Crème de la Crime. The sixth, *Blood Money*, will appear this year.

Mary Andrea Clarke is also a Crème de la Crime author, when she isn't being a civil servant. Her second pre-Regency Crimson Cavalier mystery, *Love Not Poison*, will be published in 2009.

Ann Cleeves won the inaugural CWA Duncan Lawrie Dagger in 2006, with *Raven Black*, the first in her Shetland Quartet. *White Nights*, the second in the series, was published by Pan Macmillan in 2008.

Lesley Cookman writes pantomimes as well as crime novels. Her Libby Sarjeant series and her non-fiction book *How to Write a Pantomime* are published by Accent Press.

Natasha Cooper found her niche as a crime writer after several historical novels. *A Poisoned Mind*, the ninth in her Trish Maguire series about a socially-aware barrister, was published in 2008 by Simon & Schuster.

Martin Edwards is the author of the acclaimed Harry Devlin and Lake District Mysteries, the editor of a number of crime fiction anthologies and also the winner of the CWA Short Story Dagger in 2008. His novels have been shortlisted for several major crime writing awards.

Peter Guttridge is a writing teacher, crime fiction critic and fiction prize judge as well as a novelist. His satirical Nick Madrid series is published by Headline, and he is working on a non-comic trilogy exploring Brighton's criminal past and present.

Sophie Hannah is a poet and children's writer as well as the author of three psychological crime novels which have been word-of-mouth bestsellers. *Little Face, Hurting Distance* and *The Point of Rescue* are published by Hodder & Stoughton.

Kaye C Hill's accidental sleuth Lexy Lomax made her first appearance in *Dead Woman's Shoes*. The follow-up, *The Fall Girl*, will be published by Crème de la Crime in 2009.

Reginald Hill has been one of the UK's most distinguished crime writers for over thirty years. He is best known for creating the bestselling Dalziel and Pascoe series which runs to over 20 titles.

Peter James's D I Roy Grace series, set in and around Brighton, was an instant bestselling success, and is now published in 30 languages and in development with ITV as a major television drama series. The latest title, published by Macmillan, is *Dead Man's Footsteps*.

Peter Lovesey's illustrious career has spanned four decades, three crime series and numerous awards including the CWA's Diamond Dagger for a lifetime's achievement. *Murder on the Shortlist*, his collection of short stories, is published by Severn House.

Adrian Magson cut his writing teeth with short stories and features for women's magazines, published in the UK, South Africa, Sweden, Norway, Australia and the US. His five thrillers starring Riley Gavin and Frank Palmer are among Crème de la Crime's best sellers.

Val McDermid's first crime novel was published in 1987, and two decades, three series and a string of acclaimed standalones later, she is one of the most popular and bestselling authors in the UK. Her latest title is *A Darker Domain*, published by HarperCollins.

Barbara Nadel's series starring Turkish cop Cetin Ikmen is published by Hodder Headline. She takes a keen interest in the rights of people with mental health problems.

Chris Nickson is a freelance music journalist, specialising in world and folk music. Born and raised in Leeds, he lived in the US for 30 years before returning in 2005 to live in north Derbyshire. His short story *Home* was the north midlands winner of the Criminal Tendencies 2009 competition.

Grandmother of nine **Sheila Quigley** achieved a six-figure deal for her first crime novel set on the Seahills estate in Houghton-le-Spring in 2004. She is currently working on a new novel, *Thorn in My Side*.

Sarah Rayne's mesmerising psychological thrillers are published by Simon & Schuster UK. *Tower of Silence* was shortlisted for the Theakston's Crime Novel of the year in 2005. Her most recent title is *Ghost Song*.

Professional actress **Linda Regan** always wanted to be a crime writer. Crème de la Crime helped her dream come true. *Dead Like Her*, her third D I Paul Banham novel, comes out this year.

Zoë Sharp's hard-hitting series about female bodyguard Charlie Fox has achieved success on both sides of the Atlantic. The latest title, *Third Strike*, is now available from Allison & Busby.

Caroline Shiach, winner of the international Criminal Tendencies competition with *Does It Always Rain in Manchester?*, is a consultant haematologist. Her lifelong love of crime fiction led her to have a go herself – and she turned out to be rather good at it.

Musicologist **Roz Southey** turned to crime in order to tell some of the stories which didn't fit into her PhD. *Secret Lament*, the third in her series starring 18th century musical sleuth Charles Patterson is published this year by Crème de la Crime.

Andrew Taylor is the only author to have won the CWA Ellis Peters Award twice: in 2001 for *The Office of the Dead* and in 2003 for the Richard and Judy bestseller *The American Boy*. His latest novel, *Bleeding Heart Square*, is published by Penguin. He also won the CWA's prestigious Diamond Dagger in 2009.

The National Hereditary Breast Cancer Helpline is based in Derbyshire's beautiful Peak District. This unique and nationally available service was founded in 1996 to offer support and information to women concerned about their risk of breast cancer because of family history. Visit **www.breastcancergenetics.co.uk**.
The Helpline is supported by the Genesis Appeal.

The Genesis Appeal is the only charity in the UK entirely dedicated to the prevention of breast cancer. Based at Europe's first purpose-built breast cancer prevention centre, the Genesis Appeal funds vital research into prevention and early diagnosis; their aim is to create a future without breast cancer. Currently one woman in ten in the UK will develop this terrible disease; the Genesis Appeal aims to make 1 in 10 none in 10. Visit **www.genesisuk.org**.

The National Breast Cancer Coalition is an American grassroots organization dedicated to ending breast cancer through the power of action and advocacy. Along with its research and education arm, the National Breast Cancer Coalition Fund, the Coalition works to increase federal funding for breast cancer research; oversee how research funds are spent; improve access to high-quality health care and breast cancer clinical trials for all women; and expand the influence of breast cancer advocates wherever breast cancer decisions are made. Additional information can be found at **www.StopBreastCancer.org**.

Crème de la Crime is delighted to support the Genesis Appeal, the National Hereditary Breast Cancer Helpline and the National Breast Cancer Coalition by publishing Criminal Tendencies. The Helpline will receive £1 from the cover price of each copy purchased in the UK. The Coalition will receive $1 from the cover price of each copy purchased in the USA.

Contents

Foreword

Mark Billingham

So, here's a *real* mystery…

For reasons I cannot fathom, short stories seem to have become somewhat unfashionable with both publishers and readers. This may be a case of the public getting what the public wants or it may be the other way around, but either way it is extremely bad news for readers and writers alike. This drop in the popularity of short story collections is particularly strange because they are ideally suited to an age where time spent reading has to be snatched: journeys to and from work on the bus or the train; that precious half-hour before children get home from school; fifteen minutes before you drift off to sleep at night.

What could be more perfect than a book of short stories?

Whatever the reason for it, the decline of the short story has also meant a decline in opportunities for new writing. Traditionally, the short story was how writers learned their craft, and with good reason. There can be no better way to learn economy and to perfect style than through a form where not a single word can be wasted. The best writers are usually those who know when they have said enough and writing short stories teaches that most valuable of lessons; one which a great many writers – this one included – would do well to remember from time to time.

For me, it's probably best summed up by a comedian who once said: "If it's going badly… get off. If it's going well… get off."

Because I firmly believe that (A) it is harder to write a

1

great short story than a good novel and (B) that any trend which sees short fiction marginalised should be bucked as a matter of course, I'm thrilled to have been involved with *Criminal Tendencies*. This fantastic collection gives many of our finest crime writers the chance to surprise their fans and, even more importantly, sets stories from the established masters of the craft alongside the work of newer writers. One such author is Caroline Shiach, whose entry, *Does It Always Rain In Manchester?* was chosen as the winner of the *Criminal Tendencies* competition and is published here for the first time together with stories from Val McDermid, Reginald Hill, Andrew Taylor and many other household names. This is the kind of well-earned leg-up that all new writers hope for and which may well become increasingly important as credit continues to get well and truly crunched and publishers become a little less willing to take risks.

Good causes may also suffer as a result of the afore-mentioned crunching, but in buying this book you are helping a *very* good one with a pound from every copy sold being donated to the National Hereditary Breast Cancer Helpline. If you would like any more information, please visit:

www.breastcancergenetics.co.uk.

So, if your tendency is towards great short story writing, here are twenty five tales in various shades of black. Murder, mayhem and Mancunian precipitation *and* it's in a good cause.

Why are you still reading this? Turn the page and get stuck into those stories.

It would be criminal not to.

Editor's note

Assembling and editing this collection of top-class crime stories has served to show me one thing and confirm two more that I've known for a long time: breast cancer touches an extraordinarily high proportion of people in some way; crime writers are an amazingly kind and generous bunch of people; and there are a lot of talented writers waiting to be discovered.

The result is something for all tastes and inclinations: past, present and future crime, tough crime and the softer kind, even a smile or two.

My deepest thanks go to everyone who has contributed to the book's success: authors, designers, competition judges, booksellers, everyone who forms part of the chain which carries a good story to an enthusiastic reader, and in this case provides much-needed support for an excellent cause.

Lynne Patrick

4

OUT OF HER MIND

Carla Banks

Words on a page, black print on white. Words on a screen, black print on a flickering monitor, safe, contained. He's the dark shape in the night, the soft footsteps that follow in the darkness, sealed away as the book is closed, fragmenting into nothing as the screen shuts down into blackness.
But now he's seeping around the sides of the screen, bleeding off the edges of the paper...
The room is empty. The light reflects from the walls, glints on the metal of the lamp. The screensaver dances, flowers and butterflies, over and over.

The summer heat was oppressive. Laura looked out of her window. The small patch of ground behind the house was scorched and wilting, and over the fence the buddleia that grew in the alleyway drooped, its purple flowers brown at the tips.

The air was still and dry. The louvres were open, but the wind chimes she had put there at the beginning of the summer hung motionless. She tapped them with her finger, the gentle reverberation giving her the illusion of coolness.

"You going to sit there all day?"

Laura jumped and turned round quickly. It was David.

"You going to be sitting in front of that thing all day?" He resented the hours she spent in front of the screen.

"I was just..." She gestured towards the monitor where the screensaver danced in a pattern of butterflies. "It won't come right. I need to..." She couldn't explain, but she knew she needed to keep on writing.

He was impatient. "It's beautiful out there. I'm not going to be stuck in on a day like this. I'm going out. Are you coming?"

She looked round the room. Her study was stark with its north facing window and bare walls. Her desk was tucked away in a corner. It was quiet. It used to be safe. "I have to go on. I can't leave it now." And she couldn't.

"You aren't doing anything. You're just staring out of the window. Can't you make an effort, pretend you want my company once in a while? I might as well be married to a machine." He was angry and frustrated. It was summer, a glorious summer's day, and Laura just wanted to sit in her study, staring at the white flicker of the screen, tap tapping her fantasy world into its electronic soul.

You married a writer, she wanted to say. *That was the deal*. But there was no point. He didn't want to hear it.

"I'm going." He slammed out of the room, out of the house, doors opening and closing with noisy violence. Laura let the silence close in on her, then turned back to her desk. Her hand hovered over the mouse for a second, then she pushed it, and the screensaver cleared.

Writing running down the screen. Just words on a page. And then a shadow when the house is empty, a footstep in the corridor, the creak of someone outside the door.

It's nothing. It's imagination. He's always been there, the monster under the bed, the bogeyman in the cellar. Just a shadow to frighten children in the night.

Only the footsteps are gone now. There is no monster under the bed, no bogey man in the cellar. He used to live in Laura's mind, live on her screen, in the pages she writes. He used to hide behind the butterflies and the flowers of the screensaver. But now he's gone. He's escaped. He's somewhere else.

The butterflies used to dance on the buddleia, but now the flowers are dying and the butterflies have gone.

Laura was in the supermarket. While David was out, she could surprise him. *Look, I did the shopping!* He hated shopping. Mechanically, she took stuff off the shelves, loaded it into the trolley, a bag of salad, bread, eggs, milk, bacon. Something was tugging at the back of her mind. She could see the patterns on the screensaver moving and dancing. Waiting. She shouldn't have left. She had to hurry, she had to get back.

The supermarket aisles were long and well-lit with rows of shiny tins and boxes reflecting the light into her eyes. Reds and yellows and greens, primary colours, nursery colours. The trolley had a red plastic handle and bars of aluminium and the boxes and bottles and tins on the shelves flickered as the bars ran past them, like the flicker of the words on the screen.

The aisles were long and straight. Laura pushed the trolley faster and faster past each one. Biscuits and cakes. Tinned fruit and vegetables. Soaps and cleaning stuff.

And a movement at the far end of the aisle.

She squinted but the light reflected off the tins and the bottles, reflected off the shiny floor. She screwed her eyes up, but she couldn't see it properly. It had been – just a flicker, a silhouette moving quickly round the corner, out of view, out of sight.

She pushed her trolley into the next aisle, and her foot slipped in something sticky, something viscous, something that spattered across the shelves and dripped on to the floor, red, dark, *drip, drip*, pooling round her feet in abstract patterns.

She stopped, frozen, half-hearing the voices: "Look out,

someone's dropped a bottle of wine… better be careful… mind the glass… get a…"

She pushed past, the wheels of her trolley smearing through the red and leaving a trail on the floor behind her. "Hey!" But the voices didn't matter. She had to get back.

The queue snaked away from the checkout. She pushed her trolley to the front. "Sorry, so sorry…" as people stepped back, frowning, puzzled, too polite to object. She didn't have time to queue. She fed her purchases through and dug in her bag for her purse as the checkout girl drummed her fingers on the till and the queue stirred restlessly behind her.

"…with a filleting knife."

She blinked. It was the girl sitting at the till, her face hostile and blank. "What?"

"Forty-five. Forty-five pounds. …Did he slash her?"

"What?"

The eyes rolled in exasperation. "D'you want any cash back?"

"Oh. No."

The car park dazzled in the sun, the concrete hot under her feet, the metallic paint of the cars sending shards of light into her eyes.

Night time. He walks the streets, he waits in the dark places. A silk scarf whispers between his fingers. It's light and gauzy, patterned with flowers and butterflies. It's smooth and strong. He has something else in his hand. It's long and thin and sharp. It glints where the light catches it.

Someone is coming. The sound drifts around the roadway, loses itself in the darkness, in the wind that rustles the tops of the trees. It's what he's been waiting for, tap, tap the sound of heels on the pavement, like the sound of fingers on a keyboard, like the sound of knuckles against the door. Tap, tap, tap.

And then there will be the other sound, the sound that only the two of them will hear, the sound behind her in the darkness… the soft fall of footsteps, almost silent, lifted and placed, carefully but quickly, moving through the night.

The heatwave broke two days later. In the morning the sky was cloudless, the shadows sharp as a knife on the walls and on the pavements. The buddleia, parched, drooped down, the petals falling into the dust. Laura sat at the table crumbling a piece of toast between her fingers. The sun reflected off the polished surfaces, off the steel of the cutlery, the spoons, the knives.

David sat opposite her, immersed in the paper he held up in front of his face. Laura stared at the print, black on white, words that would blur and vanish behind the moving patterns of flowers and butterflies.

"Maniac." David closed the paper and tossed it on to the table.

Laura looked at the crumpled sheets. WOMAN… KNIFE ATTACK. She grabbed it and smoothed the page out, her hands moving in frantic haste.

WOMAN KILLED IN KNIFE ATTACK. It had been the previous night, in the car park, in the supermarket car park. The woman must have walked across the concrete that was still warm from the sun, her heels tapping briskly, the street-lights shining on her hair. Walking tap, tap, tap towards the shadows where the trees started, the trees that whispered in the night.

She went to her room and switched on her machine. Her hands hovered over the keyboard and then began to move. Tap, tap, tap. The words appeared on the screen, filled it, scrolled down and down as her hands flew over the keys. She wrote and deleted, wrote and deleted, and each time, a woman walked into the darkness where gauze and flowers and butterflies fluttered in the wind. And the light glinted on something in the shadows, just for a moment.

The day greyed over as the clouds rolled in. The air cooled, became chill. Laura typed, deleted, typed again.

"Still at it? You've been here all day."

She jumped and turned round.

It was David, trying hard to be patient. "I've made tea."

"Thanks." She wasn't hungry, but… "Thanks."

He'd made egg and chips. The chips lay pale and limp on the plate. The yolk of the egg trembled under its translucent membrane. She cut the chips into small pieces, pushed them into the egg, watched the bright yellow spill and spread over her plate.

"Egg and chips not good enough for you any more?" He was angry again. He'd made the effort and she didn't appreciate it – didn't appreciate *him*.

She couldn't explain. She couldn't tell him. "It's fine. Egg and chips is fine. I'm just not hungry, that's all."

He grunted, but didn't say anything. He was trying. He was making the effort. He shook the sauce bottle over his plate. *Smack* as he hit the base with the flat of his hand. She watched red spatter over the mountain of chips.

"Ketchup?"

She shook her head. "Did you get a paper? Is there any more about…?" *About the murder.*

"No. Stupid cow, though. What did she expect, out on her own at that time?"

What had she expected? She saw the wine spilled on the supermarket floor, the drip, drip from the shelves, the bright red of the splashes. David lifted a chip to his mouth. Ketchup dropped on to the table, *splat*.

She had to get back.

10

The dark footprints cross the paving stones of the alleyway, prints that look black and shiny in the moonlight, growing fainter and fainter with each step until they fade to nothing.

It is starting to rain. The drops make black marks on the dry flags. The drops are big and heavy, splashing out as the rain falls harder and harder. The footsteps begin to blur, and a darker colour trickles across the ground with the rain that starts to run across the path, across the alleyway, running into a black pool that gleams in the shadows. And the puddles cloud as dark streaks mingle with the clear water, running thick and black then clearer and faster, into the gutters, the drains and away.

The next morning the sky was Mediterranean blue. The sun blazed down, scorching away the freshness of the storm. The air was hot and dry. Laura's fingers flew across the keys.

David was the doorway. "It's been on the radio," he said. His voice had the lift of excitement. "There's been another."

"I know." She typed, the words spilling out of her fingers. She couldn't stop now, she mustn't stop.

…and the rainwater ran across the paving stones…

"Not the supermarket." David wanted her attention. He had information to pass on, exciting news, and he couldn't wait to tell her. "In the alleyway, Laura. They found her in the alleyway. Right behind our house! Last night."

I know. But she couldn't say it.

Three a.m. Something wakes her. She lies very still and listens. Silence. The wind whips the clouds across the moon. Light. Dark. Light. Dark. The curtains are pulled back and the trees in the garden make caves of shadow. They rock and sway. The branches of the cotoneaster scrape across

11

the window. Tap. Tap. Tap. The alleyway is full of night.

David had been out all day, came back to find Laura at her desk, the dishes unwashed, the fridge empty.

He looked at the screen. "Nothing. You've done nothing. Sitting there all day. I can't do it all."

Sorry. I'm sorry. But she couldn't say it. Her eyes moved towards the window, where the buddleia flowers drooped over the high fence. A sudden breeze made them lift their heads. A piece of tape, yellow and black, danced through the air and wrapped itself round the stems, then hung still. All day. She'd heard them there all day, behind the garden, in the alley.

Later David relented. "I've made you a sandwich."

She couldn't choke it down.

"There's no pleasing you!"

She flinched as his hand brushed against hers.

His eyes were cold. "Out. I'm going out. If you want to know."

She couldn't worry about that now, couldn't let it distract her. Nothing else mattered now. She had to get back to her desk, back to her screen.

In the distance she heard the door slam.

Laura sat in her study. The rain had started falling hours ago, and David had not come back. She read the words that filled the screen. She scrolled down, read. Her fingers tap tapped on the desk. She looked through her window. Now, it was dark outside, the back garden, and the fence, and the alleyway all in shadow, empty now and silent.

She went out into the corridor and opened the hall cupboard. The corridor was painted white, the walls satin, the doors gloss. The floor was polished. The light reflected into her eyes.

She opened the cupboard. She drummed her fingers, tap, tap against the door. She took off her slippers, and put on a pair of black shoes, strappy, with very high heels. She had to fiddle with the fastenings for a few minutes. She stood up, tall and straight. She put on her coat, a mac, light and summery. It would be no protection against the rain. She threw a scarf, a summer scarf, thin and gauzy, round her neck. Then she walked to the door. Her heels tap, tap, tapped on the lino.

The street is long and straight, with pools of light under the streetlamps, light that glints off the water as it runs down the gutters. And between the lights, only shadows. The rain drips off the trees. Dark and then light. Dark and then light.

I can't find you any more!

I can't find you any more!

She walks on. She knows he will come. He has to.

Her feet tap tap on the pavement, moving quickly from light to light. And then she hears it. The sound of soft footsteps behind her, moving fast, moving closer.

Something glints in the darkness. Something blows in the wind, gauze and butterflies and flowers.

David gets home late. As he comes through the gate, he sees a curtain twitch in the house next door. He hesitates, then walks up the path. His own front door is open. He can hear it banging as the wind blows. He catches it before it can swing shut again, stands for a moment, listening. He looks at the window where the curtain moved. "Laura?" he calls, and again, more loudly. "Laura?" Then he closes the door quietly behind him.

The house is silent.

He goes to Laura's study. The screen flickers, the flowers and butterflies locked in their perpetual dance. He banishes them with a touch, and looks at the screen, looks at what Laura was writing, looks at the words that scroll down the screen.

The street was long and straight, with pools of light under the streetlamps, light that glinted off the water as it ran down the gutters. And between the lights, only shadows. The rain dripped off the trees. Dark and then light. Dark and then light.

I can't find you any more!

And then, over and over: *No, no, no, no...* down the screen. Down and down, *no, no way, no way, no way. No..w no..w now now now.*

He reaches out and presses a key. The writing jumps, fades, is gone.

The black screen faces him.

He smiles.

TOP HARD

Stephen Booth

The lorry I'd been watching was a brand new Iveco with French registration plates. All tarted up with flags and air horns and rows of headlights, it was like the space shuttle had just landed in a layby on the A1.

I'd got myself a position no more than thirty yards away, slumped in the driver's seat of a clapped-out four-year-old Escort that had last been driven by a clapped-out brewery rep. Or that was the way it looked, anyway. It was one o'clock on an ordinary Monday afternoon. And all I had to do was wait.

The trouble was, the lorry hadn't been doing very much. So all I had to look at was a red and white sticker on the Escort's dashboard thanking me for not smoking, and a little dangling plastic ball that told me what direction I was going in. I might have been facing the soft south, but at least I was nicotine free.

I already knew a few things about this French truck by now, of course. I'd counted its sixteen wheels and admired the size of its tail pipes. I'd seen the sleeping compartment behind the cab, which contained a little ten-inch colour telly, a fridge and even a microwave oven for warming up the driver's morning croissant. I knew that its forty-foot trailer was packed full of leather jackets, jeans and denim shirts – all good stuff that's really easy to shift. And I also knew that somebody was going to be really pissed off about that trailer very soon.

Well, it definitely looked like a solid job so far – good information, and a plan that might actually come together for once. And that's saying something in this part of the world. So all I had to do was sit tight and wait for the action. Yeah, right. It's funny how things can start out really good and solid in the morning, and then turn totally brown and runny by tea time. It's one of my own little theories. I call it the Stones McClure Vindaloo Lunch Rule. It's as if the bloke with the beard up there likes a bit of a joke now and then. And this was going to be one of his joke days. Well, I might just die laughing.

Meanwhile, sitting in a tatty motor was in danger of ruining my image – the Escort just wasn't worth looking at. Well, that's the point of it, I suppose. There were an incredible 85,000 miles on the clock of this thing, which proved it hadn't been handled by a used car dealer recently. The floor seemed to be covered in empty sweet wrappers, the mouldy debris of a cheese sandwich, and dozens of screwed-up bits of pink and white tissue. The inside panels looked as though they'd been trampled by a gang of miners in pit boots. The cover had fallen off the fuse box, and a tangle of wires and coloured plastic hung out of it, for all the world as if I'd just botched a hot-wire job. The car smelled of stale beer, too. Maybe a pack of free samples had split open some time. Or maybe a brewery rep just goes around smelling like that. You can take low-profile a bit too far sometimes.

In a word, it just wasn't the sort of motor that folk round here are used to seeing Stones McClure in. My style is more poke than parcel shelf, if you know what I mean. More turbo charge than towbar. Not to mention a spot of F and F across the fake fur seat covers.

For the last few minutes I'd been dozing a bit, clutching my plastic bottle of Buxton Spring Water in one hand and a half-eaten Snickers bar in the other. Don't believe that means I had no idea what was going on. I've got this trick of keeping one eye half open at all times, like an old tom cat. It's saved me a lot of grief on jobs like this.

One-fifteen. I sat up to take a quick look round. Along the road a bit there was a roundabout where the traffic was grinding its way on to the A614 towards Nottingham or heading west on the A57 into Lincolnshire. Apart from a roadside cafe, there was nothing around me in the layby – just empty fields on one side, and a bit of Sherwood Forest on the other. I mean there was nothing apart from four lanes of traffic thundering by on the A1, obviously. But the drivers weren't taking notice of much. They were busy fiddling with their Blackberries and Bluetooth, or counting the miles ticking off as they hurtled towards their next meeting or their latest delivery of widgets. This is what vehicle thieves rely on. Nobody sees anything going on around them when they're on the road.

Well, people never learn, do they? That's my second rule. And thank god for it, because this is what keeps blokes like me in beer and Meatloaf CDs for life.

I glanced at my watch. Shouldn't be long now. Earlier on I'd watched the driver who brought the lorry disappear into the cafe, shrugging his shoulders at the smell of hot fat drifting from the window of Sally's Snap Box. He was a short, thickset bloke wearing blue overalls and a five o'clock shadow. You could practically hear him singing the *Marseillaise*. This bloke's load might be headed for Leeds or Glasgow. But it wouldn't make it to its destination. Not today.

It was the load that was important, you see. Thieves don't target brand new trucks for their own sake. If you're planning to cut a vehicle up for spares, you go for an old Bedford or something. There's a big export market for old lorry spares. But if you're nicking the load, it's a different matter. That's where the really big business is – at least £1.6 billion worth a year, they say. And people will do anything to tap into dosh like that.

For the sake of authenticity, I was tuned in to a local radio station on the Escort's battered old Motorola. But the presenter had just stumbled off into one of those endless phone-in segments they seem to like so much. Grannies from all over the county were passing on tips for getting cocoa stains out of acrylic armchair covers, or swapping back copies of *People's Friend* for a second-hand budgie cage. It was dire enough to kill off my remaining brain cells – the few that last night's booze had left intact.

And then – bingo! An unmarked white Transit van slowed in the inside lane of the A1 and pulled slowly into the layby in front of the French truck. Action at last.

I have a really good memory for registration numbers, but the plate on the Transit was a new one to me. That was no surprise, though. It would have been nicked from a car park in Worksop or Mansfield some time during the past hour, and that was someone else's worry.

From my position, I could just see a bloke jump down from the passenger side of the van. He had the collar of a red ski jacket turned right up and a woollen hat pulled low over his face, making it impossible to get an ID on him. As soon as he'd slammed the door shut, the Transit pulled out into the traffic again and disappeared south.

I stayed low in my seat. I ate a bit of my Snickers bar. The chocolate was starting to melt on to my hand and my fingers were getting sticky. I wiped them with a windscreen wipe out of little packet that I found in the door well. I would have stuffed the used wipe into the fold-out ashtray, but it was already jammed full with more crumpled bits of tissue, all yellow and crusty. Anonymity is fine, but I draw the line at catching some disgusting disease for the sake of camouflage.

The bloke in the cap was fiddling with something I couldn't see, right up close to the near side of the Iveco's cab. No one took any notice of him, except me. Then he looked round once, took a step upwards, and was gone from sight.

I speed-dialed a number on my mobile, then waited a minute or two more until I heard the rumble of a diesel engine and the release of air brakes. As I started the Escort's motor, I glanced in my rearview mirror and saw a large figure emerge from the cafe. It was a bloke so big that he had to duck and walk out of the door sideways to avoid bringing the side of the caravan with him. He lumbered up to the side of the car, hefting something like a lump of breeze block in his left hand. And suddenly it was as if the sun had gone in. Oh yeah, meet my sidekick, Doncaster Dave. He's my personal back-up, my one-man riot squad. A good bloke to have watching your arse.

Dave had been stuffing himself with sandwiches and cakes in Sally's at my expense. Well, it's better than having him sit in the car with me. He gets twitchy when there's food nearby, and he'd probably enjoy the phone-in programme and laugh at the DJ's jokes. And then I'd have to kill him.

"Come on, come on."

Dave was starting to go into the monkey squat necessary for him to manoeuvre his way into the passenger seat, when the door of the cafe flew open again and a second figure came out. This one was dressed in blue overalls, and it was gesticulating and shouting. The sight of the lorry pulling on to the A1 seemed to infuriate him and he ran a few yards down the layby, yelling. Then he turned and ran back again, still yelling. This was far too much noise for my liking. And definitely too much arm waving. Even on the A1, he might get attention.

I could see Dave speaking to him, and nodding towards the Escort. The bloke came eagerly towards me, and I sighed as I wound down the window.

"*Mon camion*," he said. "My truck. It is being stolen."

"Let him in, Donc, why not?" I said. So Dave opened the back door of the Escort without a word. The Frenchman climbed in, and Dave squeezed into the front. The breeze block in his hand turned out to be the biggest sausage and egg butty you've ever seen, dripping with tomato sauce. The car filled with a greasy aroma that would linger for days. It didn't go too well with the stale beer either.

The Iveco was already a couple of hundred yards away by now, and the Frenchman began bouncing angrily.

"What's up, monsieur?" I said, as I indicated carefully before pulling out. I was waiting until I spotted some slow-moving caravans to sneak in front of. Getting on to the A1 from a layby is a bit dicey sometimes – you can easily end up with a snap-on tools salesman right up your backside, doing ninety miles an hour in his company Mondeo.

"We must follow the thieves. They steal my truck."

"Dear, oh dear. It happens all the time, you know. You can't leave anything unattended round here."

"Hurry, hurry! You are too slow."

I shook my head sadly. Well, there you go. You give somebody a lift, do them a favour, and the first thing out of their mouths is criticism of your driving. The world is so unfair.

"It's always been like this, you know," I said helpfully. "This bit of the A1 was the Great North Road. You know, where Dick Turpin used to hang out? You've heard of Dick Turpin, have you, monsieur?"

"*Comment?* What?"

"Highwayman, you know. Thief."

This is straight up, too. Well, the original Great North Road is a bit to the east, but it's been well and truly bypassed now. Some of it has deteriorated to a track, fit only for horses and trail bikes. But make no mistake. This whole area is still bandit country.

"Then there was Robin Hood," I said. "Robbing from the rich to give to the poor. Oh, and we had Mrs Thatcher, of course, who got it the wrong way round."

The Frenchman wasn't listening to my tour guide bit. He was gesturing down past the gear lever towards the bottom of the fascia, in the general direction of my mobile phone, a pile of music CDs, and the world's worst in-car stereo system.

"Yeah, you're right, it's crap, this local radio. *Le crap*, eh? I don't know why I listen to it. What do you fancy then, mate? Some Sacha Distel maybe?"

I poked among the CDs as if I was actually looking for *Raindrops Keep Falling On My Head*. It wasn't likely to be there. Not unless there was a cover version by Enya or UB40. Whoever normally drove this Escort had different tastes from mine. No doubt about it.

"How about this? This is French." I held up Chris Rea's *Auberge*. "*Auberge.* That's French, right?"

I slipped the cassette into the deck, and Rea began to sing about there being only one place to go. It's really funny how you can always find Chris Rea tapes in sales reps' cars. I reckon they have them so they can play *The Road to Hell* and feel all ironic.

"No, no. You must call for help," the trucker shouted in

my ear over the music. "Roadblock. Stop the truck."

And then he reached forward, trying to grab the phone. Dave barely moved. He gave the Frenchman a little flip and the bloke hit the back of his seat like he'd bounced off a brick wall.

"Sorry, mate, but the signal's terrible round here," I said. "It's all the trees. Sherwood Forest, this is."

The lorry driver called me a *cochon*. I failed French O-level, but even I know that isn't polite.

"Look, I'm really sorry it's not Sacha Distel, but I'm doing my best, right?"

As we approached the big roundabout at Markham Moor, the Iveco was already halfway up the long hill heading southwards, growling its way past the McDonald's drive-thru and the Shell petrol station. I could catch up with the lorry easily. No need for lights and sirens – which was lucky, because we didn't have any.

But the sight of the red and yellow arched signs across the carriageway put me in mind of something.

"Hey, it's a bit like a scene in that film, what's it called? You know, with John Travolta and the black bloke in a frizzy wig. What do they call a Big Mac with cheese in France?"

Dave's ears pricked up at the Big Mac, but he didn't know the answer.

The Escort's steering juddered and the suspension groaned underneath me as I twisted the wheel to the right and we swerved into the roundabout, across the A1 and towards a little B road that leads past the Markham Moor truck stop. As we passed, I couldn't resist a glance into the truck stop for professional reasons. On the tarmac stood two orange and white Tesco lorries, a flatbed from Hanson Bricks, and a Euromax Mercedes diesel, all backed up against a couple of Cho Yang container trucks. There was a load of NorCor corrugated boarding, and even a Scania full of Weetabix. To be honest, though, I couldn't see anyone shifting fifty tons of breakfast cereal too easily. Not in these parts.

The Frenchman started gibbering again and pointing to the main road, where the back of his lorry had just vanished over the hill.

"*Non, non*. Turn round. That way. The thieves go that way."

"It's a short cut, mate. What do they call a Big Mac with cheese in France?"

"*Merde!*"

Then he began to poke his finger at Dave's shoulder. Well, that was a mistake. Dave stared at him, amazed, like a Rottweiler that finds a cat pulling its whiskers. His immense jaws opened and his teeth came down on the round, stubby thing in front of his face. It disappeared into his mouth with a little spurt of red, and he began to chew. The Frenchman pulled back his finger fast, in case it went the same way as that sausage.

We passed through a couple of little villages before I turned on to a road that was more mud than tarmac. A track led us over the River Maun, past some derelict buildings, through some woods, over another river and into more woods. The trees closed all around us now, dark conifers that wiped out any hope of a view.

But in the middle of the trees a space suddenly opened up on a vast expanse of wasteland – acres and acres of black slurry and weed-covered concrete. There were old wheel tracks down there in that slurry, and some of them were two feet deep. This was one of our dead coal mines, whose rotting bodies lie all over Nottinghamshire these days – a memory of the time when thousands of blokes and their families lived for the seam of coal they called Top Hard.

Finally we ran out of road and pulled up by a series of slurry lagoons. These lagoons are pretty deep too, and I wouldn't like to say what the stuff is that swirls about down there.

"OK, Monsieur Merde. Out."

The Frenchman looked from me to Dave, who helpfully leaned back to unfasten his seat belt. The trucker flinched a bit, but looked relieved when the belt clicked open. He got out and looked at the devastation around him, baffled.

Well, this little bit of Nottinghamshire is no picnic site, that's for sure. We were on the remains of an old pit road, where British Coal lorries once trundled backwards and forwards all day and all night. In some places there are old wagons dragged off the underground trains, filled with concrete and upended to stop gypsies setting up camp in the woods. But there are always ways in, if you know how. Up ahead was a bridge where you could look down on the railway line that had carried nothing but coal trains. The lines are rusted now, but the coal is still there, way below the ground. Top Hard, the best coking and steam coal in the country. Top Hard made a lot of the old mine owners rich.

Yes, this was once the site of the area's proudest superpit. A few years back, when it was still open, a report came out with the idea of making it a Coal Theme Park, preserving the glory days of the 1960s. There would have been visits to the coal face, a ride underground on a paddy train, and maybe a trip to the canteen for a mug of tea. They had a dry ski slope planned for the spoil heap.

You'd need a heck of an imagination to picture this theme park now. The buildings have been demolished, and the fences are a futile gesture. There's just the black slag everywhere and a few churned up roadways where they came to cart away the debris of a way of life.

The Frenchman stared at the lagoons, then turned round and looked across the vast black wasteland of wet slurry behind him. It would be suicide to try to walk through that lot. He shrugged his shoulders and waited, his eyebrows lifted like a supercilious customs man at Calais. Suddenly, his complacency annoyed me.

"Take a look at this then, mate. What do you think? Pretty, isn't it? This is what's left of our mining industry. Coal mining, yeah? It may not mean much to you. You grow grapes and make cheese in France, right? But coal was our livelihood here in Nottinghamshire once. Blokes went down into a bloody great black hole every day and got their lungs full of coal dust just so that we could buy food after the war. You remember the war, do you? When we kicked the krauts out of your country?"

Of course he didn't remember the war. He wasn't old enough. Nor am I, but I've read a history book or two. I know we bankrupted ourselves fighting the Germans, and it was the miners like my granddad who worked their bollocks off to get this country out of the mess afterwards. And their sons and grandsons carried on going down those bloody great holes day after day to dig out the coal. Decades and decades of it, with blokes getting crushed in roof falls and burnt to death in fires, and coughing their guts out with lung disease for the rest of their lives.

And this is what thanks they got, places like this and a score of other derelict sites around Nottinghamshire, Derbyshire, Yorkshire. Maggie Thatcher betrayed us, the whole country let us down. Even our own workmates stabbed us in the back. It was 1984. Write it on my gravestone.

Somewhere north of Newark the French truck would be picking up speed on the flat. In a few minutes it would it hit the bypass and turn off westwards on the A46. Within the hour it'd be in a warehouse on an industrial estate outside town, and it would be nothing to do with me at all. All thanks to Slow Kid Thompson.

Oh, I forget to mention Slow Kid, didn't I? Slow Kid Thompson is one of my best boys. He's got a lot of talents, but his number one skill is driving. If Slow can't drive it, it hasn't got wheels. Today, he'd just delivered our first big load, a job worth quite a few grand to us all. After years of doing small-scale business, shifting dodgy goods and re-plating nicked motors, we were finally moving into the big time. That Iveco represented the start of a new life.

"You're lucky, monsieur. I'm feeling in a good mood."

By now the Frenchman had gone as quiet as Doncaster Dave. I guess it had finally dawned on him that we weren't going to help him catch his stolen lorry after all. Maybe he'd realised that there'd be no nice British bobbies rushing up to arrest the villains who'd ruined his day. No high-speed pursuit, no road blocks, no one to pull him out of the brown stuff.

Oh yeah, that's another thing I forgot to mention – you just can't rely on anyone these days. I call it the Stones McClure Top Hard Rule.

WORK EXPERIENCE

Simon Brett

It should have been a straightforward job. Louis had cased the joint. Milton was set up as the getaway driver. The actual burglary was to be done by Hopper, who's the best lock-man in West London, and me, Chico. And everything would have been fine if Hopper hadn't insisted on bringing his young nephew Terence along.

Seems it's something they're very keen on at schools these days. 'Work Experience' they call it. Usually the kids go along with their parents to get a taste of the workaday world, but with Terence's dad in Parkhurst for the foreseeable, that was never going to work out, was it?

Apparently the boy done some Work Experience with his mum, who does location catering for television programmes. Terence had helped – or more likely hindered – her for a week when she was cooking for the crew on one of them reality shows, you know, hidden cameras, members of the public looking stupid. Called *Danger: Men At Work*. Title doesn't mean anything to me. I'm not into telly. Anyway, that Work Experience must've been a waste of time. Location catering isn't going to be much use to the boy. Never going to be a career for a grown man, is it?

So Hopper, who's always had a strong sense of family, said Terence should come along with him on this job.

Terence is at that awkward age, all elbows and Adam's apple. He wears t-shirts with meaningless slogans on them, hoodies, and garments which have never quite decided whether they are shorts or trousers dangling off his thin backside. And he has like permanently grafted on his head a baseball cap, which he'll wear at any angle other than the natural one with the peak in front.

Hopper didn't mention the idea of bringing Terence along until right at the end of the planning meeting. He must have known none of us would like the idea, and hoped to shuffle it in unnoticed when we was all getting ready to leave.

Up until that point everything had gone very smoothly. Although I say it myself, that was mostly down to me. I'd picked up the information about the place, and I'd given Louis some very good suggestions before he checked it out. I was flattered that during the planning meeting more than one of the others referred to it as 'Chico's job'. I hadn't been with the gang as long as the rest, and it gave me the feeling they were beginning to accept – even respect – me.

I'd heard about the place from a mate of mine down the Red Cow. Blob, he's called. And I must say, when he told me, my first reaction – like anyone's would have been – was that the job was a total non-starter. I mean, one thing you learn pretty early in this line of work is to keep clear of the Filth. I've nothing against coppers individually – I'm sure a lot of them are kind to animals and good to their mums – but as a general rule I've made it my business to avoid them. So when Blob says that the flat he's recommending is right over a police station... well, I thought he was about ready for the old Care in the Community.

Next he comes up with some proverb about the best place to hide being nearest the light, which still sounded well dodgy to me, but I kept listening. And I'm glad I did, because the more detail he give me, the more I knew the job was a real peach. Soft, juicy, ripe for plucking.

Fact is, this police station was a redbrick Victorian block, built in times when the old cash flow wasn't so strapped. Offices downstairs, second storey all police courts and meeting rooms. That floor hadn't been used for some time, and during another cost-cutting round in the nineteen-seventies, some bright spark had had the idea of turning it into a residence (known waggishly round the station as 'Evening Hall') and flogging it off.

This was duly done and the flat was bought by some geezer who was an expert in antiques. Specialised in gold and silver coins, and according to Blob, the place was full of them. Owner spent a lot of time abroad, buying from other dealers. And this was the sweet bit... place had no burglar alarms, no grilles on the windows, nothing. Geezer reckoned being sat on top of a cop shop was security enough. Apparently felt so confident the stuff'd never get nicked that he hadn't even insured it. (Which, incidentally, is not something I'd recommend.) Reason I can sleep easy at night doing the work I do is that I know in most cases anything I purloin will be covered on the old insurance. So really what I commit is victimless crimes... though strangely some of the people whose stuff I take don't see it that way. Nor, for some reason, do the insurance companies. Or the police. Odd, that.

Anyway, like I said, Louis cased the joint. We always work that way – get a place looked at by someone who's not going to be involved in the actual thieving. Louis's good for that kind of work. Seeing him for the first time, it'd never occur to you that he'd ever broken the law in his life. And certainly not that he's the brains behind our outfit. We don't have a leader as such, but Louis is the one we all refer to, check stuff out with. You'd never know it, though. He looks like a retired schoolteacher, all thick glasses and shapeless corduroy. And he's got this bumbling way about him. No one's surprised when he takes wrong turnings and walks into places he shouldn't. That's how he played it when he was casing the police station. Told us all about it at the planning meeting.

"It was my intention," he says, "to make a cursory preliminary examination of the exterior, and to that end I wandered about in the manner of a superannuated gentleman whose mental faculties were challenged by the task of finding the main entrance."

(Another thing about Louis, he does tend to use a lot of long words. Rest of us don't always understand all of them, but most of us usually get his gist.)

"My scrutiny confirmed our most optimistic expectations. Though the police station itself is guarded by a plethora of CCTV cameras and other security devices, there is nothing to monitor who enters or leaves the first floor flat."

"Except," objected Milton, who, despite the contrary impression given by his looks, reckons he's quite quick on the old logic, "surely anyone who gets up to the first floor entrance is going to have to go through the police station's surveillance system? Unless you're suggesting we use a helicopter."

Louis holds up a hand to quieten him, like Milton was some kid talking out of turn. The way he done it suggested the old boy really must have been a schoolteacher at some point, before he saw the light and come over to our side.

"What you say is correct. And any attempt to gain access to the upstairs flat by its main entrance would be extremely hazardous."

"You suggesting we smash in through the windows then?"

"Milton, Milton, if you have a fault, it is that you tend to be too precipitous. You want everything to happen immediately.

Which, while an excellent and desirable quality in a getaway driver, is an instinct which must at times be curbed during normal social intercourse."

"Er...?" says Milton, who's never been as good at getting Louis's gist as the rest of us.

"What I am asking is that you allow me to make my report in my own style. And at my own pace." This was said in a way that must have made a good few fourth formers cower over the years. It certainly had the effect of shutting Milton up.

"Having ascertained the security situation on the exterior of the building," Louis went on, at his own pace, "I then decided I should extend my investigation to the interior. Not wishing to raise suspicions, I developed the already-assumed persona of a somewhat confused elderly gentleman. My cover story was to be that, while entrusted with the care of my grandson's gerbil, I had inadvertently allowed it to escape through my open back door, and I was hoping to enlist the assistance of the police to secure the rodent's recapture.

"When I entered the building I discovered that there was a queue of other complainants, and the desk sergeant was preoccupied by a large lady, bearing a more than passing resemblance to Boadicea, who was insisting that, unless her neighbour could be persuaded to clip his leylandii, blood would flow.

"After some minutes of sitting waiting, I rose and, with a mumbled explanation about prostate trouble, asked a passing WPC to be pointed towards the gentlemen's lavatory.

"I was directed through a door into a central area where, serendipitously, the male and female conveniences turned out to be placed either side of a substantial staircase. The space was occupied only by a few filing cabinets and some broken-down chairs. It wasn't anyone's office, just a glory-hole on the way to the police cells and the station's back entrance.

"Anyway, at the top of the staircase I could see a wall not included in the building's original design, into which was set another door. This, I felt certain, must give access to the flat upstairs. Exaggerating my assumed decrepitude – just in case anyone should come in and see me – I climbed the stairs, which were dusty with disuse, as was the small strip of landing in front of the wall. And the good news is that the lock on the door up there is of such simplicity that it would take someone of Hopper's talents a matter of seconds to open it with his bare fingernails."

Our lock-man accepted the compliment with a modest smile. Louis also smiled and placed his hands flat on the table to indicate that his report was finished. Milton was still cowed by the schoolmasterly reprimand he had received, so I was the one who asked the obvious question. "You're saying we should make our way into the flat from *inside* the police station?"

"You have a very acute understanding, Chico. That is exactly what I meant."

We were all silent for a moment. Then I showed I was prepared to ask another obvious question. "But won't the Filth notice? I mean, look at us. Say it's just Hopper and me does the job. The only way we two would look right in a cop shop is with handcuffs on."

"Dressed like that you would indeed, Chico. But were you to don the habiliments of a member of Her Majesty's Constabulary, you would present a much less incongruous picture."

OK, I'd never heard the word *habiliments* in my life before, but I was still getting Louis's gist. "You mean we dress up as coppers?"

"Indubitably."

Hopper and me exchanged looks. One thing neither of us likes doing is committing more than one crime at a time. A burglary of gold and silver coins is one thing, but doing it while impersonating a police officer... well, that's dead iffy.

"What about me?" asks Milton. "Won't people smell a rat when they see two coppers legging it into the getaway car?"

"No, they won't," Louis purred. "They will think it the most natural thing in the world."

"How'dya mean?"

"Milton, Milton, what could be more natural than for two police officers to get into the back of a Panda car driven by another police officer?"

"You're saying I'm going to be in fancy dress and all?"

"Yes, Milton."

"And I'm going to hotwire a police Panda?"

"Yes, Milton."

There was another silence. Long one, this time. Then I says, "Come on, Louis, tell us how it's going to work."

So he told us. We asked a lot of questions, we pulled the plan apart, tested it for weaknesses. And at the end, not for the first time, we all agreed that Louis was a blooming genius.

It was then that Hopper shuffled in the idea of his nephew Terence coming along for Work Experience.

I thought teenagers was meant to be silent. Grumpy, always going off to their bedrooms in a huff, shutting the world out with their IPods, never giving their parents or any other adults the time of day. Well, that evening, soon as Terence, escorted by his uncle Hopper, joined Milton and me in the car on the way to the job, it was clear he didn't fit the moody teenage stereotype. Blab, blab, blab all the time with him. I tell you, spend half an hour with that boy and you'll come away with permanently bent ears.

Another drawback was his after-shave. Smelt like a bloomin' spice-rack, ponged out the whole car.

We didn't involve him till the day of the job. Louis said the less the boy knew the better, and I was with him on that. But blimey, if we'd answered all the questions he chucked at us, he'd soon've known more about the job than we did.

He wanted to know where we was going, he wanted to know why the three of us was dressed as coppers, he wanted to know if we was armed… coo, he didn't half go on.

Eventually Hopper told him to put a sock in it, with the additional sanction that if he didn't, Terence would get a mouthful of his uncle's sock, with foot and boot attached.

But that only kept him quiet for a few minutes, then he was off on the natter again. But at least he'd taken on board that we didn't want to talk about the job. So he decided to delight us with reminiscences of his previous Work Experience instead. You know, this week he'd done with his mum on the old location catering.

So Terence burbles on about that for a bit. I hardly listen. Don't care for the television much myself… well, except for the sport, obviously.

Mind you, young Terence's got a ready audience in Milton. Every moment he's not out on a job Milton spends glued to the telly. He knows all about all the shows, so he's dead impressed that Terence has met all the people on this reality show his mum was catering for – *Danger: Men At Work*.

"Ooh," Milton says, "I loved the one where they filmed in the fast food restaurant. That waitress didn't know they'd got the hidden cameras on her, did she? What a prat she looked. Do you know, Terence, if people have ever asked them to stop filming?"

"No," the boy replies. "They all love it. Being on telly, showing what good sports they are, everyone likes that."

Like I say, I've never seen the show, so none of this means much to me. But Milton got very excited when Terence shows him this printed pass he'd been given, printed with *Danger: Men At Work* in big letters, so that he's allowed on the set or the location or whatever they call it.

Anyway, the two of them are going on ninety-nine to the dozen, and we're getting close to the police station what is our destination. So I tell Milton to stop the car, because now it really is time to tell Terence what his role is going to be in the evening's proceedings.

And we've found a proper job for him, not just answering phones and photocopying, which I gather is what most kids on Work Experience do. Louis's idea, needless to say. He come up with it soon as he heard from Hopper how old Terence was. He says, "Perfect. This could not be more serendipitous." He likes that word. Blowed if I know exactly what it means, but I get the gist. Means on the good side of bad, anyway.

Louis's planned for us to do the job at eleven o'clock. He says that's the time the police are most stretched. There's a lot of ugly stuff goes down when the kids who've been binge-drinking all evening get turfed out of the pubs. So every cop who can be spared is on the streets, trying to stop the paralytic youngsters from topping each other. Which means there's less of the Filth in the station and those that are there tend to be preoccupied with emergencies.

It was an emergency that Louis had planned to use as our cover. And Terence's Work Experience would mean him being the centre of that emergency. He took his instructions like a lamb, I must say. Gabby he may have been, but the boy was up for anything. I mean, I daresay some kids his age might have objected to being covered with tomato ketchup and minestrone soup. Not Terence. He agreed without a murmur.

Now, perhaps I should explain about the tomato ketchup and minestrone soup. With the ketchup you're probably ahead of me – yes, it was meant to look like blood. But for the purposes of Louis's plan, Terence didn't just have to look as if he was injured, but like he'd thrown up over himself as well.

We done a bit of experimentation before we plumped for the minestrone. Back in the old days I remember best thing to use to look like puke was called Sandwich Spread. But could we find it on the shelves down Tesco's? Could we hell.

Then Hopper remembered something that'd been served up at his school dinners called Macedoine of Vegetables. He said one kid threw up in the playground after eating it, and you couldn't tell the difference between what he'd thrown up and what they'd just all eaten. But with Macedoine of Vegetables we also drew a blank down Tesco's. What's happening to all our fine old traditional British foods? Louis even tried going a bit upmarket to Waitrose, but again no dice.

So it was a can of minestrone soup we ended up with. And to make Terence not only look but smell liked he'd thrown up, Louis give us this idea of sprinkling the boy with parmesan cheese. Always niffs a bit of vomit, the old parmesan. And, thank God, it was a stronger smell than the boy's after-shave.

When we was just round the corner from the police

station, Milton stopped the car (one he'd hotwired earlier in Ladbroke Grove – we were only going to use the thing for this part of the job, then abandon it). And we set about making Terence look like he was a kid who'd overdone the old booze and got into a fight. Wasn't difficult. Boy was so scruffy to start with, he didn't need much extra. Just the tomato ketchup as if it had gushed from his nose, minestrone soup down his front and he was done.

Hopper and I splashed a bit of the same on our uniforms, to look like we'd been struggling with him, then we took our leave of Milton. His job was to go round the back of the station and hotwire one of the Pandas ready for the getaway.

As we emerge from the car, Terence reaches into the pocket on his hoodie and pulls out a camcorder. Expensive bit of kit, no bigger than a paperback book.

"What's that for?" asks Hopper.

"You don't mind if I film what we're doing, do you? You know, so's I've got a record."

"You film us," says Hopper, "and the only record you'll have is a criminal one. Will you get it into your thick head, Terence, that in this line of business the last thing you want is a record of what you're doing. Because that could easily become evidence, and we don't want to make the Law's job easy for them, do we?"

The boy looked a bit crestfallen, but he didn't argue and put the camcorder back into his pocket.

It's at this point that Hopper and me give Terence his instructions and each of us grab him by one arm.

Now, I reckoned, if there was a dangerous bit of the plan, we were going to hit it in the police station's reception area. Louis's view was at that time of night we'd have no problems. There'd only be a desk sergeant on duty and chances were they'd be busy with some other emergency. All we had to do was make it from the main entrance to the door leading to the staircase area, and our troubles'd be over.

We weren't worried about the old CCTV. Hopper and I pulled the peaks of our police hats down, and we made Terence, for once in his life, wear his baseball cap the right way round. So his ugly mug was pretty well hidden and all.

Soon as we round the corner and can actually see the police station, we slot into acting mode. Terence goes back to full-on struggling and a bit of sozzled mumbling, while me and Hopper make with a few remarks like "That's enough of that, young man" and "You'll feel differently after a night in the cells", for the benefit of any passing witnesses. We've agreed that, once we're actually inside the police station, we'll stay schtum. Don't want to draw attention to ourselves, do we?

When we get through the door, we think it's all going to be kushti. There's a rowdy shout-off going on between three drunks and the desk sergeant, who's far too busy with them to notice our little threesome. So we beetle across to the other door.

Get a bit of a shock when, just before we reach it, blooming thing opens. And out comes this well dishy WPC. She takes in the situation immediately and, wrinkling her dainty little nose at the niff of Terence, says. "Looks like he's going to have a night sobering up in the cells."

Which is good. Means our cover has worked. Even a genuine cop thinks we're the real deal.

"God, he smells disgusting," she observes.

And it's a pity she says that. Because what none of us had taken into account in our planning for the job is the vanity of youth. Boy like Terence is very sensitive about how he smells – that's why he soaks himself in that disgusting after-shave. And he can't bear the thought of this dishy WPC thinking he's niffy. So he does a knee-jerk reaction and says – forgetting that he's meant to be smashed out of his skull – he says in perfect, polite English, "Oh, it's not me that smells, it's the parmesan."

Well, the WPC looks rather suspicious at that and, though we're through the door before she has time to say anything else, Hopper and me recognise that this has got the job off to a bad start. Always going to be a risk bringing a Work Experience kid along with us.

Anyway, this isn't the moment to tear the boy off a strip. Through the door, up the stairs and, as Louis had promised, Hopper opens the door easy as if he'd had his own house key.

We're inside the flat's sitting room, and no one's seen us except for the WPC. We listen for sounds of pursuit, but there's nothing. We breathe sighs of relief, we've got away with it. I still don't say anything to Terence, but his uncle gives him a quick dressing-down. Then we get out our torches and concentrate on the loot.

Bloody hell, Blob's information was good. Everywhere our torchbeams go, there's gold and silver coins. Glass-fronted display cases all over the walls and on every other surface. We get out the nylon bags we've brought for the purpose and start filling them up with the clinking stuff. We're not greedy, but there doesn't seem much point in leaving any of them behind.

When all the display cases are empty, we do a quick shufti round the rest of the flat, but there's nothing. All the collection's in that one room. Not that we're complaining, mind. The haul we've got, once it's been converted into readies by a specialist friend of mine on Westbourne Grove, will keep the lot of us in clover for a good few years.

I look through a window down to the parking lot at the back of the station. I flick my torch on and off with the prearranged signal. Headlights flash on one of the Pandas. Milton's got our getaway car ready. Job very nearly done.

Then the phone in the flat rings.

Hopper and I stand still as statues, as if the handset could, like, see us if we moved. We grin at each other sheepishly and relax. The phone rings on and on.

And then – bloody hell – Terence only goes and answers it, doesn't he?

"Hello," he says.

Hopper's across the room in nanoseconds. He's snatched the receiver from the boy's hand and ended the call. And he just stands there, looking at his nephew and shaking all over, too furious for his mouth to form words. Finally he manages to say, "Why the hell did you answer it?"

"I thought it might be important," the boy replies limply. "My mates at school who've done Work Experience say most of it's answering phones." His uncle just glares at him. "And photocopying," adds Terence.

I'm in no mood to hang around. What should have been a straightforward job is now becoming a dead complicated – not to say dangerous – one. "Come on, move!" I say. And me and Hopper are out the door to the staircase. We don't say a thing more to Terence. He's got himself into this mess. He can get himself out of it.

But he's not the only one in a mess. Soon as we emerge on to the staircase, we can't help noticing that the area down the bottom of it is full of the Filth. And we're standing there clutching nylon bags full of gold and silver coins. If you're ever wanting to explain the meaning of the expression 'caught red-handed', you could do worse than describe the situation we was in at that moment. And all thanks to trying to give young Terence some Work Experience.

The dishy WPC's there. I reckoned she alerted the others. And there's a very senior-looking cop – at least a Chief Superintendent, I reckon – standing there holding a mobile phone. I'd put money on it being him who just dialled the number of the flat.

"So," he says, all silky-like. "Caught red-handed."

Proving the point that I just made.

Neither Hopper nor me can think of anything very bright to say by way of come-back to this, so we just stand there, totting up the likely sentence for combined burglary and impersonating a police officer. We've both got a bit of previous, so the tariff could be pretty harsh.

There ensues what I think Louis would describe as an impasse. We don't move any further down the stairs, the Filth don't come up to get us. A Mexican stand-off without the guns. Hopper and me have a nasty feeling we know how it's going to end, though. The chances of us getting past the massed cops and out to Milton's Panda are about as strong as a Premier League footballer speaking English.

Given the direness of our situation, we'd both forgotten about Terence. Then we hear the door behind us open and there he is.

He's got his camcorder up to his eye, like he's filming everything. Round his neck he's wearing the identity pass he was bragging to Milton about in the car.

And Terence says to the cops, "Good evening, ladies and gentlemen." They look at him dead suspicious. They aren't about to go soft on him because of his youth. They reckon he's as much a part of the gang as Hopper and me. And he's going to go down the same way we are.

But then Terence says, "You'll be glad to know that your station has been selected to appear on *Danger: Men At Work!*"

The reaction to this is really amazing. The Filth's faces which a minute before were all stern and forbidding, suddenly break out into grins. Laughter even. All of them want to show what good sports they are. They can take a joke.

"Yes," Terence goes on, "you don't know it, but what you're doing is at this moment being beamed by hidden cameras to the viewing public of Great Britain. You have been the victims of a *Danger: Men At Work* set-up. I and my colleagues…" he gestured to me and Hopper "…are in fact actors… but I don't think you can deny that you were about to arrest them, weren't you?"

Filth shuffle their feet a bit at this, and the Chief Superintendent geezer admits that yes, the thought had crossed his mind. Then he roars with laughter, still desperate to show what a good sport he is.

"And now," Terence continues, "our hidden cameras will catch your reactions as my colleagues and I go through to the parking lot, where another actor is waiting in a hotwired police Panda car!"

They think this is even funnier. Terence has been walking down the stairs as he speaks, and we've been moving ahead of him, so we're all three at floor level by now. Carefully Terence puts his camcorder down on the newel post of the staircase, so that it's facing right at the Chief Superintendent. The Chief Superintendent looks directly into the lens and beams like his daughter's got married on the day he won the lottery.

"Gangway, please," says Terence, and the Filth obediently

move to give us a route out to the parking lot.

How long they stay grinning at the non-existent cameras we don't know, because as soon as the three of us are in Milton's Panda, he puts his foot down and we're out of there.

Everything else went smooth as you like. We met up with Louis, got the coins converted into legal tender and went our separate ways. In my case that meant taking the missus to the Seychelles for six months.

For the first time ever we split the loot five ways rather than four. Reckoned Terence deserved his share. Granted, he was the one who got us into a very nasty hole. But we couldn't help being impressed by the way he got us out of it. None of it's wasted, you know, Work Experience.

BEFORE THE FALL

Maureen Carter

"Thank God you're here, sarge. He's threatening to jump."
A line of sweat glistened above the young officer's lean top
lip; his voice held an uncharacteristic catch. Detective
Sergeant Bev Morriss divined the signs. For rookie PC
Daniel Rees this was a first: pavement huggers as they're
known in the biz.

"Over my dead body," she muttered. They stood shoulder
to shoulder on a patch of slightly tacky tarmac. Squinting
against the fierce midday sun, her gaze followed the none-
too-steady line of Rees's finger. Her strikingly blue eyes put
the azure sky in the shade. Not that she was aware of that –
she'd blanked everything bar the young man hunkered on a
flat roof four floors up, trainers just jutting over the edge.

"What d'we know, Danny?"

"Not a lot." Rees turned his mouth down. "Says he'll take
a dive if anyone goes near. He was chucking bricks a minute
ago."

Hand shielding her eyes, Bev focused on the hunched
figure, playing in her head various ways the incident could
pan out. "How long's he been up there?" She caught
her breath surreptitiously. The sprint from the hastily
abandoned police motor now straddling a nearby kerb had
led her to make a mental note or three: join a gym, re-join
old gym, attend any gym. Rees was fitter than a surfing
whippet.

"Not had time to ask around yet, sarge." The hankie he
dabbed round his neck was already damp. Summer in the
second city. Constable Rees, tall and dark, was losing his

cool. "We got the callout ten – twelve minutes back."

She nodded; knew that. The 'we' included fire and ambulance crews on standby down the road. She'd clocked them as she cruised past looking for a space. The alert had gone out over the police radio, Bev happened to be in the vicinity, offered to take a look. Her partner Mac Tyler was hooking up, soon as. The turnout might be overkill but better safe…

It wouldn't be pretty if Batboy spread his non-existent wings. The mean-looking pebbledash structure wasn't one of Small Heath's poxy high rises, but taking four floors without a lift wasn't a good move.

"One of this lot might know something." Rees jabbed a thumb over his epaulette. Gawpers were gathering behind a police cordon that was still being erected round the ugly squat block. Bev presumed the defunct building had housed council offices, tenant support, something of that ilk. Whatever, the show was gratis and the audience was rapt.

"Spectator sport, Danny." She delved in a voluminous bag for aviator shades. "Free fall… better than the Olympics."

Sunglasses in situ, she checked out the crowd. Several faces and craned necks were vaguely familiar. The Coppice estate – known round Highgate nick as the Cop-it – was little more than an annexe to Winson Green prison. She noted a couple of uniforms mingling with the jobless, feckless – and in at least two cases legless – voyeurs. The officers were jotting names, numbers, addresses, covering the basics. Anything earth-shattering would be filtered back pronto. Earth-shattering? Maybe not.

"I reckon he wants his mam." The grating vocals emanated from behind. Bev and Rees whipped round so fast they almost collided. An old woman had slipped through the police tape and now stared skywards, scrawny arms folded tight across a faded Playgirl t-shirt. Her rust-coloured perm framed a face like a sepia doily.

"No worries. We can sort that... Mrs...?" Bev paused, but the prompt wasn't delivered. The old dear hadn't wrested her glassy-eyed gaze from the roof. Bev registered fluffy mauve slippers and thick Norah Batty tights. Wrinkles must live close by, probably one of Batboy's neighbours, which meant a squad car could whisk the mother to the scene before you could say trained negotiator. Bev rubbed her hands. Sorted.

The old woman gave a derisive sniff. "She's gone AWOL."

Or maybe not. She stifled a sigh. "I'm DS Morriss. Bev Morriss." She flashed her trust-me-I'm-a-detective smile. "And you are...?"

"Six kids. And she buggers off just like that." Fingers clicked like snapping twigs.

A tinny *Greensleeves* issued from an ice cream van; frying onion odour wafted in the sultry air. Bev took a calming breath. "Look, love..." She tapped the woman's arm. "If you can just give us..."

"Be with some bloke..." Dazzling dentures had come adrift. A darting worm of a tongue nudged them back in line.

Bev's fists were balled. The clock was ticking and the jammy dodger wannabe was still up there. "If you can just give us the boy's name, love." Priority. Establishing communication. Police procedure. Common sense, really.

"Cheap tart." The old woman could've been talking to herself.

"Enough already." Bev stowed the sunglasses in her Guinness-coloured bob. "Give, lady. Who's the lad? Where's he from? What the freak's he playing at?"

Wrinkles blithely curled a crimped lip. Bev moved in close, recoiled at eau de old lady. "Listen up, grandma… If that kid jumps… on your head be it." Rapid blink. Mental cringe. *I can't believe I said that.*

"Yeah, well, that's one way o' putting it." The flicker of a grin ran across the old girl's lace-face. Bev's stunning oratory had won the booby prize: Wrinkles looked as if she was about to share.

Or might have – but for a communal gasp from the crowd. Twenty plus heads angled back. The youth, now standing, teetered precariously, arms flailing, baggy combats flapping. Put Bev in mind of an octopus on heat. Like she'd know. Then a glint from a Zippo lying on the gravel caught her glance – and a pack of Embassy shot overhead. Didn't take Sherlock. Some joker on the ground must've thought Batboy needed a smoke. The lighter had been lobbed first, grabbing for it had almost sent the lad over the edge. When balance was restored, the crowd's released breath could have powered wind farms.

"Knock it on the head, you lot," Bev yelled. "Go and have a word, Danny. You were saying, Mrs…?"

"Parton. Dolly. And 'fore you ask… I don't."

Thank God. "And the kid is…?"

"Kevin Skipton. His mates call him Skippy." A not helpful image sprang to mind; Bev banished it and focused on Dolly's words. "Lives in one of them maisonettes on the Grove Road? Kev's the eldest. Lad's only sixteen, but he looks out for the little ones; makes sure there's food on the table, clothes on their backs."

Yeah. Bet he's got a tree-house in Sherwood Forest. Bev lifted a sceptical-stroke-cynical eyebrow. "Sounds a regular little Robin Hood."

Dolly shrugged. "OK, he thieves a bit, but only to feed

the kids. Mind, the youngest's just a bab. Kylie-Anne." An indulgent smile faded fast. "Sort of crap name's that?"

"So." Bev joined the dots. "The mother's legged it and Kevin's cut up? Reckons this'll get her back?"

"Summat like that."

Books. For. Up. Turn. Bev had Batboy pegged as a loser, but not in the family break-up sense. Rough on the lad, that. Not that topping himself was any answer. Talk about defeating the object. Empty threat, then? On the other hand, if he lost his footing and fell, he'd be more than a crazy mixed-up kid. He'd be a crazy mixed-up dead kid.

She looked again at the boy on the roof: the hunched shoulders, pinched features, lank mousy hair; dirt-streaked face. Poor little sod. Most teenagers on the Cop-it carried blades, but Skippy carried a cross the size of a cathedral. He'd had to play ma, and presumably pa, to a bunch of snotty-nosed siblings. Skippy's skinny shoulders weren't just hunched, they were bowed. And his world had come crashing down anyway. God forbid the lad followed.

Bev cleared her throat. "Is there a dad in the picture, Mrs Parton?"

"Be a team photo," she sneered. It figured – in this neck of the woods family values were on a par with Aldi price cuts. "No," the old woman said. "The mam's not much cop – but she's all they've got."

"Any idea where she is?"

"Ain't you the detective round here?"

Bev did her detecting bit, and within minutes patrol cars were en route to half a dozen properties across the city; addresses elicited from Dolly where the errant Sharon Skipton might be shacked up. It wouldn't take long and no one on site was going anywhere. Least of all Kevin.

In between taking and making calls, liaising with Highgate, Bev had shouted up offers of food, drink, a mobile; tried getting him to open up. Lad had barely opened his mouth.

"How goes it, boss?" Mac Tyler. For a guy the size of a grizzly, Bev's DC was amazingly light on his feet.

"Whoop-de-do-not." She brought him up to speed, asked what had taken him so long.

Mac waggled enigmatic eyebrows, took a warm KitKat from one pocket, an ice-cold coke from another and handed them over with a conspiratorial wink.

"Ta, mate." She took a few glugs, pressed the can against her forehead. The goodies were from the newsagent's on the corner. Mac wouldn't have been shopping just for sustenance. "And?" she asked.

"The lad was banned from going in. Owner says he lifted more stock than a pick-up truck."

Fitted with the old lady's story. Bev frowned, glanced round. Where was Dolly?

Mac loosened his collar with a stubby finger. "A door at the back's been forced." And he'd had time for a recce. "I mentioned it to the rookie. Suggested he keep an eye? The press boys are sniffing round out there."

"Tell me about it," Bev drawled. The media were chomping at the bit out front, too.

"How we playing it, boss?"

She'd had a word with the guv. Detective Superintendent Bill Byford wanted a watching brief. No percentage forcing the issue. "Softly softly," Bev said. "No rush, is there?"

And then movement and a flash of colour on the roof caught her glance and everything went into overdrive.

"Tell me that's not what I think it is." She narrowed her eyes but it was still there.

A baby in a yellow romper suit was being dangled in

midair; Kevin Skipton was doing a Wacko Jacko. Was it Kylie-Anne? Kev's kid sister? The spectators' buzz descended into sudden absolute silence. Bev's mind raced as fast as her heart. It was think-on-feet time.

Then time ran out.

It seemed to happen in slow motion with a soundtrack of gasps and screams. The sickening crunch of the impact; the scarlet splatter and spray. Blood soaking through the tiny yellow jumpsuit. Every horrified gaze was on the crumpled bundle. For what seemed an age no one moved; bodies, expressions frozen in shocked disbelief.

It took Bev several seconds to recognise the smell. Her senses were primed for blood. Not the fumes she was inhaling. Her brain needed a few seconds more to collate the data. Then she scowled, spitting feathers. It was a frigging joke. The baby gear had been wrapped round a doll and a load of paint. The lad must've poured it into something flimsy, a plastic bag maybe. Why the hell…? If the tosser was just having a laugh, she had a damn sight better punch line.

"Right. You little sod…" But when she raised her furious gaze to the rooftop, Skippy hadn't so much flown as done a runner.

It was more sprint than marathon. The kid must've realised he'd not get away. When Bev, breathing hard, arrived at the back of the building, Kevin Skipton was indeed hugging the pavement. Danny Rees, she found out later, had brought him down with a rugby tackle, but it was Dolly Parton's slipper that was now planted across the lad's nape.

He gave out a plaintive, muffled, "Let me go."

"Let me go *please*." Dolly pressed down with her foot. "Please!"

3 1613 00396 9568

CALUMET CITY PUBLIC LIBRARY

"Never did know when to stop, did you, Kevin?" The old woman released the foothold, turned to Bev. "He's not a bad lad."

"Scuse me while I get his knighthood." She tapped a Doc Marten on the gravel. Mac ambled over, helped the youth to his feet, then frisked him. The only thing Kevin carried was a bit of extra weight.

"I tried talking him out of it," Dolly mumbled.

Bev chewed her lip, arms folded. "Give, granny. Ten seconds. Or you're both down the nick."

Blink of an eye and she gave. "Ernie Watson was after a decoy. Said Kev could earn himself a bit of pocket money if he created a bit of a stir."

Bev exchanged glances with Mac. Ernie 'Tools' Watson was a small-time villain with a big payroll. He used a lot of kids in the business; made Fagin look like a child protection officer. Ernie had apprentice dealers, carriers, tea-leafs, you name it, all over south Birmingham. The cops had been on his case for a couple of years. "Decoy for what? When? Five seconds, lady."

Dolly gave a resigned sigh. "Hold-up at the Eight-till-Late."

"And?"

"Don't say nothing," Kev pleaded. "He'll go ballistic."

"Cuff 'em, Mac." Bev made to leave.

Dolly reached out twiggy fingers. "Birches Arcade. Chippie one side, hairdresser's the other. It's takings day."

Not rich pickings then: it was a row of shops on the estate. Still, gift horse, mouth and all that. First things first, though...

"Danny, get the cars round there," Bev ordered. "And stand the emergency crews down." She glanced at Mac, who was already on the phone to Highgate rustling up reinforcements. Hands on hips, she treated Skippy and the old woman to a glare apiece. "Decoy I can just about get my head round. But that freaking charade…"

"Tools come up with the idea," Kevin mumbled. "I just had to make it convincing."

"Don't hold out for an Oscar, kid. And the sob story?" Bev glowered at Dolly. "That was a load of balls?"

The old woman found her slippers fascinating. "It just sort of came out."

Bev sighed, shook her head. "Mac, when you've finished…" The troops on Sharon Skipton's trail needed calling off. Waste of frigging time.

"Kev is good with the kids, though. We're a close family."

"Oh, well. That's all right then." Like she meant it. "Whose idea was the bloody doll?" she snapped.

Kevin lifted a tentative hand. "Saw that on the box. *The Bill*? *Casualty*? Something like that. Looked good, didn't it?"

"Not as good as your CV's gonna look, kid. Let's think… Breaking and entering, criminal damage, conspiracy, wasting police time, aiding and abetting, perverting the course… you getting the picture?"

"He'll get a damn good hiding an' all when I get him home."

"Home?" Bev narrowed her eyes.

"Shurrup, gran." Kevin's trainer toed the ground; his face was puce.

"You are joking?"

"Course I'm his gran. Looking out for him, wasn't I? Didn't want him getting in trouble…"

"Glad that worked, Dolly." Bev groaned, pictured the paperwork. She was sorely tempted to let him walk. He was only sixteen. No previous. No weapon. No one was dead.

He'd likely just get a caution. He wasn't the sharpest knife in the canteen, but maybe he'd learn a thing or two from this fiasco.

"Boss." Mac slipped his phone in a pocket, beckoned her over. "A word."

She skewered Skippy and his gran with another hostile glare. "Don't move an eyelash. Either of you."

Mac had just spoken to Danny Rees. It was what you'd call a partial result. Danny and four other officers had apprehended three goons coming out of the Eight-till-Late. Ernie Watson hadn't shown, he'd sent his minions, but if Kevin coughed…

Bev sauntered across. "OK, Skippy. Here's the deal." She didn't actually say, Spill the beans and save your bacon, but that's what it came down to. His gran's hefty two penn'orth plus dire warnings tipped the scales: Tools Watson was no match for the formidable Dolly Parton. Kevin agreed to give a detailed statement later in the afternoon and evidence during the trial.

"Thanks, officer." Dolly tucked her arm affectionately into the boy's. The warmth seemed genuine on both sides. "Come on, love. Let's get home. Your granddad's no match for them kids."

Bev watched them walk away, chatting and having a laugh. The lad was lucky having Dolly to look out for him, keep him on the straight and narrow. It might all go pear-shaped, but when the case came to court, hopefully Kevin would be in the witness box, not the dock.

Job done, sort of, Bev and Mac headed for their motors. She kicked a stone, apparently deep in thought.

"OK, boss?"

"Nah," she sniffed. "Well pissed off."

"Why's that?" He ripped a ring pull on a can of Red Bull.

"Missed a great line, didn't I?"

"Yeah?"

"Hawaii Five-O? The rookie?" She flashed a grin. "Never got to say, Book 'em, Danno."

"Lucky that. His name's Danny."

"Pedant."

HANGMAN

Mary Andrea Clarke

The Crimson Cavalier knew there would be no second chance. The shot had to count. Eyes narrowed against the unaccustomed daylight. The scaffold stood prominent, centre of the excitement of the clamouring crowd.

A cheer went up as a balding, middle-aged figure mounted the steps of the scaffold, waving to surrounding well-wishers. A hush fell as he started to speak. His words were brief, thanks to all for coming to see him turned off, and a cheery farewell which seemed incongruous with the grim setting.

The Crimson Cavalier watched solemnly as the macabre ritual began. As the man's parting words ended, his hands were bound. The rope was slipped over his head.

Now was the moment. A quick glance over the shoulder ensured that the horse was still tethered at a safe distance, ready for a speedy escape. Careful to keep out of sight from the vantage position just inside the prison walls, the Crimson Cavalier levelled the pistol. Eyes closed fleetingly and a brief prayer was offered before taking aim.

The report of the gun startled everyone, not least the man with the rope around his neck. The lever had barely been pulled, releasing the trap door. From a short drop which left him struggling for breath came a longer fall to the ground, as the pistol ball caught the rope, causing enough damage for bystanders near the scaffold to complete the job. As the executioner looked for the source of the shot, pandemonium ensued. The Crimson Cavalier noticed the glint of a knife near the rope, and had the satisfaction of seeing two figures from the crowd move forward to support the limp figure. The unevenly swaying and roaring crowd made it difficult to tell whether they had moved him away from the scaffold. There was nothing more the Crimson Cavalier could do and it seemed sensible to take advantage of the chaos to slip away through the general melée. Then a shout went up over the hubbub.

"The executioner's dead! The hangman's been shot! Murder! Murder!"

The Crimson Cavalier froze, head turning back slowly, hovering on the verge of going through the gate. No, it was not possible. The shot had been a precise one; it could not have caught anyone.

Could it?

"The Crimson Cavalier! Look! There! By the gate!"

There was no time to ponder the issue now. The hand of an obliging stranger pushed the Crimson Cavalier through the gate; a miracle Biblical in nature closed the crowd behind and opened it in front. A path cleared, and the horse tethered within sight of the gates of Newgate Prison seemed easily within reach. The grubby urchin deputed to watch the animal deftly caught the tossed coin, and the boy watched as the lithe figure mounted with impressive speed, turned the beast and rode off.

Galloping through the murky back streets, the Cavalier heard no sounds of a hue and cry, though there were occasional surprised glances from the poverty-stricken populace. As the horse grew breathless, it seemed prudent to slow down. The animal dropped to a canter, guided into the less well populated areas to afford its rider a chance to think.

The daylight gave too much exposure. They required cover, and quickly. The villages and woods at the edge of

London were still too far away. There was nothing to be done but keep to the less appealing, and, hopefully, less well investigated areas while negotiating the way. Luck held, and horse and rider reached the woods without mishap. Once under cover of the trees the rider pulled up, pausing to give both a chance to draw breath.

And after a quick glance around to ensure no one was within sight, it was a flushed young lady who pulled the mask from the lower portion of her face, and opened it out to wipe her glistening cheeks and forehead.

Miss Georgiana Grey closed her eyes briefly, took a deep breath and re-folded the dark cloth to tie it back around her face. It seemed Harry Smith was safe – but at what cost? Had she helped to save the life of one man only to take that of another? How could it have happened? She had known it would take an inordinate amount of luck to shoot straight through the rope, and had fired well over Harry's head to catch it. She had not seen anyone standing behind. Could the executioner have moved suddenly when Harry dropped?

Georgiana gave herself a shake. This was neither the time nor the place to ponder the matter. The authorities might not be close upon her trail, but they would not let the killing of an executioner pass lightly. A chance encounter with someone who had seen her progress from the prison could set them in her direction. She leaned forward to pat the horse's neck.

"Good girl, Princess. Come, let's move."

A tug at the reins set them forward again. It seemed a little odd to be negotiating this route with the sun peeking through the trees, but they soon reached their destination.

The area around the Lucky Bell tavern was quieter than Georgiana was accustomed to. A tavern patronised by highwaymen was not an establishment one would normally expect a gently reared young society lady to frequent, but her career as the Crimson Cavalier had brought her a number of encounters not normally within the preserve of ladies of quality.

Georgiana was expecting that she would have to knock on the door, but by good fortune the proprietor Cedric was outdoors, apparently having taken out an empty beer barrel. Catching sight of her, he halted. Georgiana saw him turn his head and call indoors. A woman of comfortable proportions came out, wiping her hands on an apron. Cedric stepped forward to greet their guest.

"In you come, lad. We heard what happened at Newgate."

"Already?"

Cedric nodded. He and his lady stood back to allow Georgiana in ahead of them. Booted, gloved and masked, with no attempt made to remove the three-cornered hat adorned with its bright red scarf, the Crimson Cavalier stepped across the threshold.

All talk ceased. There were just a few patrons in the taproom, but Georgiana was conscious of all eyes on her. The silence hung heavy, similar to the atmosphere at Newgate in the moments before the execution. Suddenly a man stood up, walked slowly over to the newcomer and held out his hand. As Georgiana grasped it, she found it almost shaken from her arm. Others followed suit. A general flood of conversation and congratulations broke out, and a bemused and rather touched Georgiana accepted the thanks and good wishes of her fellow highway robbers, who shook her hand, gripped her shoulder and slapped her back in recognition of her morning's work.

"Drinks all round," said Cedric. "Harry's upstairs. A couple of the lads brought him in, on the hangman's cart yet."

"Well, he won't be needing it," said a burly man with masked eyes, tossing back the remains of his drink before seeking more.

A shout of laughter went up.

"How is Harry?" asked Georgiana.

"Winded, fair woozy, but alive, thanks to you," said Cedric.

Georgiana shook her head. She felt uncomfortable accepting such acclaim.

"I didn't shoot the hangman," she said.

"No matter," someone spoke up.

"Oh, aye. One less of them and Harry's still breathing."

"Come upstairs, lad," said Cedric. "He'll be glad to see you."

Georgiana followed Cedric up the narrow wooden stairs to a small bedchamber at the back of the establishment. Harry lay on the bed, fully clothed but for his boots. Two men were with him; Georgiana recognised the friends who had taken him from the rope. They gave her a nod, the one nearer the bed stepping back with the brandy he appeared to have been administering to the patient. Harry recognised her, and he struggled to sit up. Georgiana moved quickly forward and pushed him down gently, shaking her head.

"Thank you, lad," rasped Harry. "I'm told 'twas you that saved me."

"Not entirely," said Georgiana.

The man holding the brandy shook his head. "We could never have got him down if you hadn't hit the rope," he said.

"Fair bit of shooting," said his companion, his tone respectful.

"Aye, that it were."

Georgiana acknowledged the compliment with a nod, then turned back to Harry.

"How are you?"

"My throat's afire and my head's busting. But I'm still here."

"You've always had the devil's luck, Harry," said his friend with the brandy.

"That's true," said Harry. "'Tis not the first time I've nearly hung." He held out a hand to Georgiana. "Thank you, lad."

Georgiana nodded. "Try not to let it happen again," she said.

Harry gave a burst of laughter which resulted in a fit of coughing. The sound of activity outside the room prompted one man to swiftly put a kerchief over Harry's mouth to stifle the sound while the other listened at the door. Cedric's voice could be heard outside but Georgiana could distinguish no words. It seemed the man at the door could because his eyes widened and he moved back into the room with the speed of a cat. Georgiana found herself unceremoniously bundled under the bed with an injunction to stay quiet. Cedric's voice became clearer as she heard the door open.

"I don't know what you're talking about," he said. "The Crimson Cavalier! Don't he have a horse and rob carriages? Well, I don't see no horse nor carriage in here."

"Funny," said a voice unfamiliar to Georgiana. "Well, well," it continued. "The man who should have been hanged."

From her position under the bed, Georgiana could see scuffed brown boots uncomfortably close.

"Hiding a criminal, then?" came the voice again.

"He's dead," said one of Harry's friends.

"You cut him down?" asked the interrogator.

"'Cause he was dead," said Harry's other friend.

"Who said so?" demanded the newcomer.

"Well, look at him. He ain't moving."

There was silence for a moment. The new arrival spoke. "Surgeon's supposed to certify him dead."

"I didn't see no surgeon. Jack, did you see a surgeon?"

"No."

"There you are, then, no surgeon."

"Probably ran off when the shooting started," said Jack.

"Expect so," said his friend.

"We wanted to bury our mate," Jack continued. "Did you expect us to leave him there for the crows?"

"Harry paid the extra. He didn't want no sawbones cutting up his insides."

The newcomer spoke again. "What about the Crimson Cavalier?"

"What about him?" said Jack.

"We think he shot the hangman."

"Then you'd better find him," said Jack's friend.

"Not here," said Jack.

"No," said his friend.

"He was seen coming here," persevered the stranger.

"Do you see him?" Jack asked.

Silence.

"Oh, be off with you, nark," said Jack. "Have some respect for the dead."

"All right," said the newcomer. "But someone shot Bob Flint doing his duty, and when I find out who…"

"You'll hang him," said Jack's friend.

Jack guffawed.

"Come on," said Cedric, "let's leave these gents in peace to mourn their friend. You can have a drink, then be on your way."

Georgiana sensed some resistance and saw the feet of the stranger shuffle to the door. She caught a glimpse of the another booted foot kicking it closed, and thought she heard an oath muttered. There was tense silence for a moment or two as each waited for a sign of the returning visitor. When none came, a figure bent down next to the bed and Georgiana was hauled out with as little ceremony as she had been pushed in. It was with some difficulty that she kept her mask on. His companion was retrieving the blanket which he had hastily thrown over Harry.

"Sorry, lad. Nothing else we could do."

Georgiana shook her head. "No. Thank you." She frowned. "Bob Flint? The hangman. But surely..."

Jack nodded. "Aye, that's it. You're not imagining things. Bob Flint was one of us."

"Nothing worse than a turncoat," muttered his friend.

"Lads, lads," said Harry, sitting up.

"We'd best get you out," Jack said to Georgiana. "Let me see if the nark's gone."

Georgiana waited while he checked outside the door. All seemed quiet apart from the patrons in the tap room. Jack put a finger to his lips and went out, jerking his head for Georgiana to follow. She nodded, turning only to wave farewell to Harry. Jack went slowly ahead of her down the stairs, pausing about halfway to listen. Apparently satisfied with what he heard, he continued.

As far as Georgiana could see, the patrons in the tap room were the same ones who'd greeted her on arrival. There was no sign of any stranger.

"The boy took your horse around the back," said Cedric.

"Thank you," said Georgiana. She handed Cedric a coin and prepared to depart.

"Hold on," said Jack. "Where's Ned?"

Georgiana paused. Cedric frowned and looked around the room.

"He was in the corner," said Cedric.

"Well, he's not now," said Jack. He frowned. "Didn't Ned used to work the road with Bob?"

Cedric nodded slowly. "He did, now you mention it." It was Cedric's turn to frown. "Ned's brother was the first one Bob Flint hanged."

Georgiana was surprised at this. She had discovered a code of loyalty among the highway fraternity. The betrayal of a former partner seemed particularly nasty.

"Ned took it bad," said Jack. "Got careless. No one would work with him after that. Nearly got Harry killed once." Jack looked towards Georgiana. "I'll ride with you to the woods."

Georgiana was astonished. "There's no need."

"There is," Jack insisted. "He's dangerous, and if 'twas he who shot the hangman he's trying to lay the blame on you."

The two left the tavern, riding side by side in silence, both sets of eyes and ears alert. Silence reigned and it began to seem their fears were groundless.

A twig snapped.

Georgiana and her companion looked at each other, and hands went to pistols. Neither saw any movement; only the breathing of their own horses broke the quiet. Her hand relaxing on her own pistol, Georgiana turned to bid Jack farewell.

The shot rang out suddenly, whistling past her ear as she moved her head. The horses whinnied their unease, and Jack's reared up suddenly. Jack held on, steadying the animal, until Georgiana could grab its reins. Another shot flew past them.

Two figures appeared from the direction of the woods, both with pistols levelled. Georgiana recognised the heavy-set legs and scuffed brown boots of the man who had been looking for the Crimson Cavalier. The other seemed familiar. Jack's call of "Ned!" confirmed it.

Ned ran towards them, his pistol waving wildly.

"He killed the hangman!" he shouted. "The Crimson Cavalier."

Her own pistol in her hand, Georgiana reined Princess in and aimed a swift kick at the pistol in Ned's hand as he came running towards her. Her aim was true. The pistol fell and Ned himself lost his balance. His companion moved forward to his aid. Jack slid from his mount and plunged forward to grab his legs. The man fell, and Jack pinned him to the ground, arms behind his back. Georgiana took some cord from Princess's saddle bag and approached the still unsteady Ned. He knelt on the ground, eyes glazed, and offered little resistance as Georgiana tied his hands.

"There's the hangman's killer," said Jack, one knee on his captive's back. "Your friend there. Ned. Bob Flint hanged his brother."

"But…"

"Never mind 'but', you nark. That's your man, not the Crimson Cavalier."

Jack pulled his prisoner up roughly, keeping a firm hold on one arm. He jerked his head, signalling to Georgiana to bring her prisoner over. Ned's dazed condition made it an easy enough task. Jack pulled his pistol and thrust his captive forward.

"Take him," he said, "but try to touch my friend here and you'll be food for the crows yourself."

The man looked warily at the pistol, then at Jack and the Crimson Cavalier. He moved forward obediently, taking

Ned's right arm so Georgiana could let go of his left. She walked back to Princess and mounted. Jack followed suit.

Georgiana stretched out her hand to Jack. He shook it warmly.

"A good brawl," he said.

"Yes."

"Good day to you, friend."

"Good day."

The Crimson Cavalier threw a final glance towards the lawman and his prisoner, standing bemused at the scene. Then she turned her horse and rode into the wood.

GAMES FOR WINTER

Ann Cleeves

He flew into Stillwater in late January at sunrise on a clear day, so his first view was of flame-coloured mountains and forests heavy with snow and tinged with pink. There was no wind, and the ride in the small plane from Juneau was as smooth as sailing on a lake. Although in summer there was a boat every week, in winter flying was the only way in. Stillwater was as remote as any island.

They touched down earlier than the schedule and there was no one to meet him. The pilot lifted down his bags on to the runway, then got back into the plane and took off. Mark watched it until it flew away over the horizon. It was very cold standing there, and brilliantly clear. No noise, not even birdsong. The runway and a couple of huts and one road running off into the woods. A backdrop of mountain. The blinding light reflected from the ice, and sharp black shadows.

A dog barked, and a woman bundled in a parka which made her look as fat as she was tall came out of the closest hut.

"Hi there." The dog had followed her and was dancing around her legs. "You're the new teacher." Close to, he saw she was middle-aged but striking. Red hair under the hood, a wide Cheshire cat mouth.

"Yes," he said, aware of how English his voice was, thought that even one word sounded clipped and pompous. "Mark. Mark Arden."

"Well hi, Mark. Pleased to meet you. Sally-Ann Larson. My daughter's in eleventh grade. Let's go into my office and

I'll get you some coffee then phone around and find out what's happened to your ride. Welcome to Alaska."

He met Sally-Ann's daughter the next day in school. She was sitting on the front row in the class for the older students. The school took children from kindergarten through high school. There were forty of them all together, three full-time teachers. Mark was an extra, part of a cultural exchange programme. Usually he taught in an inner city comprehensive in Newcastle, not very far from the suburb where he'd been brought up. He was twenty-six and needed a challenge. There'd recently been a messy separation from the girlfriend he'd had since college.

Beth Larson was sixteen, blonde and freckled, though as she stood to recite the Pledge of Allegiance, feet apart, hand on her heart, she looked so earnest that he thought she seemed younger. She had the same wide mouth as her mother. As they sat down he saw a moose in the school yard, grazing leaves from a nearby tree. It shook its head, and the loose skin which hung like a collar round its neck moved too. The kids took no notice.

He asked them to introduce themselves in a piece of writing, "as if you were introducing the characters in a story." When they read out their work he thought how different they were from the students he'd taught at home. One boy boasted about his skill with tractors, another described a summer fishing trip. Beth placed herself in the kitchen at home helping her mother baking for her father's birthday party. *He works most of the week in Anchorage,* she wrote, *so it's always special when he comes home.*

Mark thought it was as if he'd gone back in time. These children seemed to belong to his grandparents' generation. In some respects, however, the settlement's philosophy was surprisingly contemporary, liberal. He'd expected a backward community. Redneck. Hunting and shooting and isolationist. But many of the residents of Stillwater had moved there from the city because they were looking for a better way of living. They were idealists, who'd cleared a patch in the forest and built a house out of logs for themselves and their families. They cared about their community and their environment. In the dark winter evenings they attended book groups and nature groups. They watched arty films in the school hall and put on plays. They didn't bother much with the television because the reception was poor and anyway most of it was trash, but many did listen to the World Service on the BBC.

In the summer, he supposed, it would be different. Then tourists came to camp in the National Park and took boat trips into the bay to see the wildlife. The hotel would open again. But in the dark nights of winter the people of Stillwater made their own entertainment.

Mark lived with Jerry Brown, a young man from Seattle who worked as a ranger in the National Park. They shared a little house which was reached by a track through the trees. It had a porch looking over a bit of cleared meadow to a frozen stream. Jerry had moved to the community two years before and adored it. He said it was the only ethical way to live. He had a share in the Larsons' cow and took his turn at milking her. He led the conservation group. At home he was relaxed and friendly. He liked to drink beer and smoke a little dope, play very loud rock music. After all, he said, there was no one to disturb, only the bears, and it was probably a good thing to discourage them. He seemed to Mark to be as naïve and friendly as the children.

Mark walked to and from school, unless there was heavy snow. He enjoyed the exercise, the sting of the cold against his face and in his lungs. One afternoon he walked home and stopped by the jetty to look over the bay to watch the setting sun on the glacier. Cormorants stood on the wooden railing. The lights were coming on in the scattered homesteads on the opposite shore. Despite the cold, he must have stood there longer than he'd realised, because when he turned away from the view to continue, he saw it was almost dark. There were stars and a moon like a thin, tilted smile. Someone was walking down the straight road towards him. It was Beth Larson. She stood beside him, looked out at the jetty.

"We swim from there in the summer."

He felt uncomfortable being there with her. She was standing very close, whispering almost into his ear.

"It must be cold." He knew he sounded ridiculous and stamped his feet to cover his embarrassment. The temperature had dropped as the light went.

"Sometimes we go skinny dipping…"

He imagined her in the summer sunshine, with her gold hair and gold skin, flashing like a fish through the water.

"You should get home," he said. "Your mother will be expecting you."

"She's visiting Mary Slater. You know how they talk. She won't be home for an hour. The house is empty. Come back. You could help me with my school work." Though her voice made it clear that wasn't at all what she had in mind.

He actually considered it for a moment. He wondered later what had stopped him and decided it had nothing to do with ethics. A fear of being caught.

"No," he said. "I don't think that's a terribly good idea."

"You will," she said. "By the end of the winter when the boredom's set in, you'll be begging me by then. Only I might have changed my mind."

Then she ran off, her boots making only a rustling sound

in the new snow. She disappeared into the darkness and he could make himself believe that the encounter had been a figment of his imagination. Back at the house Jerry was caring for an injured surf bird he'd picked up from the shore. He had put it in a cardboard box and was feeding it pilchards from a tin. Mark would have liked to ask his advice about Beth Larson, but he seemed engrossed in his task and the moment never seemed to arise. Although Mark's students in Newcastle had been precocious, none of them had propositioned him, and he told himself he must have misinterpreted what had occurred.

That night he dreamed of Beth Larson. In the dream it was summer and he was swimming with her. She rose out of the bay, pulling herself up on to the jetty, and water dripped from her hair and ran over her body. He was about to reach out and touch her when he woke. In class the next day she was sitting in the front as usual, serious and polite. He found it hard not to look at her, to remember that she had been available to him. He lost himself in daydreams.

The following weekend it was Valentine's Day and all the community came together for a pooled supper and party. All the adults at least. The kids weren't invited. The food was supposed to have an erotic theme and they'd had fun with hot dogs and mounds of rice curved like breasts and strangely shaped fruit and vegetables. All very innocent, no doubt, but Mark felt uneasy. The evening wasn't what he'd expected. He had thought these people would lead simple and unsophisticated lives, had imagined himself even as a missionary from civilised world. But even though they wore jeans and hand-knitted sweaters and thick woollen socks they talked about artists and writers who were only names to him. They made *him* feel like the country cousin, gauche and uneducated.

It didn't help that he found it hard to concentrate on the conversation. They were talking about a student who'd drowned in a boating accident. It was almost exactly a year since his death. The water had been so cold, they said, that he'd had no chance to survive. The shock would have killed him in seconds. Jerry, who was there too, made little effort to join in. He sat on the floor, leaning against the wall, a can of beer in his hand, watching them. Even in this setting he was a scientist. Mark did try to take part in the discussion, but the party was being held in the Larson house and he was distracted. He imagined Beth upstairs in her room. When the heating pipes gurgled, he pictured her taking a shower, the water trickling over her shoulders into the tub. There was no water pressure in any of the houses in Stillwater so it would dribble slowly, across her belly and between her legs. Finally he made his apologies and left. Jerry offered to drive him, but Mark said he preferred to walk.

Outside the cold took his breath away, and he stood for a moment gasping, snorting out a white vapour through his nose. The stars were hidden by cloud and there were occasional flurries of snow. The lights from the house saw him through the trees to the road and then he switched on his torch. There was no sound except for the squeaking of his feet on the compacted snow, and that seemed very far away because of the fur hat pulled over his ears. He walked on, past the school and the gas station. Everywhere was in darkness. He was approaching the turn-off, the track which led to Jerry's house, when he heard the sound behind him, a roar which made him think of an avalanche or water released from a dam. Here, surrounded by trees, it didn't occur to him in that first second that the noise might be man-made.

Then he realised it was the sound of an engine being revved very hard, revved to screaming point. Headlights flashed through the trees. In the dual beams he saw that it was snowing more heavily now. He jumped off the track into the trees just in time as a white pick-up screeched past. He had stepped into a drift and the snow had gone over his boots and inside his socks. He was climbing out when the pitch of the engine changed and the headlights were turned again towards him. The truck only paused for a moment, then roared back down the road, the way it had come, spraying loose snow from the wheels, sliding when the driver touched the brakes to round a corner. Mark could not tell whether or not he'd been seen. He had the ridiculous thought that he might have been a target.

At school on Monday, he called Dan Slater back after class. The Slaters were the only family in the community to have a white pick-up, and the parents had been at the Valentine party. Outside the other kids were standing around in the yard. That was unusual. It was too cold, even in daylight, just to hang out. Their presence unnerved Mark, though they couldn't possibly hear what he was saying. Dan was fourteen, very young for his age. He had problems with simple reading and writing. At home they would have said he had special needs.

"Were you driving your father's truck on Saturday night?"

Dan blinked, looked out of the window, stared at the ceiling.

"Sure," he said. "He lets me."

"You were driving very fast. You could have hurt yourself."

Outside the kids seemed to lose interest. They were starting to drift away. Mark felt more confident. He'd worked with dozens of students like Dan. He spoke gently.

"Weren't you scared, driving like that? What made you do it? It wasn't a race."

"Not a race, no. Sometimes we race. But not last time."

"What then?"

"It was a game."

"What sort of game?"

"I guess it was a dare."

"Who dared you, Dan?"

But Dan wasn't prepared to talk any more. He pulled the strange, little boy faces he made when he was concentrating in class, shuffled his feet and stared out of the window. Finally Mark let him go.

When Mark got home Beth was waiting for him. They never locked the door, and she was inside the kitchen, sitting on the rocker in front of the stove, moving backwards and forwards. He'd been surprised to see smoke coming from the chimney as he'd approached, had thought Jerry must be back earlier than usual from work. She'd taken off her boots and her outdoor clothes, put a cassette into the recorder. When he opened the door she stood up. She'd changed from the clothes she'd been wearing in school. Her jersey had a slash neck and was very tight. Her jeans could have been sprayed on.

"I thought I'd give you a second chance," she said. "I've seen the way you've been looking at me in class."

He stooped to unlace his boots. He knew he should make a lighthearted remark and send her on her way. Nothing too heavy. He had to live here for the rest of the year. He couldn't afford to upset her or her parents. But he was flattered too. Excited. She walked towards him, moving her hips in time with the music and she grinned, thinking in his moment of indecision, that she had him hooked.

"Is this a dare too?" he asked.

"What do you mean?"

"Like Dan stealing his father's pick-up and racing round the tracks."

She didn't answer.

"You do know Dan could have killed himself?"

She began to struggle into her coat. Although the grin seemed fixed to her face, there were tears on her cheeks. She tried to push past him, but he stood with his back against the door, pressing it shut. He took her by the shoulders, felt the bones under her thick coat, remembered other bones, another woman. He whispered into her ear, as she had whispered to him on the jetty, and his voice was seductive too. "Just how far would you have been prepared to go, Beth? What exactly did they dare you to do?"

"Nothing," she said. "It was just a game." She scrambled out of his grasp and he let her go, feeling suddenly ashamed. The last of the sun caught her hair as she ran away down the track.

That night he dreamed of her again. In the morning her school desk was empty.

"Does anyone know where Beth is today?" he said, looking around the classroom. They stared back at him, challenging him to ask more. Whatever game was being played, they were all in on it.

"Her mother phoned in to say she's sick." It was Peter, the boy who knew about tractors. He was thickset and sullen and Mark had come to the conclusion that he knew little about anything else.

"Who told you that?"

Peter shrugged, not caring whether or not he was believed.

While the children were eating their lunch, Mark went to the Larson house. Sally-Ann would be working in the booking office on the airstrip and Beth's father was in Anchorage. On his way there he wondered why he was going. Was he looking for an excuse to see Beth on her own? He decided he was worried about her, though what on earth did he think could have happened to the girl?

He found her outside. She was in an open-sided barn splitting logs with an axe. Mark watched her from the yard. The axe was heavy, and she struggled to lift it, but her aim was exact and the blow was powerful. He thought how strong she must be, stronger than him. The wood split with one go and the splinters scattered, bouncing on the concrete floor. He could smell the resin from where he stood.

"I thought you were sick," he said. He waited until she was resting. He didn't want to scare her while she had the axe in the air. It would have been easy to cause an accident.

She didn't bother replying.

"Tell me about these games," he said.

"Why?" Her voice was bitter. "Do you want to play too?"

"I want to understand."

"It's winter," she said. "Boring. We have to do something."

"It has to stop. Someone will get hurt. Tell them. If it doesn't stop, I go to the principal. And to your parents."

She turned angrily to face him, allowing the axe to crash to the floor.

"People have already been hurt," she said. "They won't stop."

But the next day she was back in school and he thought he'd handled the situation well. She'd have passed on the message to her friends. There would be no more foolishness.

He stayed at school late that evening for a staff meeting, and then to prepare a lesson for the following day. He was the last to leave the building and it was already dark, though there was enough of a moon for him to follow the road. Past the gas station, Jerry's was the only house. There had been a slight thaw and he'd been aware all day of the sound of melting snow dripping from roofs and trees. Now it had started to freeze again but he felt as if he was being followed by the same persistent sound. He stopped once and still it seemed to be there, coming from the trees on either side of the road. When he shone his torch there were strings of icicles on each branch, quite frozen. It began to unnerve him and he wondered if it wasn't water after all, but the scratching of animals in the forest. There were brown bears. Everyone had stories about them, stealing food from outhouses, staring in through windows. They were only dangerous, people said, if they were cornered. He had never quite believed that. He walked more quickly. The sounds came nearer, gathering around him, closing him in.

Close to the turn off to Jerry's house, panic made him stumble. As he pulled himself to his feet, he swung the torch behind him and saw two figures on the road. They were wrapped in coats and hoods so he couldn't tell who they were. Each had a stave in one hand, a piece of wood as thick and solid as Beth's axe handle. They banged the sticks in rhythm on the frozen path.

"Hi!" he called, relieved at first to have company. "Who is it?" But before he had finished speaking he had realised that they weren't there to help him. He turned to continue on his way, but another moving shape had appeared on the road ahead of him, blocking his path. For a moment the scarf he was wearing slipped and Mark recognised Peter, the tractor driver.

More figures approached, moving through the forest. He circled, shining the torch crazily around him, catching glimpses of them, hooded like ghosts. The noise they made didn't come from the natural sound of footsteps or crackling undergrowth. Each held a stick which he knocked against tree trunk or branch, disturbing the snow lying there and shattering icicles. It formed a strange percussion, at once hollow and brittle, which grew louder and louder. Mark jumped from the road into the trees and started running, sucking in the icy air in huge, howling gasps.

Roots tangled about his legs. The ground was uneven. There were frozen pools and outcrops of rock. Branches whipped into his face and upper body. And always he was aware of the noise around him and behind him. At last, when he was too exhausted to continue he curled into a ball behind a pile of dead undergrowth. His muscles twitched from the exertion and he was still wheezing, but he forced himself to stay silent. He listened.

The dull thud of wood against bark had stopped. There were footsteps but they seemed to be dying away. Desultory scraps of conversation grew more distant. Someone laughed. It seemed that the game was over. It was too cold and uncomfortable for them. They'd had their amusement. They'd go home to a wholesome supper, an evening of computer games. And in the morning they'd sit at their desks daring him to speak of what had happened. He'd overreacted of course, which was just what they'd wanted. He'd made a fool of himself. He had believed that they meant to hurt him. He wasn't sure he could forgive them. Especially, he thought, Beth had betrayed him. She would have to pay for his humiliation.

Although it seemed as if he'd been running for miles, when he could think more clearly, he saw that he wasn't far from home. There was a faint light at the end of a clearing which must be their house. If he'd not panicked he could easily have made it back to safety before the children caught him up. Jerry would be cooking. He'd promised potato pancakes with apple sauce. It was the night, Mark thought, to open that bottle of scotch he'd brought with him. What a sight he must look, all scratched and bruised. He began rehearsing a story of the incident in his head. How could he explain it? As a joke at his own expense, perhaps. The rookie Brit teacher spooked by a bunch of kids.

They were all waiting for him in the house. He didn't realise until he'd pushed open the door and by then it was too late. Peter came round behind him and wedged it shut. They were sat on the floor round the walls, the sticks and baseball bats propped beside them. They had all kept very quiet, like the guests at a surprise party. He wondered if there had been the same nervous giggling. Now nobody laughed. They looked up at him and stared.

"Come on, kids," he said. "This is a joke, right?"

"Not a joke," Beth replied sternly. "A dare."

"You should go. Jerry will be here any minute."

"I'm here already," Jerry said. He slipped out from the bedroom. He looked as he always did when he got in from work. Relaxed and gentle. He wore a plaid shirt and jeans and held a can of beer in his hand. "It's my dare. I get bored in winter too."

"You dared them to frighten me off?"

"Oh no," he said. "They dared me. To get rid of you. Without too much fuss. Before you could tell anyone about our games." He looked around at the staring children. "What shall it be, guys? A boating accident like last time? Or something more imaginative?"

The children picked up the sticks and began to batter them, the same rhythm over and over again, against the wooden floor.

PUSH!

Lesley Cookman

Push!
She seemed to have been pushing for hours, although it was probably only a few minutes. As she rested briefly before the next effort, the unrelenting fluorescent light above her burned bars of brightness on her closed eyelids.

Push! She felt the veins standing out on her neck and heard the thud of her own heartbeat echoing behind her eardrums. Something will burst in a minute, she thought in an almost detached manner, and it will all be his fault.

Another rest period. She moved wearily, trying to find a better position.

Push! All this, for a few minutes of sweaty, illicit, passion. Or, to be truthful, several hours of it, if you added it all up, all those encounters behind the long row of filing cabinets during the lunch hour and in the stationery cupboard at any time. Then there had been the under-ground car park, the back of his car, and even one spectacular occasion on the last train from Waterloo.

Push! She had to keep going, despite the weariness in her thighs, her swimming head and this awful weakness that followed each monumental effort.

Push!

When was it she'd realised that something was wrong? She let out a panting breath and tried to remember. November, it must have been. When they'd been organising the Christmas party. That was it. She could see him now, his tie loose, his hair sticking out at the side of his head.

Funny, she'd never noticed how thin it was getting.

"You realise I'll have to bring the wife?" He was tucking his shirt in, not looking at her.

"To the party?" She struggled upright from her uncomfortable position against the metal shelving.

"She'd be a bit surprised if I didn't. Comes every year." He smoothed his hair down, licking his palm in a way that made her feel faintly sick.

She bent down so that he couldn't see her face, and pulled up her tights. She would have to go into the Ladies on her way back to Bought Ledger, get cleaned up. "You didn't bring her on the summer outing," she said, her voice muffled.

"I didn't tell her." He pushed the knot of his tie back up to his Adam's apple, stretching his neck like a turkey. "Come on. I'll see if the coast's clear."

She straightened up and watched him peer furtively round the door, amused at his futile precautions. The whole Accounts floor and half the Sales department knew about them. She didn't know why he didn't just bring in a mattress and hang a Do Not Disturb notice on the cupboard door.

Push!

He'd begun to avoid her after that, during the day, at least. She was furious with him, but more so with herself when one day after weeks of ignoring her, he'd followed her halfway home and dragged her into the alley next door to Mr. Singh's All Nite Take-Away – and she'd let him. Pathetic. But she couldn't refuse him. As soon as his hand had slid up under her skirt her knees had buckled and that was that. Up against a wall in an alleyway, like the silly teenager she had been only a few short years ago.

Push! Perspiration was dripping down her forehead and off

her nose now, and she really didn't think she could go on much longer. Love, she supposed it was. What else would have her in this ridiculous position now? Had his wife felt like this? A sudden rush of fellow feeling for the vague, grey personage in the suburbs overwhelmed her and two hot salty tears dripped on to her dry lips.

He had left the room some time ago; she had watched him go, hurriedly, not looking back. Had he left his wife the same way? Rushing off for a quick grope with her, or one of her predecessors, for of course she now realised that she hadn't been the first, not by a long chalk.

Push! Something had changed, she could feel it. She must be nearly there. Panting, she stopped pushing. Nearly over.

She had told him on Valentine's Day. Told him she'd had to move out of the flat, couldn't go back to Mum. He'd looked past her out of the window and said couldn't she do something about it? He'd help, give her money. She'd thrown his coffee at him.

The next time she'd seen him, he was having his trousers wiped down tenderly by that brunette from Sales. The expression on his face had said it all.

There was a buzzing in her ears, now, and she felt distinctly lightheaded. She tried to concentrate on the reason for her being here; stop herself drifting away entirely on a sea of pain. She saw again the caressing hand slide over the smooth dark head bent before him in a parody of submission, and knew again the sharp spike of jealousy that seemed to pierce her chest and leave her breathless. As she was breathless now, with this never ending pushing.

She'd got used to spying on them. He no longer used

their stationery cupboard, but the cleaner's cupboard in the basement. And his car, of course. In fact, he'd become almost blasé about the car, leaving it parked out in the open, right underneath the office window.

And now, suddenly, it was easy. One more little push and it was sliding. She could feel it, sliding out and away from her – release at last.

The filing cabinet made a satisfying crash as it finally came to rest on the car parked below the open window, and if she squinted, it looked almost as if it could get up and walk away on the two legs protruding from the bottom.

NEUTRAL TERRITORY

Natasha Cooper

He chose Amsterdam as the neutral territory for the handover. I don't know why, except that it's easy to get to and we'd never been here together.

I came a couple of days ago to acclimatise and find my way about. I didn't want to get lost and be late for this rendezvous. Already I feel at home. It's a lovely place. An old, eccentric guidebook has been leading me along the prettiest canals and showing me the most welcoming of the tiny cafés. Brown cafés they call them because of all the smoke stains on the walls and ceilings, like the ones around me now. They're cosy and no one minds how long you stay, or stares at you even when you're a fifty-year-old woman on your own with nothing but your thoughts for company.

Being on my own isn't quite what I expected, you know. It's not like being free. At first I thought it would be. When you're divorced you can say what you want, and eat what you want, and choose what to wear without worrying you'll be told you look like an old hag, or are showing too much flesh, or whatever else he's decided he can't bear on the day. If you've never lived as we did, you won't understand, but believe me, it's amazing to be shot of it. At first.

Then the emptiness begins to stretch you out and tempts you to believe it wasn't as bad as you thought, that you were making a silly fuss, just as he always said. You wait for the phone calls that never come. Nothing happens unless you organise it, and you're too tired to do much after work. You soon learn that when you are invited out it's always for kitchen supper, not the kind of dinner party that's reserved for couples. You see pity in faces that used to be eager or admiring. You can feel your daughters dreading a call for sympathy from fifty miles away.

That's why I was so glad when all this started. I really had begun to think I'd exaggerated the bullying. Then I got his solicitor's letter, accusing me of stealing his grandmother's emerald. He should have known me better. Granny Mansell might have liked carting a vulgar great flashing green square around on her finger, but I never did.

In any case, knowing he set such store by the ring, I handed it to him, along with all the other jewellery, the day I said I couldn't go on. He swore at me and flung the whole lot in his sock drawer. Months later, when he finally agreed to leave, he packed up his stuff and missed the ring. It wasn't my fault. I didn't even know it was there. Lucky I didn't sell the chest of drawers, really. Of course, he had to blame me for what he'd done. As always.

This is better. I'm winning. You see, I have to keep fighting the fool that lives inside me like a parasite, eating up all the rage I need to keep me upright. Sometimes I've lain half-asleep in the early morning and dreamed of how he might come banging on the door, begging to be let back in, apologising for everything he did, telling me he understands at last and wants to make it right. I have to kill those dreams fast.

This genever would probably help stiffen my sinews. I never liked gin in the old days; it was his drink. But here, where you have it neat and cold, it's different. The taste's tangy, with something spicy and something fruity, and the cold burns as it goes down your throat.

Here he is at last. With her. Walking into the café as if he owns it. She is gorgeous. Much prettier than I ever was. And pregnant.

Will he pull out a chair for her and see she's comfortable before he looks around for me? Will he give her the tenderness I once thought he might learn?

"Annie, I've already told you why I don't want you here." His voice is just the same, abrupt but full of fake-patience, and it makes me shudder. "Go to the cafe next door. I'll collect you when I'm done with this."

Her voice is quieter, so I can't hear the protest. But I can see it in all her body language. She's swaying and puts out a hand to touch the wall, as though she needs its solidity to hold her up.

"Oh, for pity's sake!" he shouts and almost pushes her down into a chair. "Waiter! Waiter! Bring her some water. And I'll have… a beer. Any kind."

He throws his gloves on the table in a gesture that's so familiar I'll never scour it from my memory. They fall with the usual slap. And this time one of them slithers to the floor. He looks astonished at its rebellion. Good for the glove!

I feel in my bag for the little wash-leather sack that holds the box containing Granny Mansell's emerald. It's all right; I haven't lost it.

Draining my glass, feeling the genever's burn like a spur, I get to my feet and stride across to them.

"Sarah!" he says in an accusing voice that means: how did you get here first and why have you been spying on me?

I put the wash-leather sack in front of him without a word and notice he rips it open to check I haven't substituted a plastic toy for his precious jewel, and I turn to his wife.

"My friends and sisters think if I'd told him to behave like a civilised human being when we were first married, I could have changed him. I don't know if it's true, and it's too late for me, but you've still got time. Good luck."

I give the waiter some money for my drink and walk out of the cafe. This *is* freedom.

MINDSTALKER

Martin Edwards

Sadie Kyle smiled at the door guard on her way into court, as if to say *Think I look good in black?* The man blushed; for a moment, Breen thought he was going to drop his gun. Sadie had that effect on people. She was the sexiest judge Breen had ever seen. You could imagine her pronouncing the death sentence and making it sound like a tease.

Not that this was a capital case. Four women had died over an eighteen-month span, but even so, the maximum penalty was only 'life meaning life'. Traditionalists said that a civilised society only executed those who threatened the security of the state.

Hannah, he knew, thought differently. She had no time for do-gooders. The prison ships were overflowing, she used to point out, why not dump a few of the bad guys overboard? Breen didn't argue with her: if people profiled as dangerous could be locked up without even committing a crime, how could you justify keeping a convicted murderer alive?

"Didn't take her long," Hannah whispered, her breath warm against his cheek.

Breen wondered if she was jealous of Sadie. The thought hadn't occurred to him before. Perhaps it should have done. They were both young, attractive women, scrambling up the ladder in the fiercely competitive business of criminal justice.

Sadie Kyle was a graduate of the fast-track judicial college at Milton Keynes. These days judges had to keep in close touch with the people: no more room for the greybeards of yore, denying all knowledge of popular culture. Sadie was famed for living hard and playing harder. She might have kicked her coke habit, but last night she'd probably been out at a club until the early hours.

Hannah wasn't a party animal. She was even more focused than Sadie, and that was saying plenty. *Focus*, that was the key to everything, Breen said to himself. Hannah loved the job. For her, it was a turn-on when the media described her as a career cop. "It's all I ever wanted to be," was her regular line. All her life, she'd wanted to front a serial killer inquiry, to be the one who hunted the bastard down. Now her dream had come true.

"She was out for twenty minutes," Breen murmured. "Why waste time?"

A stroke of luck, Breen thought, that this trial had been allocated to Sadie Kyle. It made sense, though: the court executives were no fools, they knew how to respond to public demand. The eyes of the nation were on this court-room and who better to preside than the most telegenic judge of them all? He'd been watching Sadie's video column these past few weeks. Justice delayed was justice denied, that was one of her themes. Judges had targets to meet; they didn't have all day to sit around deliberating. The queue of cases waiting to come to court never seemed to get any shorter. Mercifully, only treason charges led to all the palaver of a jury having to be sworn in. An inefficient hangover from the past, scarcely consistent with the need to safeguard the state from its enemies. The government was talking about reforming the law so that even capital cases could be disposed of more swiftly.

Hannah, Breen knew, yearned for the rules of the game to be modernised. If this case went the way it should, she expected promotion and a transfer to the National Security

Squad. Nothing was worse than bringing a suspect to justice and then waiting for a year only to see the case thrown out on some legal technicality. It didn't happen so much these days, but if even one guilty person went free, that was an affront to civilised values.

Sadie coughed and the courtroom fell quiet. Breen felt his heart skip a beat. What was the verdict going to be? Leave his profile aside and the evidence was thin. She turned to face the man in the dock and shook her head, as if in sorrow.

Breen relaxed. It was going to be all right.

"Taz Parlane, I'll get straight to the point. In my judgment, the evidence against you is overwhelming. I find you guilty on all counts."

Next to him Hannah hissed, "Yes!"

Even before Sadie finished speaking, the noise from the gallery was deafening. Members of the victims' families were shouting. Some punched the air in triumph, others pointed angrily at the man in the dock. A respectable man in a lounge suit ran his finger across his neck in a contemptuous throat-cutting gesture.

Sadie nodded at the security team. The woman in charge lifted her gun and bellowed, "Silence in court! The judge must be heard!"

When the commotion had died down, Sadie said, "I can well understand the feelings of those who have suffered because of your crimes, Taz Parlane. As you are aware, the views of victims' families will be sought in determining the circumstances of your sentence. I leave it to you to deduce their intentions."

Parlane stared at her, sullen, wordless. Breen wondered how heavy the sedation had been. All in a good cause.

"I intend to impose the most severe punishment available

to me. Four sentences of life meaning life under the Truth In Sentencing Act, one term for each of your crimes. You will spend the rest of your days in jail. No remission. My only regret is that at present society fails to acknowledge that, for crimes such as yours, there can be no prospect of rehabilitation and that there is frankly little point in keeping you alive." She glanced around, in the direction of the television cameras. "If I had any influence at all with our rulers, I would urge them to review the penalty in serial killing cases as a matter of urgency."

Hannah and the other detectives sitting further down the bench mimed applause. Sadie caught the gestures, gave a minute nod of approval.

"On you, Taz Parlane, I shall waste no further words. Take him down."

As the big men seized the prisoner and bundled him towards the exit, Breen sensed Hannah's body stiffening beside him. She was excited. Such a result! Tomorrow her name would be all over the net.

More noise, but this time Sadie quietened people herself with a wave of the hand. "Thank you, everyone. This has been a traumatic case, a dreadful experience for everyone – including the judge. I'd just like to thank my staff here for their tremendous support, with a special mention for security – as well-organised as ever. The lawyers have done their job with their customary calm and good humour. The police have been marvellous, as usual, coping with a tremendously difficult investigation and the usual constraints on funding and resources. A special word, though, for Detective Team Leader Hannah Dowe, whose incisive work played such a vital part in bringing the culprit to justice."

Breen squeezed Hannah's hand. "Told you her heart was

in the right place."

Sadie wasn't finished yet. "And I must express particular gratitude to the prosecution's expert witness, Professor Joshua Breen of the University of Plaistow, whose profiling testimony I found so convincing. Well, thank you, everyone. And now, if you'll excuse me, I'll take a short break before the next case begins. We reconvene in half an hour."

As the court rose, Breen and Hannah found themselves mobbed by people pushing cameras and microphones in their faces. Questions fired at them from all quarters.

"Ms Dowe, how do you react to Sadie Kyle's judgment? Why do we need to keep people like Parlane alive?"

"Professor Breen, is it true you've sold the television rights to your notes on the case?"

"A quick word for viewers of Eurocrime, Professor Breen?"

"Is it true, Ms Dowe, that you've been asked to star in a film of your career alongside Robbie Williams?"

All Hannah managed to say was, "Give me a break, he's old enough to be my grandfather," and then the minders from TV Confidential huddled around and swept them off through the back doors of the court complex into a waiting limo.

They were driven off at speed, shielding their faces. It never paid to look as though you courted attention. In the back of the car, Hannah's hand slid along Breen's leg. He watched her Nefertiti profile, felt himself stirring, wanting her. It had been quite a day. Time yet to celebrate.

First stop was TV Confidential's media centre. The journey was a nightmare. Twenty-four hours earlier there had been a suicide bombing in Shoreditch and the roads were still in chaos. A good thing they weren't going out live.

In make-up, they chatted to each other: inconsequential stuff, you could never be sure that the staff wouldn't sell titbits to rival channels and bringing a personal privacy action was such a bore. Breen had been a star for a couple of years now; he was accustomed to attention, to the point of weariness. For Hannah, the spotlight was equally familiar. She'd made her name fighting a harassment case against her old boss. The compensation had been a record sum, enough to buy her an eleven million dollar apartment in Knightsbridge. They would be going back there once the recording was done.

Vicky Singh talked earnestly to camera, telling the story of the killings. Four pretty young women, murdered in their own homes. The throat of each was slashed. No trace of sexual assault in any case, no sign of a forced entry to the buildings, no connecting link between any of the victims.

"For glamorous young detective Hannah Dowe, it was the toughest inquiry she'd ever had to handle. A case that could make her – or break her."

Breen watched Hannah. She was silent, a faraway look in her eyes. He'd come to know her very well these past few months, he could tell that she was rehearsing soundbites in her mind. "Team effort… just a small cog in a very large wheel… dedicated officers… behind the scenes… nothing glamorous… long hours… remembering the victims… focusing on the need for justice."

Disclaimers were a necessary ritual. No one would take any notice of them, no one was meant to. As Vicky said, Hannah, the public face of the inquiry, was young and lovely and that was all that mattered.

The killer, Taz Parlane. A young man who had drifted from job to job. He'd last worked a year ago, serving tables in a cannabis café. People who knew him said he was affable enough. But what could they know of his darker dreams?

"You had little or no forensic evidence against Parlane, did you, Hannah? A hair from the last victim found on his coat, it wasn't very much. The defence lawyers argued the traces could have arisen from contamination by you or your colleagues. Accidental – or deliberate."

Hannah stared, unblinking, at the camera. A style she'd perfected during the course of her personal litigation. She was a formidable witness. Unshakable.

"That was a filthy line in cross-examination. Of course, we're used to attacks on our integrity. Besides, forensic was only one piece in the jigsaw. We had so much more on Taz Parlane."

"Professor Breen's profile of the killer, you mean?"

"It fitted Parlane perfectly. And then there were the brainprints, they corroborated everything the professor said."

"But brainprinting is still controversial."

"I keep saying, Vicky, it's a mistake to confuse brain-printing with the old-style polygraph. This is about more than simple old-fashioned lie-detection. It's about analysing what goes on in the deep recesses of the human mind."

"But the brainprint only records the presence of electrical activity within the suspect's head," Vicky persisted. "Isn't there a danger, if you misread what that activity means?"

Hannah had fended off questioning from the toughest defence lawyers in Britain. She could cope with Vicky Singh.

"We're sensitive to the human rights issues, believe me, every cop is nowadays. We spend half our lives at civil liberties seminars." Her voice became husky. "But what I say is this – let's not forget the human rights of the young women Taz Parlane killed. I'm sorry, I just have to make that point. It's too easy to forget what they went through. What their loved ones are still going through."

"And yet some critics argue that…"

"Remember, the courts have agreed to admit brainprint evidence at long last. They wouldn't do that if they weren't sure it was safe. In some cases, the brainprint is the only thing the police have. Sole witness for the prosecution. But that wasn't the case here."

"Because besides the brainprint – you had Joshua Breen's profile of the culprit?"

"Without it," Hannah said softly, "there's a danger that Parlane would still be free. Free to kill and terrorise."

Vicky started talking about Breen. He struck a modest pose as he listened to her, let her wonderment wash over him. "…brilliant… wayward… not yet thirty… some say a maverick… a wizard, a shaman, a man who hunts through the minds of killers."

"All I do," he said amiably, when his turn came to speak, "is use my imagination. That's the key to understanding criminals, Vicky. Imagination."

She loved that. They always did. Forensics were over-rated. Crime scenes were fine, they bristled with clues. *Every contact leaves a trace* – where did that get you? Each trace was open to interpretation. DNA evidence was all very well. OK, so you could prove it was a billion to one that this dab of saliva or that dollop of semen came from the accused. But how did it get to the crime scene? The media had exposed enough cases of incompetence and corruption to put those who worshipped forensic data on to the defensive. Criminal investigators needed something more than physical stuff. They needed to stalk the culprits, get inside their heads.

"You tracked Parlane, didn't you?" she asked. "You followed his every thought. That's your gift, to fathom the dark side of the human condition."

He gave a shrug, offered a disarming smile. She was quoting directly from his publishers' latest press release. He liked that. "I'm no miracle worker, Vicky. Just a trained psychologist, wanting to do his bit for law and order."

Her smile was coquettishly disbelieving. She wasn't as pretty as Hannah, he thought, or Sadie Kyle come to that. Even so…

She paused, lowered her voice a little. "There's just one thing. People say that there's a personality cult surrounding the new breed of profilers. You're all handsome young men, perhaps the image thing even gets in the way…"

"The work always comes first," he interrupted. "Publicity is only a means to an end. If my appearing on television helps to bring just one killer to book, all the sleepless nights will be worth while."

"Jo Swann, Alex Penberthy, Rachel Davis, Su Baptiste. Four women with everything to live for." Vicky's tone was sombre. "So why did Parlane kill them? You seemed so sure his motivation wasn't sexual."

"As I said in court, he loved the taste of power. Power and control." He leaned forward, warming to his theme, his knees almost touching hers. "He wanted to have their destinies in his hands. On another day, in another mood, who knows? He might have let them live."

Vicky was concentrating on him; her lips were slightly parted. He could tell that she found him attractive. She was supposed to be a tough interrogator, but she was giving him an easy ride. He'd read something about her ending the affair with the network controller who had given her this job. Might as well ask for her contact details when the recording was over. You never knew.

Hannah was becoming impatient, shifting in her seat, glancing at the clock on the studio wall. It was a long time since Vicky had asked her a question.

"At the end of the day," she interrupted, finally, "we're all working together. This isn't about me, or Professor Breen. It's all about a team of committed professionals."

"Of course," Vicky said smoothly.

The look in her eyes said *But none of us truly believes that, do we? My viewers certainly don't. We're all celebrities nowadays. At least we are if we want to have a hope in hell of making something of our lives.*

She didn't put any more questions to Hannah. Five minutes later, the interview was over. At the bar upstairs, he let Vicky flirt with him when Hannah departed to the loo. She gave him her card and suggested he call her.

"Only one thing," she said. "You'll have to promise not to try reading my mind."

"Too late," he said. "I already have."

She laughed and said, "Sadie Kyle took a shine to you, anyone could see it."

"I hope you're not suggesting her judgment was anything other than impartial," he said easily.

"She knows it's all about conviction rates. Meeting government targets, topping the league tables. Judges are no different from cops."

Hannah came back, gave Vicky a sharp look. "We'd better go."

Breen smiled at Vicky, said thanks for everything, and offered his hand. She gripped it tightly, held it a moment too long.

Outside, Hannah said, "She fancies you."

He frowned. "You said that about Sadie Kyle this morning. What is this? You never used to be so – so *paranoid*."

"I'm not. I just don't think you should encourage these women."

"Encourage them? Come on…"

The quarrel spluttered along after they got back to her place. She opened a bottle of Bollinger, but even a couple of glasses weren't enough to make either of them lighten up. The elation of a guilty verdict had never subsided this quickly, he thought. There was no excitement like the excitement of testifying about someone's evil crimes, but already Parlane's conviction was a distant memory.

Hannah was harping on about Sadie Kyle, about the weight she'd put on his profile of the murderer's behaviour. The clues that lay within the culprit's own personality.

"You needed that profile," he said irritably. "Without it, you didn't have a hope of fastening the crimes on Parlane."

"You're forgetting the brainprint."

He shrugged, to show what he thought about brainprints. "Please."

"And we had the hair," she said, her voice rising in anger.

"Yeah, planted on the coat by Rudd or Mettomo or Carter, or one of the other guys who wants to get inside your knickers."

She swore at him, but he wasn't fazed. "You needed the profile," he repeated. "I made this happen for you, Hannah, let's leave it at that, huh?"

Later, in the darkness of her bedroom, he wondered if he'd made a mistake. On balance, he thought not. The Parlane case was a good result. For him as well as for Hannah.

He watched her as she slept. The duvet was on the floor, she was wholly uncovered. Naked and defenceless. Not unlike Su Baptiste, the night she was murdered. Poor Su:

he could imagine, he could precisely imagine, what must have gone through her mind when, the moment she turned her back on him, her killer put the knife to her tender throat. He thought about it often, more often than he should.

Power and control.

He wondered who had killed her. Parlane? Unlikely. Finding a stranger-killer, these days it was like looking for a needle in a haystack. There were thousands of bad men out there, ticking like bombs. So many of them ready to explode.

As he studied the curves of Hannah's body, an idea slid into his mind, wicked and tempting. Risky, so risky, but at least it would give him the fix that he craved.

Savage death of murder cop. He could see the headlines now. Poor Hannah, she made enemies too easily, that was her problem. No shortage of suspects. He'd be distraught, pledged to help find the culprit.

Who would take the rap, though? That was the question. Something to puzzle over, worry at, until he came up with the answer.

His imagination working, he caressed Hannah's warm flesh. A gentle motion, helping his thoughts to focus. He was doing what he loved best. Taking a walk through the mind of a murderer.

THE MAN WITH THE PRAM

Peter Guttridge

Anna can't clear her throat and it's really upsetting her. She tries to cough but the air doesn't leave her lungs. She wonders if she's picked something up from the parakeets. Some kind of bird flu. She's frightened to see them. She doesn't expect to find parakeets nesting in trees on the banks of the River Thames. She doesn't know much about birds – her part of Poland doesn't have a big variety – but she knows parrots belong somewhere tropical. This part of the Thames has many things going for it but tropical climate isn't one of them.

The Man With The Pram tells her about the parakeets. He appears by her side as she sits on the bank of the river. She's reading Jan's copy of Stefan Grabinski's horror stories when she hears the flutter in the tree canopy above her. Green, long-tailed birds dive. She flaps her hands, dropping the book.

Jan is Anna's boyfriend, if a boyfriend is somebody who rams himself into her as she lies, legs awkwardly akimbo, jammed between the toilet and the bath in the mouldy-smelling bathroom of the tiny house. It is hard to find privacy when you live eight to a room.

The middle-aged man is beside her, picking up her book. He hands it to her, glancing at the cover.

"Better than Kafka, I think," he says. "One of my favourite writers – in translation, of course. Finding horror in our quotidian reality."

He plonks down beside her on the bench. She sees a pram parked beside him. "*The African Queen*. Bogart and

Hepburn – simply fabulous. Filmed down the road." He sees her puzzlement. "These parakeets escaped from the film set. They've been breeding ever since. They're more aggressive than our own birds. In consequence they dominate west London."

He reaches behind him and fusses with the baby in the pram for a moment – she hears a little gurgle of pleasure. He shrugs. "That's the story anyway."

She wants to ask him if the baby is his, but she's choking.

"It's important to fit in," he says from far away.

The hairdresser tells her the man's name is Bernard but everyone calls him The Man With The Pram. Her hairdresser is a tiny old man, much the same age as most of his customers. He gives Anna the old person's rate for a trim. He must see she doesn't have much money.

"I'm guessing you don't live in Little Kensington," he says as he drapes a sheet around her and moves her hair out of her eyes. He sees her look. "These streets here, this little enclave, is Little Kensington in estate agent-speak. When I first set up shop here it was just Sheen like the rest of the area. We had proper shops on this lane then – grocer, butcher, fishmonger. Now you can buy expensive drapes and frocks and get your furniture reupholstered, which is lovely. But unless you're a moth you're going to starve to death."

He glances out of his window.

"Morning, Bernard," he calls.

Anna follows his look to see across the road the bald man in his fifties, podgy and stooped, pushing a pram past a French kitchenware shop. The man, presumably because he is intent on his task, doesn't respond. The hairdresser turns.

"One of the few remaining locals. The Man With The

Pram." He resumes his place behind her. "A bald man with dandruff – who says God doesn't have a sense of humour?"

She tries to cough again but it fades somewhere in her chest.

"Pretty much all the locals have moved away now – the place has been going up street by street. There was a problem with the first street to be refurbished. Every house on the terrace knocked through the front room into the living room and the entire street fell down. That's a joke."

Anna is only half-listening because she sees Milla across the street too, coming away from her cleaning job. Wearing Anna's ankle bracelet again. The one with the heart on it. The one Jan gave her.

Anna sees The Man With The Pram in the pub at lunchtime. The river is low and he sets the pram beside one of the tables at the water's edge. He walks slowly up the single flight of stairs to the bar.

"I live the life unlived," he says to Anna. "The other path – the one I might have gone down – I do go down. I live both lives."

She looks at him.

"You'd like your usual?" Sinead, the other barmaid, says.

Anna is distracted by the yummie mummies coming in for lunch. She wonders if they have ever earned their own money. Why does she even wonder? Anna works in a tea shop in the morning then the pub for the rest of the day. She serves the same women in both, sometimes on the same day.

Anna wants babies. That's all she wants. Everything else is secondary. Which fits her perfectly for living in Little Kensington. Little Kensington is a breeding ground. Every single woman of child-bearing age is pregnant or has already borne children. Every woman who comes into the pub is either with child or with children. In Little Kensington's half-dozen streets wealthy executives settle to seed their young wives, most of whom have been their secretaries.

"It's important to fit in," the Man With The Pram says, far away.

But Anna doesn't fit in. She can't afford to live on this side of the railway track. And the botched abortion means she may not be able to have children of her own.

Anna listens to four women lunching on the balcony. Three are pregnant and one has a baby in a buggy. She expects them to be talking about digestion but they seem to discuss babies. Except that when the woman with the baby goes to the toilet she hears one of the remaining women say that their friend has 'issues'.

Anna hears this word often on a lunch-time television programme called *Loose Women*. She assumes it is slang for diarrhoea just as she assumes the title of the programme is something to do with bowel problems.

When Anna arrives in England and knows too little English to do more than night-cleaning offices, she spends hours watching daytime TV hoping to improve her English. And discovers that all the women in the daytime adverts talk about is digestion and bowels.

Constipation or diarrhoea seem to be the only options for women. There is something called a slow digestive tract, something else called *bifida activa regulari*. There's a lot of talk about pro-biotics. A lot of women feel sluggish. Or bloated.

"Do you want to go out tonight?"

"I'm not in the mood. I feel bloated."

Anna worries that she might catch a short-tempered bowel if she eats what English women eat.

She still can't cough. Can't remember what coughing is.

Anna is tall and slender with long blonde hair. Czeslaw says she would be beautiful if she were less morose. The film on the television is *Invasion of The Body Snatchers* and is about these things from outer space who come to earth and replace humans with people grown in pods. A seventies remake of a fifties Cold War classic, Czeslaw says. It is a metaphor for Western capitalist society.

"It's a metaphor for communist society," Stefan says irritably, "where everybody must conform."

"It's about communism *and* the West," Jan says, clearly peeved that Czeslaw is flirting with Anna. "But it's not a metaphor – it's *cinema verité*." Jan comes from the same town as Kieslowski, Poland's greatest film director, and claims to have got drunk on vodka with him more than once. He is obsessed with *A Short Film About Killing*, in which an alienated young man murders a taxi driver. "Have you seen the people on the other side of the track." He turns to Anna, who is absently kneading her stomach. "They're pod people, aren't they, Anna?" Then he tries to put his hand up her skirt. Czeslaw smirks.

Jan wants to be a writer but in the absence of any detectable talent he's a hod-carrier and general labourer on house refurbishments in the streets of Little Kensington.

He leaves for work in the morning with Milla, who cleans in the same streets. At home, in her short skirts, she flirts with Jan. She waves her leg in front of him to show him Anna's ankle bracelet with the heart on it and laughs when she sees he is looking up her skirt instead.

"I got a new watch," Jan says. He is going back to Poland with a lot of money. Anna and Jan only have sex once. He promises to pull out. It doesn't matter. The botched abortion changes a lot of things for her.

107

Milla coos over the watch, giving him the eye. He waves it in front of Anna. One half of the round face is black, the other white. There is no indication of hours, minutes or seconds. She looks at the watch and at him.

"Day and night watch. A new way of measuring time. It splits the universe in two, into opposites."

Anna frowns.

"What time is it now?" Milla says.

He almost sneers.

"Anyone can buy a watch that shows the time. You need to be pretty discerning to buy one that doesn't."

Anna looks at him a long moment. He is as mad as Stefan Grabinski.

Nothing in England makes sense to her, although she worries that is a sign of her own alienation. The women in Little Kensington remind Anna of another film she has seen. Another remake according to Czeslaw, another piece of *cinema-verité* according to Jan. In it Nicole Kidman lives in an American community called Stepford, full of pregnant women.

When Anna goes door-to-door looking for cleaning work a number of the Little Kensington women are rude. She is puzzled by their rudeness until one of them says:

"I know you Russian girls with your blonde hair and your legs up to your ears have come to Britain to snag wealthy husbands but you're not snagging mine."

She wants to knead her stomach but she must clear her throat.

The river rises and the Man with The Pram brings his baby inside the pub, parking his pram by a table on the balcony. He coos into the pram, from which issue gurgles and cries. He comes to the bar to order another drink.

"Don't you think Sleeping Beauty would have terrible

breath after all those years? Not much fun for the Prince kissing her."

Anna looks at him.

"Probably dying for a pee too."

Her hair is in her eyes. She can scarcely see through it.

At seven in the morning Anna stands in front of the railway crossing barrier waiting for the train to go by. On her way to her new cleaning job. Jan goes to Poland and, Czeslaw believes, Milla goes with him, taking Anna's ankle bracelet. Czeslaw suggests Anna takes over Milla's cleaning job in Little Kensington.

Her hairdresser stands with a little dog on a lead some yards away. Beyond him a nervous rider is sitting astride a big horse skittish at being held at the crossing, eyeing the dog uneasily.

Anna hears the roar of the car approaching the bend behind her too quickly, then the screech of its brakes as the driver sees that the railway barrier is down. There is the whine of a higher-pitched engine too. She turns in time to see the car buck to a halt and watches as the motorcyclist too close behind goes into its rear.

The biker is thrown over the handlebars and lands beside her hairdresser with the dog. The dog, yapping, lunges. The horse, startled by the screech of the car, the motorcyclist hurtling from his bike and the yapping dog, rears up. Its rider falls gracelessly into the large hawthorn beside the crossing.

"Bloody hell," her hairdresser says, dragging his dog back from the cyclist.

The train trundles by.

The horse, whinnying, backs up against a parked car, its hooves slithering on the smooth tarmac. The old man is trying to get to the rider in the bush but his dog is running round his legs straining at its leash.

The old man disentangles himself and loops the leash over the crossing barrier. As he heads for the rider, flailing in the bush, a bell rings. Anna is looking at the dog attached by the leash to the barrier as the barrier begins to rise.

She is squinting through the curtain of her hair at something swaying above her. The sky.

She is late for work because of the kerfuffle over the dog hanging from the crossing bar and the riderless horse careening down on to the south circular. She hurries past the big cars hitched up on the kerb and rings the doorbell.

"There's a disgusting smell coming from next door's back garden," her new employer says. "Go and find out what it is, will you?"

The Man With The Pram lives next door. Jan is doing work for him before he returns to Poland. Milla cleans his house. Says there is no wife.

Anna knocks on the Man With The Pram's door. It opens so abruptly she thinks he must have been waiting behind it. She steps back in surprise.

"Go through, go through," he says, ushering her into the kitchen. He gestures at the garden beyond the open French windows. She walks into a slash of sunshine. The rest of the garden is shadowed by tall trees and thick hedges.

"Our secret garden," he says. "We're overlooked on every side but no one can see us."

He is behind her. She can smell him. Not sweet exactly. Sickly. Something old and fusty, if she'd known that word in English.

Then she smells something else. The thing in the garden. She knows the phrase 'the smell of decay' but that always sounds dessicated, dry, sandy. This is slimy, gaseous. She puts her hand over her nose.

"I don't really smell it," he says, standing beside her now. He points to a humped pile of leaves beneath a hawthorn. She can see something brown and furry poking out from the leaves. "The heat of the compost will rot it down quickly enough."

She looks at him, uncomprehending.

"It's a fox. Crawled in here to die. Probably hit by a car. The heat of the compost will rot it down quickly. I'm expecting good rhubarb when it's done." He has yellow teeth when he smiles. "If I were Damian Hirst people would pay a fortune to see it."

She hears the sound of a phone ringing back in the house.

"Excuse me," he says.

His pram is in the garden just a few yards from the pile of leaves covering the dead fox. She thinks of the poor baby assailed by that horrible smell. As if her thought triggers it, the baby begins to squawl.

She looks back into the house but can't see him. She moves cautiously over to the pram. Looks down. The baby's face is contorted as it emits cries but the rest of it doesn't move beneath its blanket. She reaches down to stroke its face. Its rubbery face.

She jerks her hand away and as she does so sets swaying a silver chain dangling from the hood of the pram. As she is trying to process the fact that the baby in the pram is a prosthetic one, she is also thinking that the glittering thing is an ankle bracelet with a heart on it. She steps towards the mound of leaves, looks back at the dangling thing and sighs when she realises it isn't her ankle bracelet.

An arm comes round her throat and on the scrawny wrist she sees a watch, its round face half white and half black.

"It's important to fit in," a voice says into her ear. She feels something sharp at her throat. She tries to cough.

She is lying with the curtain of hair over her eyes. The river is flooding: she is wet. Is this an asthma attack? She hates that she can't get her breath. She hates that she is in a constant present with no past.

And no future.

THE OCTOPUS NEST

Sophie Hannah

It was the sight I had hoped never to see: the front door wide open, Becky, our babysitter, leaning out into the darkness as if straining to break free of the doorway's bright rectangle, her eyes wide with urgency. When she saw our car she ran out into the drive, then stopped suddenly, arms at her sides, looking at the pavement. Wondering what she would say to us, how she would say it.

I assured myself that it couldn't be a real emergency; she'd have rung me on my mobile phone if it were. Then I realised I'd forgotten to switch it on as we left the cinema. Timothy and I had been too busy having a silly argument about the movie. He had claimed that the FBI must have known about the people in the woods, that it must have been a government relocation programme for victims of crime. I'd said there was nothing in the film to suggest that, that he'd plucked the hypothesis out of nowhere. He insisted he was right. Sometimes Timothy latches on to an idea and won't let go.

"Oh, no," he said now. I tasted a dry sourness in my mouth. Becky shivered beside the garage, her arms folded, her face so twisted with concern that I couldn't look at her. Instead, as we slowed to a halt, I focused on the huddle of bins on the corner of the pavement. They looked like a gang of squat conspirators.

Before Timothy had pulled up the handbrake, I was out of the car. "What is it?" I demanded. "Is it Alex?"

"No, he's asleep. He's absolutely fine." Becky put her hands on my arms, steadying me.

I slumped. "Thank God. Then... has something else happened?"

"I don't know. I think so. There's something you need to have a look at."

I was thinking, as Timothy and I followed her into the house, that nothing else mattered if Alex was safe. I wanted to run upstairs and kiss his sleeping face, watch the rhythmic rise and fall of his Thomas the Tank Engine duvet, but I sensed that whatever Becky wanted us to see couldn't wait. She had not said, "Don't worry, it's nothing serious." She did not think it was nothing.

All our photograph albums were on the floor in the lounge, some open, most closed. I frowned, puzzled. Becky was tidier than we were. In all the years she had babysat for us, we had not once returned to find anything out of place. Tonight, we had left one photo album, the current one, on the coffee table so that she could look at our holiday pictures. Why had she thrown it and all the others on the carpet?

She sank to the floor, crossing her legs. "Look at this." Timothy and I crouched down beside her. She pointed to a picture of Alex and me, having breakfast on our hotel terrace in Cyprus. Crumbs from our bread rolls speckled the blue tablecloth. We were both smiling, on the verge of laughing, as Timothy took the photograph.

"What about it?" I said.

"Look at the table behind you. Where the blonde woman's sitting."

I looked. She was in profile, her hair up in a ponytail. She wore a sea-green shirt with the collar turned up. Her forehead was pink, as if she'd caught the sun the day before. Her hand, holding a small, white cup, was raised, halfway between the table and her mouth. "Do you know her?"

asked Becky, looking at Timothy, then at me.

"No."

"No."

She turned a page in the album and pointed to another photograph, of Timothy reading *Ulysses* on a sun-lounger beside the pool. "Can't you read John Grisham like everybody else?" I'd said to him. "We're supposed to be on holiday." In the pool, the same blonde woman from the previous photograph stood in the shallow end, her hands behind her head. I guessed that she was adjusting her ponytail before beginning her swim. She wore a one-piece swimsuit the colour of cantaloupe melon.

"There she is again," said Becky. "You didn't talk to her at all, in the hotel?"

"No."

"Didn't even notice her," said Timothy. "What's this about, Becky? She's just another guest. What's the big deal?"

Becky sighed heavily, as if, by answering as we had, we'd confirmed her worst fears. I began to feel frightened, as if something unimaginably dreadful was on its way. "She doesn't look familiar?"

"No," said Timothy impatiently. "Should she?"

Becky closed the album, reached for another one. This was one of our earliest, from before Alex was born. She flipped a few pages. Cambridge. Me, Timothy and my brother Richard outside King's College, sitting on a wall. I was eating an ice-cream. The day had been oven-hot. "Sitting next to you, Claire," said Becky. "It's the same person."

I looked at the blonde head. This woman – I was sure Becky was wrong, she couldn't be the same one – was turned away from the camera towards her bespectacled friend, whose face was animated. They looked as if they were having a lively conversation, utterly unaware of our presence. "You don't know that," I said. "All you can see is her hair."

"Look at the freckles on her shoulder and arm. And her earring. She's wearing the same ones in Cyprus – gold rings that are sort of square. Not very common."

I was beginning to feel a creeping unease, or I might have pointed out that rings could not be square. "It's a coincidence," I said. "There must be more than one blonde woman with freckly arms who has earrings like that."

"Or it's the same woman, and she happened to be in Cambridge and then Cyprus at the same time as us," said Timothy. "Though I'm inclined to agree with Claire. It must be a different woman."

Becky was shaking her head as he spoke. "It isn't," she said. "When I looked at the Cyprus photos I noticed her. I thought I'd seen her somewhere before, but I couldn't place her. I puzzled over it for ages. Then later, when I was standing by the shelves choosing a DVD, I noticed the picture in the frame."

All our eyes slid towards it. It had been taken by a stranger so that all three of us could be in it: Timothy, Alex and me. We were in the grounds of a country house hotel just outside Edinburgh. It was the week of the book festival. Many of our trips over the years had revolved around Timothy buying books. Behind us were two large sash windows that belonged to the hotel's dining room. Clearly visible at one of them was the blonde woman from the Cyprus photographs. She was wearing a blue shirt this time, again with the collar turned up. Her face was small, but it was unmistakeably her. And the earrings were the same, the square hoops. I felt dizzy. This had to mean something. My brain wouldn't work quickly enough.

"That's why she looked familiar," said Becky. "I've seen that photo millions of times. I see it every time I come here. Alex is just a baby in it and… I thought it was an amazing coincidence, that the same woman was wherever you were in this picture four years ago and also in Cyprus this summer. It seemed too strange. So I got the other albums out and had a look. I couldn't believe it. In each one, she's in at least nine or ten of the photos. See for yourselves."

"Jesus." Timothy rubbed the sides of his face. When he removed his hands there were white spots on his skin. I began to turn the pages of another album. I saw the woman, once, twice. In Siena, at a taverna. Walking behind me in a street market in Morocco. Three times. She stood beside Timothy outside the Tate Modern, again with her short-sighted, frizzy-haired friend.

"But… this *can't* be a coincidence!" I said, expecting to have to convince Becky, or Timothy. Nobody disagreed with me. I felt sharp, piercing fear.

"What does it mean?" Timothy asked Becky. He rarely asked anybody for advice or an opinion, let alone a nineteen-year-old babysitter. His lips were thin and pale. "She must be following us. She's some sort of stalker. But… for nearly ten years! I don't like this at all. I'm ringing the police."

"They'll think you're crazy," I said, desperate to behave as if there was no need to take the matter seriously. "She's never done us any harm, never even drawn herself to our attention. She's not looking at us in any of the photos. She doesn't seem aware of our presence at all."

"Of course not!" Timothy snorted dismissively. "She'd try to look as innocent as possible as soon as she saw a camera coming out, wouldn't she? That's why we've not spotted her until now."

I turned to Becky. "Is every album the same?" I didn't

have the courage to look.

She nodded. "Some, she's on nearly every page."

"Oh, God! What should we do? Why would someone we don't know want to follow us?"

"Timothy's right, you've got to tell the police," said Becky. "If something happens…"

"Christ!" Timothy marched up and down the lounge, shaking his head. "I don't need this," he said. "I really don't."

"Tim, are you *sure* you don't know her?" An affair, I was thinking. A jealous ex-girlfriend. I would almost have preferred that; at least there would have been a rational explanation, a clarifying link.

"Of course I'm sure!"

"Do you want me to stay?" asked Becky. What she meant was that she was keen to leave.

"She's not some woman I've slept with and discarded, if that's what you're thinking," Timothy snapped.

"You have to tell me if she is," I said. Neither of us cared that Becky was listening.

"Have I ever done anything like that?"

"Not that I know of."

"Claire, I swear on Alex's life: not only have I never slept with this woman, I've never even *spoken* to her."

I believed him. Alex was sacred.

"I should go," said Becky. Our eyes begged her not to. She was a symbol of safety, the only one of the three of us who was not dogged by a stalker. We needed her normality to sustain us. I had never been so frightened in my life.

"I'll drive you," said Timothy.

"No!" I didn't want to be left alone with the photo albums. "Would you mind if we phoned you a cab?"

"Of course not."

"I said I'll drive her!"

"But I don't want you to go out!"

"Well, I want to get out. I need some air."

"What about me?"

"I'll be back in half an hour, Claire. Why don't you ring the police while I'm gone? Then we can talk to them when I get back."

"I can't." I began to cry. "You'll have to do it. I'm in no fit state."

He frowned. "All right. Look, don't worry. I won't be long."

Once he and Becky had left, I went upstairs and looked in on Alex. He was sleeping soundly, his hair covering his face. Despite my pleas, I found that I felt less afraid once Timothy had gone. I thought of one of our honeymoon photographs, one that could not possibly contain the blonde woman: Timothy in our en-suite bathroom at the Grand Hotel Tremezzo. He insisted on lavish holidays. Perhaps that was why we were always short of money. That and his book-collecting.

In the picture, there is a mirror in front of him and one behind, reflecting an endless row of Timothies, each smaller than the last, each holding the camera to his eye, pressing the button. They dotted an invisible line that led from the foreground to the background. I knew why the picture had sprung to mind. It was the principle of magnification: seeing my own panic reflected in Timothy's eyes had added to my paranoia.

I went downstairs and began to look through all our photographs. This time I was methodical, unsuperstitious. I found the blonde woman with the upturned collars and the square hoop earrings again and again: on a boat, in a park, walking along a canal tow-path. Sometimes she was right behind us, sometimes nearby. Who was she?

Why was she following us? I had no way of knowing. Neither would the police, not with only our photo albums to work from. Of course, they could track her down if they wanted to – they could appeal on television and somebody who knew her would be bound to come forward – but the idea of them doing such a thing was laughable. She had committed no crime. Stalking was against the law, I was fairly certain of that, but the direct accosting of one's prey was surely a prerequisite. What, I wondered, would the police have to say about a stalker so unobtrusive that, were it not for Becky's meticulous eye, we might never have become aware of her? Her presence in our lives, unnoticed for all these years, felt more ghostly than criminal. I was suddenly very aware of myself, my thoughts and my actions, and looked around the room, up at the ceiling, half expecting to find someone watching me.

I concentrated on the woman's face, trying to see a character or a motive behind it. She was either beautiful in a classical, well-proportioned way, or very bland-looking; I couldn't decide. I found it unsettling that, however hard I stared, I couldn't commit her face to memory; it was almost impossible to take in as a coherent whole. I looked at her features one by one and judged each of them regular, flaw-less, but together they made no lasting impression. I'd had this feeling before, usually about famous people. Sharon Stone, the late Jill Dando. They too had faces one could study in detail and still not know what they looked like.

In one photograph our blonde ghost was touching me. Her shoulder was pressed against mine in a crowded wine bar. Hay-on-Wye? No, Cheltenham. Another of Timothy's literary holidays. I was holding a tall cocktail, dark red and fizzy, like carbonated blood. I pointed to it, an apprehensive expression on my face. Timothy had labelled the photo 'Am I really expected to drink this?' He assigned titles to all our pictures; his parents did it too. It was a Treharne family tradition.

The blonde woman had a book in her hand. It was on the edge of the picture, some of it missing. I screwed up my eyes to read the title. *The Octopus* – that was all that was visible. My heart jolted. "*The Octopus Nest*," I whispered. It was a novel I hadn't thought about for years. Timothy used to own it, probably still did. He'd tried to persuade me to read it, but I gave up. Sometimes it is apparent from the first page of a book that nothing is going to happen. A Timothy book.

I slammed the photo album shut and rang his mobile phone. It was switched off. I paced up and down the lounge, desperate to talk to somebody. I nearly rang Becky's mobile, but I didn't want her to make excuses when I asked her to babysit in the future. If I started to talk to her about obscure novels with strange titles, she'd think I was insane. Timothy had said he'd be back within half an hour. This could wait half an hour.

I forced myself to calm down, sit down, and think about how I was feeling. Was this surge of adrenalin justified? Seven years ago, the blonde woman had been in a wine bar, holding a novel that Timothy once raved about. It was a link, but then, I reminded myself, I did not need to look for a link. A woman we didn't know was in the backgrounds of dozens of our photographs; wasn't that connection enough?

Still, I was too agitated to do nothing. I searched all the bookshelves in our house. There was no copy of *The Octopus Nest*. I tried Timothy's phone again, swearing under my breath, furious with impatience. How could he not have remembered to switch it on? He knew what a state I was in. Irrationally, I took it as an omen that it would take him much longer to return, that he might never come back. I needed to occupy myself, to drive away these groundless fears. That was when I thought of the internet.

I rushed to Timothy's study and switched on the computer, certain that Amazon would have *The Octopus Nest* listed. I wanted to know who it was by, what it was about. It might lead nowhere, but it was the only thing I had to go on. In none of the other photographs did our ghost have any identifiable accessories.

The Octopus Nest was available from Amazon, but not easily. Delivery might take up to six weeks, I read. This didn't matter to me. I didn't necessarily want a copy of the book. I just wanted to know more about it. The author was a K V Hammond. I clicked on the small picture of the novel's cover, a white background with one black tentacle running diagonally across it.

The book was number 756,234 in the Amazon chart. If Timothy and the blonde woman hadn't bought it all those years ago it would probably have been number 987,659, I thought, half-smiling. I was surprised I was able to joke, even inside my head. Somehow our ghost didn't seem quite so threatening, now that I had seen her holding a book that Timothy had once thought highly of, though I didn't understand why this should be the case. The optimist in me reasoned that she hadn't done us any harm in nearly a decade. Maybe she never would.

No description of the novel was offered. I had bought books from Amazon before, and there was usually a short synopsis. I clicked on the Google button and typed "K V Hammond" into the search box. The first result was the author's own website. Perhaps here I would discover more about *The Octopus Nest*. I drummed my fingers on the desk, impatient for the home page to load.

A photograph began to appear on the screen, from the top down. A blue sky, a tree, a straw hat. Blonde hair. Gold, square hoop earrings. I gasped, pushing my chair away from the computer. It was her. A letter welcomed me to her site, signed 'Kathryn'. Only minutes ago it had seemed out of the question that we would ever know her identity. Now I knew it beyond the slightest doubt.

I tried Timothy's mobile again, with no luck. "Please, please," I muttered, even though no one could hear me, even though a mechanical voice was already telling me to try again later. I felt as if Timothy had let me down badly, deserted me, though I knew he was probably too preoccupied to think about a detail such as whether his phone was on or off. He would be back soon, in any case.

Fear and excitement rioted in my mind, my whole body. I had to do something. Now that I was in possession of certain knowledge, calling the police did not seem such an absurd proposition. I didn't want to go into the whole story on the phone, so I said only that I wanted to report a stalker, that I knew who it was, that I had evidence. The woman I spoke to said she would send an officer to interview me as soon as possible.

Willing the computer to work faster, I moved from one section of Kathryn Hammond's website to another. She had published no books since *The Octopus Nest*, but her newsletter said she was working on her next novel, the story of fifty years in the life of a ventriloquist's dummy, passed from one owner to another. Another Timothy book, I thought. The newsletter also informed fans (it seemed to take for granted that everyone who visited the site would be a fan) that Kathryn and her sister – the frizzy-haired woman, I assumed – were going on holiday to Sicily early next year.

For a second, I felt as if my blood had stopped moving around my body. We were going to Sicily too. In February. Kathryn Hammond and her sister were staying at the Hotel Bernabei. I had a horrible suspicion we were too. My terror returned, twice as strong as before. This was as real, as inexplicable as ever.

I rummaged through the drawers of the desk, thinking I might find a letter from Timothy's travel agent or a booking confirmation. There was nothing. I flew round the house like a trapped fly, opening drawers and pulling books off shelves. I couldn't understand it; there had to be some paperwork somewhere relating to our holiday.

I was crying, about to give up, when it occurred to me that Timothy kept a filing cabinet in the garage. "Why not?" he'd said. "The thing's hideous and the house is too cluttered." I rarely went into the garage. It was dusty and messy, and smelled of damp, turpentine and cigarettes; since Alex was born, Timothy hadn't smoked in the house.

I had no choice but to go in there now. If the police arrived before Timothy got back, I wanted to be able to show them our holiday details and Kathryn Hammond's website. What more proof could they ask for? Even as I thought this, I was aware that it was not illegal for a novelist to go on holiday to Sicily. Terror gripped me as it occurred to me for the first time that perhaps we would never be able to stop her following us, never force her to admit to her behaviour or explain it. I didn't think I'd be able to stand that.

The cabinet wasn't locked. I pulled open the first drawer. A strangled moan escaped from my mouth as I stared, stunned, at what was inside. Books. Dozens of them. I saw the title *The Octopus Nest*. Then, underneath it, *Le Nid du Poulpe*. The same title, but in French. Numb with dread, I pulled the books out one by one, dropping them on the

124

floor. I saw Hebrew letters, Japanese characters, a picture of a purple octopus, a green one, a raised black one that looked as if it might spin off the cover and hit me in the chest.

Kathryn Hammond's novel had been translated into many languages. I pulled open the next drawer down. More copies of *The Octopus Nest* – hardbacks, paperbacks, hardback-sized paperbacks, book club editions.

"Fifty-two in total."

I screamed, nearly lost my balance. Timothy stood in the doorway of the garage. "Timothy, what…?"

He stared blankly at me for several seconds, saying nothing. I backed away from him until I was against the wall. I felt its rough texture through my blouse, scratching my skin.

"I was telling the truth," he said. "I've never spoken to her. I don't know her at all. She doesn't even know I exist."

The doorbell rang. The police. I'd said only that I wanted to report a stalker, that I knew who it was, that I had evidence.

THE VICAR OF CLOPWOLDE'S DAUGHTER

Kaye C Hill

"I *knew* this was a mistake."

Detective Inspector Milo jumped down from the five-bar gate with a thud.

"But I'm sure the footpath back to Clopwolde is meant to be over a stile in the corner of this field." Lexy Lomax, her heart sinking, squinted through the gathering gloom.

"Yeah? Well – I don't know how to break this to you, Lomax, but there is no stile. Also, this field is strictly private, according to that sign on the gate. We shouldn't even be in it."

Lexy rolled her eyes. She'd met Milo a couple of months ago, just after her move to the Suffolk coast. He'd already cautioned her twice, both times on points of the law that she felt were open to interpretation, particularly if one happened to be a private investigator. However, these mis-understandings aside, the tetchy cop had proved himself to be a formidable ally in the pursuit of justice. He and Lexy were even starting to forge a friendship of sorts, which had prompted her to suggest this countryside walk. Although, given her sense of direction, perhaps an evening down the local pub would have been a better idea.

A shrill bark broke into her thoughts.

"Sorry, Kinky." Lexy clicked her fingers and a caramel-coloured chihuahua squeezed under the gate, glaring up at her in the manner of a footsore dog who wants it all to stop now.

"It's not like there's anyone here," Lexy ventured. "Let's just go and have a quick look. We might hit on the footpath."

"No way."

She walked further into the field, ignoring Milo's exclamation of annoyance.

There was a dip in the centre, and within that an unexpected sight.

"Hey – what do you think these are?"

"I didn't think Suffolk had any standing stones." Milo materialised beside her.

"They're not ancient ones. Too neat and sculpted. Let's have a closer..."

"Shut up." The policeman suddenly grabbed Lexy and, to her astonishment, yanked her down on top of him behind a nearby thicket of broom.

"Milo, what the hell are you...?" She was half indignant, half laughing.

"Something weird's going on at those stones," he whispered. "Where's the dog?"

"Er... he's over..." Lexy had to shake her confusion away. Milo put out a long arm and grasped the affronted chihuahua. "Don't let him bark."

Above his whisper Lexy could hear chanting. They instinctively squirmed further into the thicket.

A procession of silhouetted people had arrived at the stones, holding flaming torches that seemed to bring the night with them. Long cloaks swirled, and the chanting grew louder.

After a moment of intent listening, Lexy relaxed. "It's OK. Only a coven of witches."

Milo jerked round to face her. "And that's all right, is it?"

"They're not doing any harm. Just worshipping the harvest."

"How do you know?"

"You meet a lot of people when you're on the road, Milo.

I can spot a pagan at ten paces."

"Oh. Right."

Lexy had hinted to Milo that she'd had an unorthodox upbringing, but she didn't talk about it much. Just a nugget every now and again.

The members of the coven, six men and six women, each aligned themselves to a standing stone. A seventh woman was left alone in the centre. She raised an object in her hand.

"Bodhran," whispered Lexy.

"Pardon?"

"Celtic drum. It's played with a double-ended beater."

An eerie hollow tattoo illustrated her point.

"They're not going to sacrifice a sodding goat are they?"

" 'Course they're not."

A command went up.

"So what's that mean?"

Lexy paused. "They're going sky-clad."

"Eh?"

Thirteen cloaks were stripped off.

"That."

Lexy felt the heat of Milo's embarrassment. She grinned to herself.

Squashed between them, Kinky struggled crossly, and she gripped his collar. She didn't like to think of the mayhem an irritable chihuahua might inflict on six naked men.

Hands joined, the acolytes danced around the stones. It was oddly moving, Lexy thought, seeing them so happy and artless in their natural state. Milo, she noticed, had his eyes trained on the High Priestess, the girl in the centre. You couldn't blame the man. She was as delicate as a wood nymph, with a swirl of raven-black curls, in which glinted a silver crescent moon.

"'Strewth," he whispered.

"Yeah, all right," Lexy growled.

He turned to her, eyes gleaming in the dark. "But you know who that is, don't you? It's Verity Perkins. The vicar of Clopwolde's daughter."

"No kidding! How do you know her?"

"We sing together in the church choir. Only she doesn't look like that on Sunday mornings."

Lexy shook her head in wonderment. Church choir on Sundays? Milo had more hidden depths than the Grand Canyon.

They watched in spellbound silence until, ritual over, the party put on their cloaks, took up their smoking torches, and slowly drifted towards the gate.

Self-conscious now, Lexy rolled away from the policeman's warm side. "OK. Show over. Time for the long, dark walk home."

"Let's follow them." Milo pushed his way out of the thicket, crouching low.

"Very funny."

"Trust me." He turned an unexpected crocodile smile on her.

Hissing protests, Lexy followed him across the field, a disgruntled chihuahua bringing up the rear. Hidden in shadows, they watched the worshippers pull on civvies and bundle up their robes. Ten of them rode off on cycles, lights bobbing along the lane. Two men, two cars and one girl remained.

Verity Perkins got into the passenger seat of a green Saab, clutching her robes. An athletic-looking lad swung in beside her, and without further ado they drove off.

The remaining man, a slight, bearded character, watched until the Saab rounded a bend, then patted his pockets.

There was a click, and the tip of a cigarette glowed.

Milo stepped from his hiding place, ushering Lexy with him. "Evening, Hal."

The acolyte peered intently through the night. "Inspector Milo? What brings you out here?" He seemed more amused than surprised.

"I've been out walking with a friend, and we've... lost our way."

"Tried asking a policeman?"

"Hilarious. Can you give us a lift back to Clopwolde?"

"Sure. Hop in."

"Thanks. This is Hal Pagham, by the way," Milo explained to Lexy. "Owns one of the second-hand bookshops in Clopwolde."

"Lucky we ran into you here," Lexy remarked.

"You certainly were." Hal dropped his cigarette and ground it out with a heel. "I was on my way home. Came the back way. Stopped here to check my messages."

Lexy caught Milo's eye. Lying toad.

Hal held the back door open for Lexy. "Just shove those books out of the way."

Lexy slid in, and extricated a heavy tome from under her, glancing at the title with a shrug. She opened it at the flyleaf.

'To my very own HP,' was written in precise, curly writing.

Someone must love him then.

The phone call came at eight o'clock the following morning.

"I need your help." It was a woman's voice. "My daughter didn't return home last night."

Lexy pushed open the window, letting in a salty blast straight off the North Sea. "Have you told the police?"

"No." There was a pause. "Not yet. She's nearly eighteen,

131

Ms Lomax."

"What time were you expecting her?"

"She said midnight."

"And you've tried calling her?"

"Her mobile's been switched off since last night."

"What's her name?"

"Verity. Verity Perkins."

Lexy's eyes snapped open like briefcase catches.

"Can I come and see you, Mrs Perkins?"

St Ethelred's was a large Norman church with all the works. Flying buttresses, gargoyles, iron-studded doors, lichen-encrusted gravestones. Rumour was it even had a congregation.

The vicarage was next door. Lexy was attaching Kinky's lead to an iron boot scraper outside when Cora Perkins opened the door.

She was a slim, lugubrious woman with anxious dark eyes and greying but rebellious curls. Verity was certainly her mother's daughter.

"It's all right – bring him up. We love dogs. Sadly, Verity's allergic, so we can't keep one."

Cora showed her to an upstairs study that overlooked the church yard.

"Robin will be here any minute," she said. "He's worried sick." She glanced out of the window at the silent rows of gravestones.

Lexy was struck by a sudden, morbid curiosity at what life must be like in the vicarage, surrounded by constant reminders of mortality.

As if she had read her thoughts, Cora gave a wry smile. "I get a grandstand view for weddings. I do love a white wedding."

She was keeping her spirits up. That was fortunate, bearing in mind what Lexy was about to tell her. Just needed to find the right moment.

"So – Verity?"

"She was out at a… rehearsal last night," Cora said. Her eyes slid away from Lexy's. "She's a musician in a little folk band."

She's more than that, love.

"She said her boyfriend, James Healey, would drop her back here at midnight, as usual. I heard a car pull up just after twelve and I went to the front door to meet her, but… no one there." Cora twisted her plain gold wedding ring. "I became apprehensive, and I started to look up and down the lane.

"By then, my husband had come back from locking up the church, which he does last thing every night. We spent the next hour waiting in the lane. But she didn't come. Robin stayed out looking for the rest of the night. I waited here in case she rang."

"Weren't you able to contact James and check with him?"

"No – although he's been taking Verity to these… music evenings every fortnight for a couple of months now, we realised last night that we have no idea where he lives. And we assume that all the contact numbers for him are in Verity's mobile telephone. I told you earlier, it appears to have been switched off, although I've been trying it every half-hour."

Kinky gave a sudden soft bark, and moments later the vicar swept in, clad in frowning black robes. He had a chafed, raw-looking face, although that wasn't unusual around those parts – the wind cutting across Clopwolde Bay could sand-blast a rhinoceros.

He took in Lexy, introducing himself with a single nod, then he noticed Kinky and softened. "Hello, boy. What a lovely little fellow you are."

Cora cleared her throat, and the vicar turned hastily back to Lexy.

"I know it's not usual for the parents of a missing teenager to hire a private investigator before… er… alerting anyone else. But my wife and I know who she's with, and, frankly, we're very keen to avoid any scandal. Very keen indeed. If Verity and the boy in question could just be located and my daughter returned home as discreetly as possible, we really would be most immensely grateful."

He clasped his hands under his chin in an unconscious parody of prayer.

"I should be able to track her down," said Lexy, carefully. "Bringing her back could be more of a problem, though, if she doesn't want to come."

"Just do what you can." His gaze flicked back to Kinky.

"And if I don't find her by this evening?"

"We'll have to call the police." It was Cora Perkins who spoke this time.

Hal Pagham's bookshop was called *Occult Leanings*. He was arranging a display of books in the window when Lexy arrived. In daylight, he was all hazel eyes and curly hair, with a bearded, Pan-like face. He wore a blue t-shirt with a zodiac symbol on it. Pisces the Fish. Suited him – slippery customer.

"Hello," said Lexy. "Remember me?"

He slid her an appraising look. "Of course. What can I do you for? *Arcane Mysteries Unravelled*?" He waved a book languidly at her.

"You could help me with a more up-to-date mystery.

It concerns your little gathering last night."

Unexpectedly, he grinned. "Thought you might have seen us in action. Bet that shocked Milo to his divisional blue core. Who are you, anyway? Other than being an unlikely police sympathiser?" His tone was mischievous rather than malicious. "That field is privately owned by the Forrington Coven, you know. We put those stones up ourselves. They're made of resin, of course."

"And there's me thinking we'd discovered the Stonehenge of Suffolk. I'm a friend of Verity's, Hal. Tell me this – who was the guy she left with last night? Driving the Saab?"

"Uh… that would have been James Healey," he said, grin fading. "What's this about?"

"Was James intending to drop her off at the vicarage?"

"Of course. He always does. Why? Problem?"

"Just tell me where James lives, would you?"

She felt Hal Pagham's disconcerted gaze follow her all the way down the high street.

The address he had given Lexy was an attractive Dutch-gabled house near Dunwich, set back in a private road, with unimpaired views across the marsh to the sea. Must have cost and arm and a leg. A young man was washing the Saab in the drive, wind whipping off drifts of spray from his hose. A vacuum cleaner stood nearby. The car was obviously getting the full works.

Lexy caught his eye. "Can you come and do mine next?"

He didn't get it, just gave her an alarmed stare, as if she was a local nutter.

She continued to smile at him.

"Er… can I help you?" He sounded like an Argos sales-man.

"You're James Healey, aren't you?"

"Do we know one another?"

"Nope. But I saw rather more of you than I wanted to last night."

A spasm of embarrassment, anger and fear passed across James Healey's face as he took this in. He glanced towards the house and began shepherding Lexy down the drive.

"Were you spying or something?"

"Unintentionally stumbled across your gathering," she corrected.

"What do you want? We weren't doing anything wrong. It's not against the law to worship nature."

"I know. You're fine. What time did you drop Verity off at the vicarage last night?"

"Just after twelve, like I always do. Why?"

"She's gone missing."

"What? She can't have." He stared at her in disbelief. "I dropped her at the church lych-gate."

"You sure about that? No one else picked her up?"

"No. Look, what are you – police, or something?"

"Just a concerned friend," said Lexy. "She's not shacked up with you, is she?"

He gave her a horrified look. "No way! My parents would freak. I'm meant to be studying."

"She is your girlfriend, though?"

He shook his head indignantly. "I only know her through the coven. I give her a lift there and back because she's on the way." He lowered his voice. "I'm making a sympathetic documentary about the Forrington Coven for a sociology project at uni. One of their conditions is that I join them in their Sabbat every fortnight." He looked back towards the house. "My folks are a bit funny about things like that. They wouldn't like it if they found out I've been baring all for the Great Goddess every quarter moon."

"Imagine the problem Verity has."

"Yeah – tell me about it. And she's High Priestess." He screwed up his face. "I wish I could help you more, but I just dropped her off, as usual. God, I hope she's all right. Do you need a hand looking for her?"

"I'll be in touch, if I need to." Lexy clicked her tongue at Kinky, and they set off across the wind-swept salt marshes back towards Clopwolde.

James was speaking the truth, Lexy was sure of it. Besides, she'd caught a glimpse of Mrs Healey through the living room window and she didn't look like the kind of woman who'd put up with any teenage tomfoolery under her roof.

It was an unexpected set-back. Like Robin and Cora Perkins, Lexy had been convinced she'd find the vicar's daughter holed up with young lover boy. With a bit of gentle persuasion, the girl could probably have been discreetly reunited with her parents, Lexy would have collected her fee, and the Forrington coven could continue communing with nature. She might even join them one night. One summer night.

Now it emerged that Verity Perkins really had gone AWOL. That changed everything.

Lexy reluctantly fingered the mobile phone in her pocket. She was going to have to call the vicarage and tell Verity's parents what their daughter was really up to yesterday evening, and then recommend they report her disappearance to the police. Which meant DI Milo would, at some point, have to explain to his superior officers that he had actually been a witness to events immediately prior to Verity's disappearance. And to make matters worse, he had been with that troublesome private eye, Lexy Lomax.

Lexy cringed as she tried Milo's phone. But the Suffolk

coastal atmospherics were capricious, and she couldn't get a signal. With a sudden stab of urgency, she broke into a run.

Clopwolde harbour hove into view, the yacht masts jangling and clattering in the wind like demonic xylophones.

The slender steeple of St Ethelred's pierced the skyline above the village. Lexy jogged, red-faced, straight for it, Kinky pattering laboriously behind her.

She came to an abrupt halt at the lych-gate. Just needed to check something before the curtain went up. Rapidly pacing up and down, Lexy examined the ground for any indication that Verity had got out of the car the previous night. She would have had a number of things with her. Her robes, which she had changed out of, her crescent moon head-band, the drum, the sword...

Lexy turned through the gate. Kinky had already gone in, despite a sign that clearly said No Dogs.

"Here, boy," Lexy murmured, her eyes fixed on little drifts of rice confetti and autumn leaves. Something was nagging at the back of her mind. Something from last night – something that didn't quite ring true. Distractedly, she worked her way through the graveyard towards the vicarage door, until a vigorous scrabbling sound caused her head to jerk up.

Her face contorted into a silent Munch scream. Kinky was on top of a fresh burial mound, digging like a lunatic, soil flying in all directions.

"Oi!" Her voice was a strangulated screech.

The chihuahua was pulling something white out of the soil. Lexy found herself backing into the shadow of a magnolia bush beside the vicarage porch.

Kinky jumped from the mound, a small object that

looked horribly like a bone gripped between his teeth.

"Get over here, *now*," Lexy hissed.

He sprinted straight past her.

She peered round the side of the porch. Kinky was heading directly for the vicar. Lexy pressed her eyes hard shut.

When she opened them, she saw the vicar stoop down and pick the thing up. Kinky pranced and barked. The vicar frowned over at the grave. He knew where it had come from, then. He took a furtive look around, and shoved the chihuahua's new toy into the folds of his cassock.

Disappointed, Kinky trotted back to where Lexy was half-crouching. She flapped her hands, not wanting him to give her hiding place away. Her phone vibrated in her pocket, making her jump.

"You been trying to get hold of me?" Milo's voice crackled out.

"Yes. About last night. There's a prob…"

"Can't talk for long. At a suspicious death."

Lexy felt the blood draining from her face.

"Not…?" Lexy lowered her voice. "Is it… male or female?"

"Male. Found in the river. "

"Thank god."

"What do you mean, *thank god*?"

"Verity Perkins has gone missing," Lexy muttered. "She was dropped off at the vicarage gate last night, but she never made it inside."

Milo swore loudly enough to wake the dead.

"Where are you?" he snapped.

"At the church."

"I'm just down the road, at Spinney Corner. I'll jump in the car now and… Lexy?"

But Lexy wasn't listening. She'd worked out what that

white thing was, the thing Kinky had dug out of the burial mound. The thing the vicar had quickly hidden.

"Milo." She squatted on her heels at the side of the porch, her voice barely a whisper. "I think Robin Perkins might know more than he's telling us about his daughter's disappearance."

"Eh?" She heard the car engine start up.

"He's got her beater."

There was a scrape from the other side of the porch.

"What are you on about?"

"Her bodhran beater," Lexy glanced around the corner. "You know, from last night."

A sudden movement galvanised her. She gave a wild shout, and launched into a run.

"Hey – what's going…?" Milo's voice yelled uselessly from the mobile.

Lexy had a good turn of speed, but Cora had a head start on her. She'd almost reached her husband. She must have overheard. And she had a spade in her hand.

In a futile gesture, Lexy flung her phone at Cora. It missed by a mile, but Cora went sprawling anyway. She'd tripped over Kinky, who'd cut in front of her in his quest to retrieve it. The spade clattered on to the path. Lexy launched herself on Cora, and pulled the woman's arm up her back.

Kinky's teeth scrunched down on the mobile.

"What the…?" The vicar stood over them, upright and shocked.

"Sorry about that," said Lexy, grimly. "But she *was* on her way to deck you."

"What on earth are you talking about?" Cora struggled angrily. "I was on my way to tell Robin that the Dean was on the phone."

"And the spade? How do you explain that?"

"Robin had left it in the porch. I was going to put it in the shed over there."

"Ah." Lexy relaxed her hold. "So, Reverend Perkins," she blustered. "Are you going to tell your wife where Verity is?"

"I thought that's what you were meant to be doing."

"You won't mind emptying out your pockets, though, will you?"

The vicar gave her a resigned look, and fumbled in his cassock. He held out the double-ended beater.

Kinky bounced excitedly.

"Not now," Lexy snapped.

A car screeched to a halt outside the vicarage gate, and a lanky, irate figure strode over.

"What's going on?"

"Officer," said the vicar, in falsely hearty tones. "Just a little misunderstanding."

Milo eyed Lexy, who was in the process of giving Cora Perkins a hand up. She inclined her head towards the beater, still held by the vicar.

"Where did you get this, sir?" Milo took it.

"From him." The vicar pointed at Kinky.

"But that's Verity's," frowned his wife. "Where did *he* get it?"

They all turned to Lexy.

"It was buried in that grave," said Lexy, pointing dramatically. "And if I'm right, there's something else in there, too."

Cora gave a small scream.

"No, not that," said Lexy, hastily. "I mean some more items belonging to Verity. Her cloak and bodhran and... other stuff." She saw the vicar's face. "You buried it all there last night, didn't you, Reverend?"

"Only place I could think of," he admitted.

"Can someone tell me what's going on here?" Cora demanded.

Milo nodded fervently behind her.

"I'm guessing it goes something like this," said Lexy, eyeing the vicar. "Last night, when Verity was dropped off by James, you happened to meet her at the lych-gate, Reverend Perkins, on your way in from locking up the church. You saw what she was carrying, and demanded an explanation."

"Thought she'd gone RC," the vicar muttered.

"But when Verity told you she worshipped with a Wiccan group, you panicked, and seized her stuff. At which point, I assume she ran off, threatening never to come back."

"Something like that," Robin sighed. "I quickly buried the... paraphernalia because I didn't want Cora to find out."

"Find out what?" his wife snapped. "I already know she belongs to the Forrington Coven."

The vicar gasped. "Well, why didn't you tell me?"

"In case you did something foolish, like drive our daughter away."

"I didn't intend to," he protested. "It was just something of a shock. Well, I mean..."

"The coven is perfectly harmless, Robin. Modern Wicca is a very caring belief system, entirely in tune with nature, green issues, ideals of equality and..."

"Absolutely right," Lexy broke in, before Cora Perkins announced her own conversion. "But going back to yesterday night, you were pretty sure, Reverend Perkins, that Verity had gone to James's house, and there was no real need for worry?"

The vicar nodded. "Well, that's where she is, isn't she?"

"I'll come to that. So when your wife came out looking for Verity you pretended you hadn't seen her."

"Didn't want to mention the row. I thought she'd be back first thing in the morning."

"But she wasn't. And when your wife started to talk about calling the police, you persuaded her to call me. The less fuss that was made about the whole thing, the better, in order that you could save face, and avoid any scandal."

"That was my plan," agreed the vicar.

"Trouble is, Verity didn't go to James's house."

Reverend Perkins looked up sharply. "Where is she, then?"

"I think she picked a more mature man," said Lexy, after a moment's pause. "Someone who took her seriously. Someone Verity's been secretly seeing for some time now, while she fobbed you off with tales of going out with young James Healey."

"She's right, too, whoever she is." Another voice rang out, and around the corner came a wood nymph, with a tumble of black curls. And, now Lexy came to see her contours more closely, a small but significant bump. She was arm in arm with Hal Pagham.

Cora fell upon her daughter with incoherent sounds of relief.

Hal Pagham turned to Lexy with his lazy grin, which she now saw was rather engaging.

"How did you know?" he asked.

"Yes, how did you know?" echoed Milo, weakly.

"Simple conjecture," said Lexy. "It was the inscription in that book in the back of Hal's car last night. *To my very own HP.* I thought it odd at the time that someone would be giving Hal a book on Practical Pagan Motherhood. Then afterwards it struck me that perhaps it was Hal who gave the book to someone else."

"His High Priestess, to be precise," Verity smiled. She turned to Cora. "Sorry, mum. I think it's a bit late for that white wedding you always wanted for me."

"Never too late, dear," said Cora Perkins. She turned to Hal Pagham, eyebrows raised.

"We can offer a Handfast ceremony," he said. "It's our version of a wedding. Very beautiful and moving."

"Thank you, Hal. I accept on behalf of my husband and myself."

"I don't know what the WI will think," said the Reverend Perkins gloomily.

Kinky, who had all the while been staring at DI Milo, gave a sharp bark.

"Do you mind if I...?" The vicar took the beater from the policeman's hand, and flung it across the churchyard.

Kinky sped after it, and returned with alacrity, dropping the beater at the vicar's feet.

"Good fellow," he smiled.

"I'm guessing there might be a small upside to this whole situation, Reverend Perkins," Lexy remarked, as he sent the beater flying through the air again.

"I doubt it," said the vicar. "What possible good can come out of my daughter leaving home to live in sin? Let alone everything else."

"Well, think about it, dad," said Verity, grinning. "With me and my allergies out of the way – it means you'll be able to get yourself a dog at last."

JOHN BROWN'S BODY

Reginald Hill

It's a great beach for bodies.

To the north towers the craggy height of Bale Head, the county's favourite spot for suicides whose battered corpses a decorous current lays neatly on the crescent of golden sand curving two miles south to the sharp point of Bodd Ness. Beyond this the incoming tide squeezes itself into the narrow estuary of the Bodd and rapidly becomes a bit of a bore. Most of those caught in that sudden rush (and despite the warnings, each year brings half a dozen) are swept out on the ebb and left as testaments to folly on our sunny beach. Add to this a funnel of tides widening out into the Atlantic which after a big storm has brought us bodies from as far afield as the Scillies, and you've got yourself a boddicomber's dream.

What's a boddicomber? With a capital B, it's a native of Boddicombe, the village half a mile inland where I've been living for the past twenty years. But with a small b, it's a beachcomber who's found a body. Macabre? Not really, not if you live here. Here with our tides and currents, it's almost the norm, and all the regulars in the bar of the *Drowned Sailor* are boddicombers in both senses.

All except one, that is.

Me.

John Brown.

I suppose, having married a local lass and lived here for two decades, I can claim the capital B as an adopted son of the village. Certainly after some initial caution, quite natural when an outsider sweeps a local heiress off her feet,

145

the denizens of the *Sailor* took me to their hearts and treated me as one of their own. Only one thing was needed to put the seal on the deed of adoption. But so far it hasn't happened.

For twenty years now I've been walking the beach once, sometimes twice a day, and I've never found a body.

Don't misunderstand me. They're not a morbid lot down in the *Sailor*. Bodies on the beach aren't a staple of conversation. But whenever another corpse is washed up, naturally this sparks off reminiscence of past tragedies with comparisons and contrasts and significant anecdotes as each discoverer in turn recalls *his* body. That's how they're identified, not by their own names, but by the boddicomber's name, as *Dick's body* or *Ernie's body*, or where the man in question has been fortunate enough to come across more than one, *Tony's second* or *Andy's third*.

It's amazing how possessive a boddicomber becomes. Every detail that can be gleaned from police investigations, coroner's inquests, newspaper reports, and any other source, is hoarded up and treasured. Sometimes their depth of background knowledge makes me wonder if some of them don't employ private detectives! I listen in dumb admiration. For that's all I can do, listen, though they've always done their best to include me in, and everyone was mightily pleased when the year before last Charley Trenfold's *seventh* gave them a hook to hung their kindness on. Now as soon as Charley's *seventh* is mentioned, some-one will turn to me and urge me to make my pathetic contribution. And I always do, because a man shouldn't turn his back on kindness. But oh! how the words bring back the bitter taste of *proxime accessit*, as sharp and pungent as it was on that misty morning two years ago.

I'd got up early to take a walk. To tell the truth it had

146

been one of those nights I'd spent uncomfortably in the spare room after yet another row with Lorna. God, that mattress! Once when friendly relations were resumed after an earlier exile, I'd joked that if we were going to make a habit of this, we really ought to think about getting a more user-friendly guest bed. To which she'd replied that if I had the money to spare, that might not be a bad idea. Which rapidly led to a breach of our armistice and another bout of sleepless nights for me.

This particular morning as I strolled along the path to the beach, I wondered gloomily whether my marriage was in terminal decline. For ten years after our romantic start, things had only got better and better. Lorna had been so in love that she'd assured me there'd be no problem in leaving the lovely family house she'd inherited in Boddicombe to move into my flat in town ninety slow miles away. But I knew how much she loved that house and assured her in turn that there was no need. Modern technology meant I could do my job as easily from Boddicombe as I could in company HQ, and I'd get to walk the beach nearly every day. Funny thing, love. We nearly fell out each trying to make sacrifices for the other. But I won, and for the next ten years I worked from home and as I'd forecast, there were no problems at all. Then the company fell on hard times and suddenly the flaw in my arrangement became apparent. When downsizing's in the air, it's easier to start with the faces you're not seeing every day in the executive dining room.

So I was out, but it didn't seem to matter. I'd made enough money when I was in to provide a reassuring cushion till I found a new job. Except there were no new jobs, not even when I cast my net well beyond the old ninety mile limit.

No problem, I said. If you can't find someone to

employ you, employ yourself. I already had a well-equipped home office. Now I invested what remained of my money in upgrading it to cutting-edge status, called in a few old favours, and suddenly I was an entrepreneur.

For a while it looked like it was going to work, but at best I was never more than holding my own. Slowly I ran out of favours and commissions. The e-mails fell to a trickle then dried up completely, the fax only chugged out advertising junk, the phone never rang and the postman brought nothing but bills.

Till finally I had to face up to it. I was an unemployment statistic living in his wife's house on his wife's money. Things might have been better if I hadn't felt so guilty about it. Looking back, I think I spent so much time telling Lorna what a liability I was that in the end she believed it.

But I did get a lot more time to walk the beach.

And that misty morning, as I stood on my usual high dune letting my gaze run north along the sand, I thought my luck might be on the change.

Each tide left its own signature on the beach and over the years I had grown expert at reading those scrawls of flotsam and jetsam and beached jellyfish and sea-wrack, and like all the boddicombers I was ultra-sensitive to anything whose configuration or bulk was out of the ordinary.

And this morning there was something there, right at the limit of my view, nothing more than a dark smudge in the bluey-pink wreaths the sun's warm rays were drawing off the damp sand, but definitely *something*...

I took a deep breath and was just about to descend from the dune when a voice called my name.

"John! Good morning to you!"

I turned in irritation to see Maisie Palliser climbing up

towards me followed by her overweight and panting pug, Samson.

I forced my features into something as close to a smile as I could manage and said, "Good morning."

Maisie Palliser was one of those women who get a reputation for kindness by making unacceptable offers of help and who use a much vaunted sympathy as a tool for getting under the defences of the vulnerable to the secrets below. She was Lorna's cousin, a couple of years older and unmarried. Not that she was physically unattractive. Indeed she and Lorna could almost have been twins. But Maisie, though devious in many ways, had no art to conceal her desire to dominate. There'd been a quarrel between their fathers, the two Palliser brothers, over their inheritance many years before, and as they grew up the two cousins hadn't had much to do with each other. A pity in some ways. There's nothing like a shared childhood for giving you a proper insight into character. Myself, I never cared for her from the start. How Lorna felt I never enquired, but I got an impression she wasn't all that worried about the after-effects of their fathers' quarrel. But when illness and accident removed the last of the older generation a few years back, Maisie had been so assiduous in bringing about a rapprochement that Lorna's gentler nature was quite unable to resist. The big card Maisie played was that she and Lorna were the last of the Pallisers, so family feuds must give way to family solidarity. I gently mocked this non sequitur, but it was no contest. Lorna was a sucker for sentiment, and perhaps unjustly, I date the beginning of the deterioration in my marital relationship not so much from the day I lost my job as from the day I first found Maisie enjoying afternoon tea in our drawing room. After that she became a regular visitor and soon Lorna seemed happy to admit her as a confidante. She drew the line, however, at welcoming Samson the pug, who combined a delicate stomach with insatiable greed, eating anything he could get his thieving teeth on, then after just long enough for his inefficient digestive juices to render it revolting, vomiting it back up, preferably on a chair or a carpet. Lorna was usually pretty neutral about domestic animals, but in this case she made an exception. She really detested that dog; its very presence set her teeth on edge, and in her quiet way she made it absolutely clear that Samson was not welcome in her house. So whenever Maisie visited, the pug was locked in the kitchen porch where he could do no harm.

"Best part of the day, this," said Maisie now as she joined me. "I don't see it often enough but I couldn't sleep last night. My old trouble."

She smiled bravely. What her old trouble was nobody knew exactly, but that it was exceedingly painful and bravely borne no one could avoid knowing.

"Same with you, was it, John?" she went on.

"Doubt it, Maisie. I don't have your old trouble," I replied.

It was bird-shot against a tank.

"How lucky you are," she sighed. "But I meant something must have got you out of bed early too. I sincerely hope it wasn't anything causing you physical pain."

"No. Just fancied a stroll, that's all."

"And you managed to steal away without disturbing Lorna, I'm sure. How is the dear girl? I must call round and have a chat soon. Don't worry. I won't take up too much of her time. I know how hard the pair of you work to make your business a success. Don't forget my offer. Anything I can do to help – folding envelopes, addressing labels, even a bit of typing. I can still manage to get my fingers dancing over a keyboard even with my arthritis. All you have to do is ask, John."

She knew damn well the business had given up the ghost just as she knew damn well Lorna and I spent more time sleeping apart than together, but how was I to tell her that without telling her that, if you see what I mean, opening the floodgates to a new torrent of useless advice and ersatz sympathy?

But I might have exploded if over her shoulder I hadn't seen the last thing I wanted to see: the familiar hunched figure of Charley Trenfold dropping down to the beach from the dunes between me and that distant mist-shrouded shape.

I muttered something to Maisie, I don't know what, and set out after him. I was the younger man and got plenty of exercise to keep me fit. But old Charley was no slouch either, and by the way he was striding out, he'd clearly his *seventh* firmly in his sights. It was partly the fact that his cottage stood a little way out of the village and a lot closer to the beach that gave him his boddicombing pre-eminence, but you couldn't deny that he had a nose for it, and though the idea was never openly expressed, everyone in the *Sailor* knew it was his ambition to overtake the record of the greatest boddicomber (and Boddicomber) of them all, Jacob Palliser, my wife's and Maisie's grandfather, who during the course of a long and profitable life had found a round dozen.

Fast as I moved, even breaking into a trot when I got close enough to see that the shape on the beach was undoubtedly a corpse, I couldn't overtake Charley. I couldn't even claim a dead heat. He reached the body a full step ahead, turned to look at me with a little start of surprise as if he'd been unaware of my pursuit, and said,

"Is that you, John Brown? Well, here's a sad sight for a summer's morn. Another poor soul lured by Old Nick to leap off the Head."

I didn't doubt for one moment he'd be right. Old Charley was so familiar with the general configuration of the tides and currents and the modifying effect of specific weather conditions that he could tell with amazing accuracy the likely point of entry any body washed up on our beach.

I looked down at the face of the man at our feet. There was a dreadful gash across his brow with splintered bone showing through, confirming Charley's judgement. Those who jumped off the Head usually died on the rocks below and lay there till the height of the tide picked them up and carried them away. I didn't recognise the face. The Head's reputation lured people from far and wide. But I knew from experience that over the next few weeks, Charley would somehow research chapter and verse of his life and background and the circumstances which brought him to this sad end. All of which would have been my task if Maisie hadn't delayed me. The bitch! She was my bird of ill omen even in this.

"Why don't you stay with him and I'll head back to the cottage and ring the police?" said Charley.

Reporting was the next important stage after finding. It got you officially into the records, established your claim, so to speak.

"No need for that," I said. "I'll do it from here."

I took out my mobile phone and dialled.

And that was how I got my footnote in the boddicombers' annals. Mobiles, already the common furniture of urban life, hadn't reached Boddicombe in any great numbers then. Now everyone in the *Sailor* has one. Rumour has it that Charley went out and bought one the next day. I smile whenever I see him use it, for I know it still rankles slightly that every time his seventh comes up in conversation, some kind soul, eager to bring me into things, will say, "Aye, that's the one that John Brown reported on his mobile, isn't that right, John?" and I'll get my thirty seconds of fame.

Two years on and that was still all I could lay claim to, though I seemed to spend more time walking the beach and its environs than I did at home. *Home!* It was hardly that any more. It was simply the house where I lodged by the grudging permission of the woman who used to be my wife. Why didn't she throw me out and sue for divorce? There were several reasons, not least among them being the fact that she'd been brought up as a Boddicombe Baptist. I don't know if this term has any official standing in the religious world, but I do know that the attitude of the BBs to divorce made the Roman Catholic Church look like Club Mediterranée.

As for me, why didn't I call it a day and walk out?

Again several reasons, with large among them the fact that I had nowhere to walk to. The years of desperately seeking work had made me a man old acquaintance crossed the street to avoid. And the years of not having any work had made me a man who crossed the street to avoid old acquaintance. So I'd zig-zagged to a situation where the only place I felt at home and among friends was the bar of the *Drowned Sailor*. If I walked away from this, my probable destination was a cardboard box in a shop doorway. Or Bale Head. Which would at least have meant that I got my place permanently in the mythology of the *Sailor*. But when I thought of the satisfaction it would give Maisie Palliser, I knew it wasn't really an option.

At my blackest moments I sometimes thought that my only chance of a future better than this demeaning present lay in Lorna dying. We'd never made wills. With only the two of us to consider in those early loving days, it seemed to be tempting fate to pay someone to formalise what would happen anyway, which is to say if one of us died, the survivor would get all. Well, those loving days were long gone, though deep inside of me I still nursed a weak runt of a hope that a love as strong as ours had been couldn't altogether die. Perhaps it was our common memories rather than Lorna's religion and my fears that kept us together? Certainly I can honestly say that even in those blackest moments I stopped short of wishing her dead, and I never got close to fantasising about killing her. But words have a life of their own, and one day not long after Christmas when some minor financial irritation had melted the cold courtesy between us to molten antagonism, I exploded, "Money, money, money, that's all you think about, isn't it? Well, I didn't marry you for your money, and as far as I'm concerned you can grow old and ugly counting it. I don't want any part of it!"

To which she replied, equally incensed, "That's just as well, because from now on you're not getting any more. You might make me miserable but you're not going to make me bankrupt."

And I, God forgive me, cried, "So you're rich and miserable and I'm broke and miserable. So why don't you take a dive off Bale Head, and that would solve all our problems, wouldn't it?"

I saw the shock in her face and wished it unsaid instantly. I wanted to say I didn't mean it, that we shouldn't be surprised if two people who'd loved each other as much as we had were as extreme in their quarrels as they'd been in their passion. But the door was pushed open at that moment and Maisie was standing there, saying, "Sorry, I rang the bell but no one answered so I just came in." How much she'd heard, I couldn't say. Everything, I suspected. Whatever, there was nothing for me to do now but leave with my retraction unattempted, and over the next couple of days Lorna gave me neither opportunity nor encouragement to apologise, and as is the way in these matters, I soon began to feel the fault was as much hers as mine, so why should I be the one who grovelled?

Then a few days later, returning to the house after another unproductive stroll along the beach, I heard Lorna call my name from the drawing room.

The first person I saw when I entered was Maisie, drinking tea. She gave a thin smile, which had something unpleasantly gloating in it. Once she'd been at some pains to conceal her antagonism towards me. For several weeks in the run-up to Christmas, Maisie had been all sweetness and light, indeed almost likeable. I wondered if she'd found God or taken up marijuana. Then suddenly, over the holiday period, she'd done a Scrooge in reverse and emerged at the other side even more of a foul-tempered, man-hating termagant than she'd been before.

Lorna was sitting opposite her on a sofa with by her side the lanky figure of Tim Edlington, the Palliser family solicitor. He rose to shake my hand and said something conventional like, "Good to see you again, John." But I detected a certain embarrassment in his tone which worried me. One thing I learned in business was, when lawyers sound embarrassed, you're really in trouble.

Lorna said brusquely, "John, I need you to witness my signature."

"Of course, dear," I said. "On what?"

"On my will."

I tried to hide my surprise. I doubt if I was successful.

155

"Your will?" I said. "I didn't realise... I mean, isn't it illegal, for a husband I mean, to witness…?"

"Only if he is a beneficiary," said Lorna coldly.

And now I felt real shock and I didn't even bother to try to hide it. I saw at once what was happening. She must have been deeply shocked by what I'd said. I guessed she'd confided in Maisie. Indeed, with Maisie having overheard my outburst, it would have been impossible for someone feeling as vulnerable as Lorna must have felt to resist her cousin's spurious sympathy and vicarious outrage. No doubt in her present anti-male mood she'd assured Lorna that all men were murdering rapists under the skin. And now I was being told loud and clear in front of witnesses that whatever else Lorna's death might do for me, it wasn't going to make me rich.

Maisie was observing me with her face set in a mask of sympathy which she didn't mind me piercing to the malicious pleasure beneath. Tim Edlington's embarrassed sympathy on the other hand was very real and he rushed in to fill the silence that followed Lorna's remark with an attempt at explanation.

"What Lorna and Maisie want to do, John, is repair the damage done to the Palliser estate, not to mention the Palliser family, by old Jacob's will."

He glanced up at the portrait of Jacob Palliser, founder of the family fortunes and grandfather to Maisie and Lorna. It was from him that Maisie inherited her need to dominate. From all accounts he had kept his sons under his thumb until he died, and even then he'd left a will cunningly constructed to leave both feeling cheated, dividing the property so that the younger son (Lorna's father) got the house and land which the elder son (Maisie's father) thought his due, while the elder got a controlling interest in the dairy products business which the younger had almost single-handedly built up. Some necessary concessions had been agreed, but effectively that malicious will had set the brothers at each other's throats for the rest of their lives.

"So," concluded Tim, "Lorna and Maisie have asked me to draw up mutually beneficial wills by which, when in the fullness of time one or the other of them passes on, the estate such as it now is will once more be joined together as a single entity."

He tried to make it sound like a reasonable act of conciliation but he knew that he was talking bollocks. This wasn't about old Jacob and the estate. It was about me. And it was also about Maisie, who was potentially by far the biggest beneficiary of this new arrangement. Neither brother had made much of his inheritance, but whereas Lorna's father had hung on to a good proportion of his, Maisie had seen her prospects dwindle to the small family cottage in which she lived, and a small income to go with it. Already, it seemed to me, she was looking around that handsome drawing room with a proprietary air.

I said, "Where do I sign?"

I didn't even bother to read the wills, just countersigned the women's signatures. Tim acted as the other witness. I shook him by the hand again and left the room. As I closed the door quietly behind me, I glanced up at old Jacob's portrait.

I'd never met the old man, but now I read in those piercing black eyes the scorn of a self-made man for a failure and a weakling who had not only lost his wife's love and respect but couldn't even find a single body on our bountiful beach.

Which of course was where I headed now. To rage and

brood and plot. And to look for bodies.

Does that sound crazily obsessive? I suppose it must. But somehow my failure to find a body had become a symbol of all my failures. No; it was more than a symbol. It was as if everything that had gone wrong in my life could somehow be tracked back to this one deficiency. It placed the blame fairly not on my own shoulders but on a malevolent fate or at best the vagaries of blind chance. It seemed to me that if only I could find my body and take my place as of right among the native boddicombers in the *Drowned Sailor*, all would be well. I could look the portrait of old Jacob straight in the eye, Lorna would regain her respect for me, her love, her energy and her healthy bank balance would be put at my disposal, and thus armed I could renew my assault on the world of commerce, and this time I would win…

Yes, I continued to think like this even after the business of the will. At first it had seemed to me that for Lorna to let Maisie into the act had been a deliberate attempt to add insult to injury. She knew how much I disliked and distrusted her. But more mature consideration led me to the conclusion that far from wanting to pile on the pain, Lorna had looked for a device which would give the whole business a patina of rationality. She could just have left everything to the Boddicombe Baptists. But that would have been undisguisable as anything but a wish to cause me pain. The business of reuniting the estate was the best way she could find of softening the blow, and her general demeanour in the days that followed made me think the whole affair was making her feel guilty and gave me hope that the embers of our love might still be warm enough to melt her heart which my stupid outburst had so hardened against me.

So I continued with my secret crazy dream that things could still be turned around if only I could find that elusive body. One corpse. That wasn't much to ask. Charley Trenfold had had a great couple of years and was up to eleven now, just one short of old Jacob's record. Surely the great and generous ocean could spare a single corpse for me?

Who was it who said, be careful what you pray for because you might get it?

A couple of weeks later I came home in the gloam of an overcast February evening, slightly out of breath as I'd been hurrying.

Happily, Lorna's principles which forbade her to divorce me also forbade her to starve me and she cooked our meal every night. A creature of habit, her menu was dictated by the day, without any reference to possible variation of appetite, and she set our meal on the table between seven and seven-thirty, and started to eat regardless of whether I had arrived or not.

On nut cutlet night, I didn't much mind whether I got it hot or cold, but today was pork chop day, my favourite, so I hurried to be on time even though it meant leaving the beach half an hour before high tide. I went round to the kitchen entrance as usual. But as I kicked off my wellingtons in the covered porchway, I realised that something was missing – the mouthwatering smell of grilling pork.

Puzzled, I pushed open the kitchen door. On the table I could see assembled for cooking all the ingredients of dinner. Mushrooms, tomatoes, chipped potatoes, and a succulent chop with the kidney in, the way I liked it. But no Lorna.

I went through the house calling her name.

There was no reply.

I went out to the old barn which acted as a garage. I had declined from Jag through Mondeo to Daewoo, but finally even that had gone and now our only vehicle was the aged Land Rover which Lorna claimed was all that country dwellers needed.

It wasn't there.

Puzzled and just beginning to be worried, but not wanting to give the local gossips still more material by ringing around, I walked into the village and called at Maisie's house. There was no sign of the Land Rover, and no sign of Maisie either. Only Samson greeted me on the threshold. He looked so disconsolate that I started to bend to stroke him. Then he belched noisomely and brought up a disgusting bolus of gristle and bone which spread itself across Maisie's pristine doorstep.

I walked down the street, past the *Drowned Sailor.* No sign of the Land Rover in the car park. I thought of going inside, but that would only have fed the local rumour machine. Increasingly anxious but still a long way from panic, I walked home by a route which took me past several outlying houses belonging to various friends of Lorna, hoping I'd see the Land Rover parked outside one of them. No luck, but as I passed the last of these, its owner, a farmer called Tony Simkin (two bodies to his credit, one of them a local politician who'd solved his problem with a corruption scandal by stepping off Bale Head) spotted me as he came out of his lambing shed.

"Evening, John," he said. "Fed up with the beach, then?"

Meaning it was a bit unusual for me to be taking my evening stroll along these lanes.

"Change is as good as a rest," I said.

"Could do with one myself," he said. "These early lambs are a pain. Thought I saw you driving that old heap of yours down the coast road earlier and I said to myself, there goes John and Lorna off to the movies in Lymton, lucky devils."

The ancient cinema which had somehow contrived to survive in Lymton, twelve miles north, was our nearest source of public entertainment.

"Not me," I said lightly.

"No?" He looked at me doubtfully. "Could have sworn I recognised the hat. But never mind. Here you are now. Won't you step into the house for a dram? Say hello to Betsy?"

Four months earlier, Tony's wife Betsy had left him, taking their two children. Then at Christmas there'd been a reconciliation, and Tony was still in the honeymoon period, wanting everyone who came near to call in and see what a happy united family they were.

I wasn't in the mood for happy united families so I made an excuse, took my leave, and hastened home.

Still no sign of Lorna, but Tony's possible sighting of the Land Rover was encouraging a new and reassuring hypothesis. Probably it was as straightforward as that… Lorna had simply gone to the cinema… a last minute decision… someone had reminded her there was a film she was keen to see…

But she wouldn't have gone without leaving a note…

I knew there was nothing on the kitchen table but I checked as I passed through. Our other note-leaving place was against the clock on the mantelpiece in the drawing room. I'd pushed open the door and called Lorna's name into the darkened room when I'd first missed her, but I hadn't actually gone inside.

Now I stepped in and put the light on.

No note against the clock. Above it, old Jacob sneered down at me.

I was turning away when my eye caught sight of what looked like a piece of paper on the hearth beneath the mantel. Perhaps the note had slipped. I went forward and picked it up. There was some writing on it in a familiar hand, but not Lorna's.

Mine.

It was my signature preceded by the typed words *signed by the testatrix in the presence of...*

The fire basket was grey with paper ash.

And as I stopped to take a closer look I saw something else.

A dark brown stain on the sharp corner of the raised stone hearth.

I touched it. It was dry. I scraped at it with my fingernail, raised the resulting powdery flakes to the light, sniffed at them.

It was blood.

I sank to the floor and squatted there, letting all the fragmented thoughts whirling around my head settle slowly into a meaningful mosaic.

I recalled the single chop on the kitchen table where there should have been two. And I recalled the bony gristly mess that Samson had vomited up on Maisie's doorstep.

Suddenly it was like putting a video in the VCR and pressing the *play* button.

Maisie had been here. Lorna had told her she'd changed her mind about the will. Maisie had protested. Lorna had been adamant. And being a woman who thought that deeds spoke louder than words, she'd produced the will and put a match to it and stooped to hold it over the fire basket. Maisie had tried to wrest it from her. Lorna, off balance, had fallen forward, crashing heavily, fatally, against the edge of the hearth.

And then?

I knew how Maisie's mind worked. The burnt will, signs of a struggle, her cousin's corpse... even if the inquest brought in a verdict of accidental death, there would be talk for ever more. She would judge others by herself and guess that in the eyes of many she would be marked for the rest of her life as a murderess who'd got away with it. That wouldn't bother her too much, perhaps, if she could claim the compensation of Lorna's house and money. But the will was in the fireplace, burnt beyond retrieval.

Then slowly as she sat there reviewing her options, an idea formed in her devious mind... an idea which at worst would clear her of any suspicion of involvement in Lorna's death and at best might result in her claiming the Palliser inheritance after all...

The coast road to Lymton which Tony thought he'd seen me driving along was also the road to Bale Head.

Maisie had put the body in the Land Rover, driven to the Head, and tipped Lorna over the edge.

Suicide while the balance of her mind was disturbed. I could hear Maisie at the inquest reluctantly letting herself be bullied into admitting that the wreck of our marriage and my unreasonable behaviour had brought Lorna to the edge of despair.

As for the burnt will, who had lit the flame? Who benefited most from its destruction?

I could see all eyes in the coroner's court turning towards me.

I'm sure Maisie's lawyer, especially if it wasn't Tim, could make a strong legal argument for reinstating the burnt will.

But why take a chance on the uncertainties of the law when there was another more certain way?

Maisie wouldn't find it hard when talking to the police to refer 'inadvertently' to my threats against Lorna's life: threats which had included a mention of Bale Head. Indeed, for all I knew she'd already told everyone in the village about them. The police would start looking for other evidence, and eventually they'd come up with Tony Simkin and anyone else who'd seen the Land Rover heading along the coast road.

Why had Tony had been so sure he'd seen me in the driving seat? He'd said something about recognising my hat…

I went back into the kitchen and looked at the clothes hooks behind the door.

An ancient and very distinctive old-fashioned floppy cap I often wore when driving in cold wintry conditions wasn't there. The bitch had already been thinking ahead to putting me in the frame!

I shook my head and asked myself, could even Maisie be as cunningly manipulative as that?

Of course she could! She'd know that once the police started looking closely at things, it wouldn't be long before the bloodstains in the drawing room were found, and then…

But even as I ran this frightening scenario through my mind, I knew that what I was really doing was attempting to block off my shock, my horror, my despair, at the prospect of admitting Lorna was dead.

Before I was finally going to lay myself open to that destructive knowledge, I would need to see her corpse.

And if my hypothesis was right, I knew exactly where I'd find it.

For the first time in many years, I headed down to the beach praying that I wouldn't find a body.

Two hours or more had passed since I'd come away and headed home for dinner; the tide had long turned and it was its receding roar that I heard as I clambered up the dunes. The night was pitch black, the air full of wind and sand and the smell of sea wrack and the intermittent cries of storm-disturbed birds which fell upon my ear like the desperate appeals of a lost soul. The sea itself was nothing more than a vague far-off line of dim whiteness and I could make out no horizon, sky and water blending into a single bowl of blackness. No use to stand up here on the dunes and try to pick out shapes on the beach. I needed to be down there, and even then, without a torch it was almost going to be a matter of feeling my way along the sand.

My heart sank at the grisly prospect. Then as if in answer to my prayers, I saw a beam of light wavering towards me up the dune.

It shone full in my face and Charley Trenfold's voice said, "Is that you, John? God, you're keen, on a night like this!"

You too, I thought. But I was glad to see him, both for his torch and his company.

Then I recalled Charley's famous nose for a body, and I didn't feel so glad.

I said nothing except, "Come on then. Let's get down there."

We descended and moved forward together in silence along the wavering high tide mark.

We both saw it at the same time. I suppose what went through Charley's mind was, this could be my twelfth! This could be the night I equal old Jacob's record!

What went through my mind I have no words to tell.

I let out a cry compounded of shock, of grief, of anger, of recognition, of farewell, and, shouldering Charley aside, I ran forward, stumbling in the soft sand till I fell on my knees by Lorna's body.

She lay on her face, as if asleep. I turned her over and my straining tearful eyes saw the deep wound on her brow which I knew probably came from the corner of the hearth rather than her fall from the Head.

My grief is impossible to describe. Not for a single moment did it occur to me how damning it was going to sound when Charley described the way I shoved him aside and went rushing forward. "And how could you be so certain that you had found your wife's body, Mr Brown? Unless of course you knew exactly where it was going to be found…"

Then Charley arrived, saying grudgingly, "So I suppose we'll have to call this your *first,* John Brown," as he let the beam of his torch play full on the face cradled in my hands.

And I looked at those dear pallid features in the pool of light. And I thought what strange changes death brought about. And Charley exclaimed, "My God! It's Maisie Palliser!"

It was like the breaking of a spell.

I blinked once, and what the darkness of the night, the tears in my eyes, and above all my fearful expectation had persuaded me was Lorna, instantly and unmistakably became Maisie.

And with equal speed the hypothesis I had programmed in my mind was reformatted. I guessed I'd been right in most particulars except one. It had been Maisie who, rushing forward in a fit of rage when she saw that Lorna really was destroying the will, had fallen and smashed her skull against the edge of the stone hearth. And it had been Lorna who, fearful of the consequences – the long-drawn-out legal enquiries, the rumours and gossip, the threat to her treasured privacy and her family reputation – had untypically panicked, packed the corpse into the Land Rover, and driven up to Bale Head. My hat she'd have put on merely to disguise herself, not to masquerade as me.

Where was she now?

My heart went out to her, wherever she was. This wasn't something she should have to bear alone. I needed to find her, let her know that whatever happened, I was steadfast.

Charley was busy phoning the emergency services. My role with his *seventh.*

Finished, he said, "Well, poor old Maisie. Anyone could see her disappointment over Tony had hit her really hard, but I never thought she'd take it this bad. At least she looks at peace now."

And she did. In fact death had taken ten years off her face, another reason why I'd confounded her with Lorna. But these thoughts were for later. At that moment I was just trying to puzzle out what Charley was talking about.

"Sorry?" I said. "What disappointment?"

"Didn't you know?" He sounded genuinely surprised. "I thought everyone knew. When Betsy left Tony, Maisie was right in there. You know how she was. *Anything I can do to help? Washing, cleaning, ironing, shopping… and is there anything else, Tony? Anything a big strong handsome man like you is missing…?* Well, he wasn't going to say no, was he? Not when it's there on a plate. From all accounts, Maisie got to hoping this was going to turn into something permanent, but anyone could have told her, first sniff Tony got of Betsy coming back, and goodbye Maisie! Well, that happened at Christmas. You must have noticed Maisie wasn't exactly going round wishing everyone a happy New Year!"

I listened, amazed and delighted. Wrapped up in my

own affairs, I'd been stone deaf to local gossip. It certainly explained why Maisie's mood had changed from one of relative benevolence for several weeks to one of more than normal malignancy! And best of all, it provided a motive for self-slaughter which would never be allowed into the open but which would certainly be whispered in the ears of the police and the coroner.

I said, "Charley, can I leave you to handle this by yourself? I'd like to get back and let Lorna know what's happened before someone else gets there with the story."

"No problem," said Charley. "You're right. It'll be better coming from you. Poor Lorna. Last of the Pallisers now."

"Indeed. Thanks, Charley. And by the way, sorry I rushed forward just now. No way to behave. This is clearly your body. We'd never have found it without your torch. It's your *twelfth*."

I could see he was sorely tempted but though us boddi-combing Boddicombers may not have a written code, we play things by the book.

"No," he said regretfully but firmly. "You were first there, John. She's yours."

That's what I call real moral fibre.

When I got back to the house, the Land Rover was parked outside. Lorna was sitting in the kitchen, drinking a glass of whisky.

On my way back I'd been working out how to play this. If she blurted everything out straight away, so be it. I'd do everything I could to cover things up. But in the long term, I doubted if this would do anything for our marriage. Shared guilt isn't a good basis for a relationship. What she needed was my unconditional love, not my complicity. And what I needed was hers, not a sense that she was in thrall to me.

So before she could speak I said, "I'll have one of those. I've got some bad news I'm afraid, dear."

I told her about finding Maisie on the beach. When I told her about Maisie and Tony Simkin, I could tell from her reaction that she'd missed this too. Boddicombers might like their gossip, but they can be as discreet as doctors when it comes to keeping things from people they don't think should know them, like family.

"So poor Maisie must have just cracked under the strain. I thought she'd been acting a bit odd lately, even for her," I concluded.

She sat in silence for a while. She looked pale and I guessed she was nerving herself to tell me the truth. Confession followed by expiation, that was the only route for a Boddicombe Baptist. Though if we could cut straight to the expiation, and it was painful enough, we might be able to put the confession on permanent hold...

But what form of expiation could I offer which would do the trick? How in the space of a few seconds could I weave a hair shirt fit for a guilt-ridden Baptist?

Then it came to me. Thank you, God, I thought. You've got yourself a convert.

I said, "This has been a terrible shock for you, darling. You look whacked out. Have you had anything to eat yet? Why don't I rustle up something for both of us. And then we'll go round to Maisie's."

She looked at me in fearful alarm.

"What for? I'm not sure... John, there's something..."

"To collect Samson, of course. You know how the poor beast doted on Maisie. He's going to be desolate. Someone's got to look after him, and if you don't, who will?"

"Samson? Look after Samson?"

I knew how she hated that dog, far worse than any dislike

she'd ever felt for Maisie.

"Yes. Maisie would have wanted that, don't you think? Good job you're here to do it. Maisie will rest all the easier for knowing that dear old Samson's in good hands for the rest of his days. If you aren't around to do it, then who will? No, it would be the needle, I'm afraid…"

I was laying it on thick. No other way when someone's in search of a sacrifice.

She said again, "Samson… look after Samson…"

For a moment I thought the prospect was going to be too daunting. But it was probably the very horror it roused that did the trick.

She nodded vigorously, even tried a smile.

"Yes, you're right, John. You're so right. That's exactly what Maisie would have wanted."

As hair shirts went, Samson was going to be really scratchy for me as well as Lorna, I thought as I contemplated the single pork chop and recalled viewing the remnants of its one-time partner.

"Right," I said. "So let's have a bite to eat, then I'll collect the dear little chap. Oh, there seems to be only one chop, dear."

"Yes. It's yours. You have it. I'm not terribly hungry."

She smiled at me as she spoke with more affection than I'd seen in her face for a long long time.

I smiled back at her. It was a long way back, but we were taking the first steps.

It suddenly occurred to me that while Lorna's will had been burnt, Maisie's presumably hadn't, which meant her cottage and income would be coming to Lorna. Knowing my wife, she would do everything in her power to renounce the inheritance.

That was going to be my next test in diplomacy. Already

I was seeing a way round it.

At the height of our anger, Lorna had sworn I would never get another penny of her money, and I had vowed that even if she begged me to take it, I would throw it back in her face.

Of course, in our improved relations it would be easy to go back on both of those promises. But how much easier it would be simply to agree that whatever both of us had said in the past about her money, she need feel no compunction about giving nor I about taking what had once been Maisie's.

And with that little bit of help, I could soon be back on my feet again!

Foolish overconfidence? Why so?

I was a fully fledged Boddicomber boddicomber and my luck had changed.

I took a knife and sliced the chop in half.

"No problem," I said. "Let's share."

12 BOLINBROKE AVENUE

Peter James

It was a pleasant looking mock Tudor semi, with a cherry tree in the front garden and a wooden birdbath. There was nothing immediately evident about the property to suggest a reason for the terror Susan Miller felt each time she saw it.

Number 12. White letters on the oak door. A brass knocker. And in the distance, the faint sound of the sea. She began to walk up the path, her speed increasing as she came closer, as if drawn by an invisible magnet. Her terror deepening, she reached forward and rang the bell.

"Susan! Susan, darling! It's OK. It's OK!"

The dull rasp faded in her ears; her eyes sprang open; she gulped down air, staring out into the darkness of the bedroom. "I'm sorry," she whispered, hoarsely. "The dream. I had the dream."

Tom settled back down with a grunt of disapproval and was asleep again in moments. Susan lay awake, listening to the steady, endless roar of the traffic on the M6 pouring past Birmingham, fear roaring like an icy flood-stream through her.

She got out of bed and walked over to the window, afraid to go back to sleep. Easing back the edge of a curtain, she stared out into the night; the large illuminated letters advertising IKEA dominated the horizon.

The dream was getting more frequent. The first time had been on Christmas Eve some ten years back, and for a long while it had recurred only very occasionally. Now it was happening every few weeks.

After a short while, exhaustion and the cold of the late October air lured her back into bed. She snuggled up against Tom's unyielding body and closed her eyes, knowing the second nightmare which always followed was yet to come, and that she was powerless to resist it.

Christmas Eve. Susan arrived home laden with last minute shopping, including a few silly gifts for Tom to try to make him smile; he rarely smiled these days. His car was in the drive, but when she called out he did not respond. Puzzled, she went upstairs, calling his name again. Then she opened the bedroom door.

As she did so, she heard the creak of springs and the rustle of sheets. Two naked figures writhing on the bed swirled in unison towards her. Their shocked faces stared at her as if she was an intruder, had no right to be there. Strangers. A woman with long red hair and a grey-haired man. Both of them total strangers, making love in her bed, in her bedroom. *In her house.*

But instead of confronting them, she backed away, rapidly, confused, feeling as if she herself were the intruder. "I'm sorry," she said. "I'm so sorry. I'm…"

Then she woke up.

Tom stirred, grunted, then slept on.

Susan lay still. God, it was so vivid this time, it seemed to be getting more and more vivid just recently. She had read an article recently about interpreting dreams in a magazine, and she tried to think what this one might be telling her.

Confusion was the theme. She was getting confused easily these days, particularly over time. Often she'd be on the verge of starting some job around the house, then remember that she had already done it; or rushing out to the shops to buy something she had already just bought. Stress. She had read about the effects of stress, in another magazine – she got most of her knowledge from magazines – and that it could cause all kinds of confusion and tricks of the mind.

And she knew the source of the stress, also.

Mandy. The new secretary at the Walsall branch of the Allied Chester & North East Building Society, where Tom was deputy manager. Tom had told her about Mandy's arrival a year ago, and had then never mentioned her since. But she had watched them talking at the annual Christmas party last year, to which spouses and partners were invited. They had talked a damned sight too much for Susan's liking. And they e-mailed each other a damned sight too much.

She had not been sure what to do. At thirty-two she had kept her figure through careful eating and regular aerobics, and still looked good. She took care over her short brown hair, over her make up and her clothes. There wasn't much else she *could* do, and confronting Tom without any evidence would have made her look foolish. Besides, she was under doctor's orders to stay calm. She had given up work in order to relax and improve her chances of conceiving the child they had been trying for these past five years. She *had* to stay calm.

Unexpectedly, the solution presented itself when Tom arrived home that evening.

"Promotion?" she said, her eyes alight with excitement.

"Yup! You are now looking at the second youngest ever branch manager for the Allied Chester & North East Building Society! But," he added hesitantly, "it's going to mean moving."

"Moving? I don't mind at all, darling!" *Anywhere*, she thought. *The further the better. Get him away from that bloody Mandy!* "Where to?"

"Brighton."

She could scarcely believe her luck. In their teens, Tom had taken her for a weekend to Brighton; it was the first time they had been away together; the bed in the little hotel had creaked like mad, and someone in the room below had hollered at them and they'd had to stuff sheets into their mouths to silence their laughter. "We're going to live in Brighton?"

"That's right!"

She flung her arms around him. "When? How soon?"

"They want me to take over the branch at the start of the New Year. So we have to find a house pretty smartly."

Susan did a quick calculation. It was now mid November. "We'll never find somewhere and get moved in within a month. We've got to sell this place, we've got to – "

"The Society will help. They're relocating us, all expenses paid, and we get a lump sum allowance for more expensive housing in the south. They're giving me the week off next week so we can go there and look around. I've told the relocations officer our budget and she's contacting some local estate agents for us."

The first particulars arrived two days later in a thick envelope. Susan opened it in the kitchen and pulled out the contents, while Tom was gulping down his breakfast. There were about fifteen houses, mostly too expensive. She discarded several, then read the details of one that was well within their range, an ugly box of a house with a 'small but charming' garden, close to the sea. She liked the idea of living close to the sea, but not the house. Still, she thought.

You spend most of your time indoors, not looking at the exterior, so she put it aside as a possible and turned to the next.

As she saw the picture, she froze. *Couldn't be*, she thought, bringing it closer to her eyes. *Could not possibly be.* She stared hard, struggling to control her shaking hands, at a mock Tudor semi identical to the one she always saw in her dream. Coincidence, she thought, feeling a tightening knot in her throat. *Coincidence*. Has to be. There are thousands of houses that look like this.

12 Bolinbroke Avenue.

Number *12*, she knew, was the number on the door in her dream.

The distant roar of the sea she always heard in that dream.

Maybe she had seen the house when they had been to Brighton previously. How long ago was that? Fourteen years? But even if she had seen it before, why should it have stuck in her mind?

"Anything of interest?" Tom said, reaching out and turning the particulars of the modern box round to read them. Then he pulled the details of the semi out of her hands, rather roughly. "This looks nice," he said. "In our bracket. *In need of some modernisation.* That's estate agent-speak for a near wreck. Means if we do it up it could be worth a lot more."

Susan agreed that they should see the house. She had to see it to satisfy herself that it was not the one in the dream; but she did not tell Tom that; he had little sympathy for her dreams.

The estate agent drove them himself. He wore a sharp suit and white socks, and smelled of hair gel. "Great position," he said. "One of the most sought-after residential areas of Hove. Five minutes walk to the beach. Hove Lagoon close by, great for kids. And it's a bargain for this area. A bit of work and you could increase the value a lot." He turned into Bolinbroke Avenue, and pointed with his finger. "There we are."

Susan bit her lip as they pulled up outside Number 12. Her mouth was dry and she was shaking badly. Terror was gripping her like a claw: the same terror she previously experienced only in her dreams.

The only thing that was different was the For Sale board outside. She could see the cherry tree; the wooden bird bath. She could hear the sea. There was no doubt in her mind; absolutely no doubt at all.

She climbed out of the car as if she were back in her dream, and led the way up the path. Exactly as she always did in her dream, she reached out her hand and rang the bell.

After a few moments the door was opened by a woman in her forties, with long red hair. She had a pleasant, open natured smile at first, but when she saw Susan, all the colour drained from her face. She looked as if she had been struck with a sledgehammer.

Susan was staring back at her in amazement. There was no mistaking, absolutely no mistaking at all. "Oh my God," she said, the words blurting out. "You're the woman I keep seeing in my dream."

"And you," she replied, barely able to get the words out, "Y- you - you are the ghost that's been haunting our bedroom for the past ten years."

Susan stood, helpless, waves of fear rippling her skin. "Ghost?" she said finally.

"You look like our ghost; you just look so incredibly like

178

her." She hesitated. "Who are you? How can I help you?"

"We've come to see around the house."

"See around the house?" She sounded astonished.

"The estate agent – made an appointment." Susan turned to look at him for confirmation, but could not see him or Tom – or the car.

"There must be a mistake," the woman said. "This house is not on the market."

Susan looked round again, disorientated. Where were they? Where the hell had they gone? "Please," she said. "This ghost I resemble… who – who is – was she?"

"I don't know; neither of us do. But about ten years ago some building society manager bought this house when it was a wreck, murdered his wife on Christmas Eve and moved his mistress in. He renovated the house, and cemented his wife into the basement. The mistress finally cracked after a couple of years and went to the police. That's all I know."

"What – what happened to them?"

The woman was staring oddly at her, as if she was trying to see her but no longer could. Susan felt swirling cold air engulfing her. She turned, bewildered. Where the hell was Tom? The estate agent? Then she saw that the For Sale board had gone from the garden.

She was alone, on the step, facing the closed front door.

Number 12. She stared at the white plastic letters; the brass knocker. Then, as if drawn by that same damned magnet, she felt herself being pulled forward, felt herself gliding in through the solid oak of the door.

I'll wake up in a moment, she thought. *I'll wake up. I always do.* Except she knew, this time, something had changed.

THE POMERANIAN POISONING

Peter Lovesey

ROSEBUD BOOKS
VOLUMES OF ROMANCE
Battersea Bridge Road
London SW11   *12th May*

Dearest Honeypot,
Have you gone into hiding? My telephonist has a sore finger
from trying your number, and your Grizzly Bear is going
spare. Can't work, can't think of anything else. Horrid fears
that his Honeypot has been stolen by some other bear and
taken to another part of the forest.
Put him out of his misery, won't you, and tell him it isn't
true? The weekend in Brighton wasn't so disappointing as
all that, was it? The trouble with this bear is that he's too
excitable when he gets the chance of Honey, but he remains
huggingly affectionate. He passionately wants another chance
to prove it.
Do pick up the blower and comfort your fretful

> *Grizzly*

PS Are you writing anything at present? A brilliant opportunity
has cropped up. Couldn't possibly make Honeypot any sweeter,
but could guarantee to make her infinitely richer.

310 Arch Street
Earls Court
SW5   Sunday afternoon

Dear Frank (I'd rather drop the nursery names, if you don't
mind),

As you see, I've moved from Fulham. Your letter was
sent on. Take a deep breath and pour yourself a double
scotch, Frank. I'm living with a guy called Tristram. He's
my age and could pass for my twin brother and we have so
much in common I can hardly believe it's true. We both
adore Brad Pitt, Harry Potter, Chinese takeaways, Robbie
Williams, Porsches, Spielberg, line dancing, goosedown
duvets and so much else it would take the rest of today and
next week to list it. Tristram went to public school (Radley)
and Sussex University. He has a degree in American Studies
and he's terribly high-powered. He knows Martin Amis
and Jon Snow and masses of people who come up on
the box. I know you'll understand when I say I'm totally
committed to Tristram now.

Pause, for you to top up the scotch.

Frank, I want you to know this has nothing to do with
what happened, or didn't quite happen, that Saturday night
in Brighton. I blame that stuff we smoked. We should have
stayed on g and t. Whatever, no hard feelings, OK?

I'm not sure if you still feel the same about the business
opportunity you mentioned, but I am quite intrigued, as a
matter of fact. Yes, I've been doing some writing, tinkering
away at a novel about the women's movement, the first of a
five-book saga, actually; but Tristram and I are both on the
Social so I wouldn't mind putting the novel on one side if
there's cash on tap now. But I must make it clear that it's my
writing talent, such as it is, that's up for grabs, and nothing

else. Putting it another way, darling, I'm open to advances in pounds sterling.

We don't have a phone yet – not even a mobile – and it gets expensive using pay-phones, so be a darling and write by return.

Be kind to me.

Luv,
Felicity

ROSEBUD BOOKS
VOLUMES OF ROMANCE
Battersea Bridge Road,
London SW11   23 May

Dear Felicity,
You may wonder why it took me so long to answer your letter; on the other hand, you may wonder that I bothered to answer it at all. I need hardly say that I am deeply hurt. For me, the age difference between us was never an impediment, and I rashly imagined you felt the same way. You gave me no reason to suppose there was anyone else in your life. You appeared to enjoy our evenings together. True, I caught you closing your eyes at the Proms from time to time, but I took it that you were transported by the music. You always seemed to revive in time for our suppers in the Trattoria. I find myself putting a cynical construction on everything now.
I suppose I must accept that I was just a meal ticket, or a sugar daddy, or whatever cruel phrase is currently in vogue.
As to that literary project I happened to mention, I shall obviously look elsewhere. The work required is undemanding

and I dare say I shall have no difficulty finding an author
willing to make a six-figure sum for a short children's book.
You may keep my CD of the Enigma Variations. To listen to
it ever again would be too distressful.

> *Your former friend,*
> *Franklin.*

310 Arch Street,
SW5   Wednesday morning

Grizzly Darling!

What a wild, ferocious bear you were last night! Honeypot
has never felt so stirred.

When I arrived with the Elgar and the Bacardi, I honestly
meant to say sorry and a civilised goodbye. You're so
masterful!

If you still mean what you said (and if you don't I shall
throw myself under a train) could you come with the van
some time between six-thirty and seven on Friday evening?
Tristram will be at his karate class and it will avoid a scene
that might otherwise be too hairy for us all. I haven't much
stuff to move out, darling. One trip will be enough, I'm
sure.

> Hugs and kisses,
> Your
> Felicity

310 Arch Street,
SW5

My own dearest Tristram,

Please, darling, before you do anything else, read this to the end. It's terribly important to our relationship that you understand what I have done, and why.

I've moved out. I'm going to stay with Frank, that doddery old publisher guy I told you about. Before you blow your top, Tris, hear me out. I've agonised over this for days. Darling, you know I wouldn't walk out on you without a copper-bottomed reason. Frank means nothing to me. He's a dingbat: pathetic, ugly, flabby, but – and this is the point – he knows a way to make me fabulously rich. I mean stinking rich, Tris. We're talking telephone numbers. And for what? For some book he wants me to write. He hasn't given me all the details yet. He's boxing clever until I move in with him, which is part of the deal, but I understand it's only a children's book he wants. I can finish it in a matter of days if I pull out all the stops, and then I'll be off like a bunny, sweetheart.

He insists I go and live in his house in the backwoods of Surrey while I'm writing the thing. Isn't it a drag? I'm not giving you the address because I know what you'll do. You'll be down there kicking in the door, and who could blame you? But just pause to think.

If I pass up this opportunity, what sort of future do you and I have? I mean, I know it's terrific being together, but what prospect is there of ever getting out of this damp slum? I've had enough, Tris, and so have you. Admit it.

I can almost hear you say I'm selling myself, and I suppose I am if I'm honest, but let's face it, I spent a week-end with Frank in Brighton before I met you. It's not as if he's a total stranger. And if I am selling myself, what a price!

Which is why I'm asking you to keep your cool and try to understand this is the best chance we've got. Just a short interval, darling, and then we can really start to motor.

There won't be a minute when you're out of my thoughts, lover.

I'll write again soon. Be patient, darling!

Ever your
Felicity

This dreary pad in Surrey   Saturday night

Dearest Tristram,

Has it been only a week? It feels like *months*. A life sentence with hard labour, and I've been doing plenty of that. Writing, I mean. Non-stop. The reason I can do so much is that I know every word, every letter, I write is worth mega-bucks. Guaranteed. It's crazy, but it's true. I'm on to a winner, Tris. You see, Frank – he's my publisher-friend – has told me exactly how this is going to work, and he's right. It can't miss. He and I are going to split – wait for it – a million US dollars!

For a kids' book?

Yes!

Scrape yourself off the floor and I'll tell you how this miracle works.

You know that Frank is the chairman of Rosebud Books, who publish romantic fiction, and before you knock it, remember that my only published work, *Desire Me Do*, paid for our new telly, among other things. Frank's outfit isn't exactly Mills & Boon, but he helps beginners like me to get started and I dare say it makes life more tolerable for a few thousand readers of the things.

One of Frank's regular writers was an eccentric old biddy called Zenobia Hatt. That was her real name, believe it or not. I'm using the past tense because she died four or five years ago, before I got to know Frank. Apparently there were hundreds of Hatts. Her books didn't sell all that well, but she kept producing them. And she expected to see them in the shops. Each time she walked into a supermarket and spotted a display of paperbacks, she checked to see if her latest was among them. If it wasn't, she made a beeline for Rosebud Books to tear a strip off Frank. She was always tearing strips off Frank. Even if the book was in the shop, something about it would upset her, like the cover, or the quality of paper they were using. I don't know why he continued to publish her, but he did. She always appeared with her two dogs in tow. They were Pomeranians. If you think I'm rabbiting on about nothing important, you're making a big mistake. The pommies *are* important.

Do you know about Pomeranians? They're toy dogs. Funny little things with enormous ruffs, neat faces and tiny legs. They come in most colours. You know how some old ladies are with dogs? Zenobia doted on hers.

Well, like I said, she died, and this is the important bit, Tristy. In her will, she left the house and everything she had to be divided between her relatives. That is, except any future income from her books. You get royalties trickling in long after a book is published, you see. Zenobia decreed that the future profits from her writing should go into a trust fund to pay for her dogs to be kept in style in some rip-off place in Hampstead that caters for pampered pets who have come into money. The residue was to be awarded annually as a literary prize: the Zenobia Hatt prize.

Nice idea, right? The snag was that Zenobia wasn't really in the Barbara Cartland class as a best-selling writer. The royalties paid the fees at the dogs' home for a couple of years and then the Pommies got arthritis (so it was claimed) and were put down. There was no money left, so the prize was never awarded.

End of story? Not quite. Cop this, love.

A couple of months ago, Frank had a phone call from California. Some film producer was asking about the rights to a Rosebud book called *Michaela and the Mount*, by – you guessed – Zenobia Hatt! It was a cheap romance she published years ago, so long ago in fact that it was out of print, so Frank wouldn't make a penny out of any deal. Don't ask me why, but this book is reckoned to be the perfect vehicle for some busty starlet they reckon is the next Madonna. Tris, darling, they bought it for a million bucks! The money goes into the trust and by the terms of Zenobia's will it has to be offered as this year's prize. The lot. The doggies aren't on the payroll any more, so every silver dollar is up for grabs. And who do you think is going to win?

Shall I tell you how? The point is that Zenobia didn't offer her money for any common or garden novel. She had very clear ideas about the sort of book she wanted to encourage. She had it written into her will that the Zenobia Hatt prize should go to the best published work of fiction that featured a Pomeranian dog as one of the main characters. As you can imagine, that limits the competition somewhat.

When Frank cottoned on to this, he did some quick thinking. Animal stories don't usually feature on the

Rosebud list, but he reckoned he could stretch a point and commission a book for kids featuring Tom the Pom that he'd rush through before the end of the year to scoop the prize. He'd go fifty-fifty with the writer, and that's me, sweetheart! I've signed an agreement and payday will be some time in January, when the trustees award the prize. As simple as that. No one else has time to get a book out, because the news hasn't broken yet, and won't until the film deal is finalised. You know what American lawyers are like. Well, perhaps you don't, but the trustees expect to sign the contract in October or November. *Tom the Pom* will hit the shops in time for Christmas and it doesn't matter a monkey's how many it sells, because it's certain to clean up half a million bucks.

That's the story so far, my love. Naturally I can't wait to finish *my* story and hand it over. Then there'll be nothing to keep me here. I hope to see you Friday at the latest, and what a reunion that will be…

Luv you,
Felicity

Same Place, unfortunately   Thursday

Tris darling,

I'm not going to make it by tomorrow. I showed Frank what I've written so far and he wants some changes, some of them pretty drastic. I tried pointing out that it didn't really matter if the writing was sloppy in places, so long as I finished the flaming book and it got into print before the end of the year, but he came over all high and mighty and sounded off about standards and the reputation of his house. I wondered what on earth his house had to do with it until I discovered he was talking about Rosebud Books, his publishing house. He says he doesn't want an inferior book to carry his imprint, especially as *Tom the Pom* is certain to get a lot of attention when it wins. I suppose he has a point.

So it's back to the keyboard to hammer out some revisions. What a drag!

I suppose Monday or Tuesday would be a realistic estimate.

Impatiently,
Luv,
Felicity

Purgatory   Wednesday

Oh, Tris,

I'm so depressed! I've had the mother and father of a row with Frank. I finished the book yesterday, with all the changes he wanted. He read it last night. He wasn't exactly over the moon, but he agreed it couldn't wait any longer, so he would hand it over to his sub-editor. I said fine, and would he kindly drop me and my baggage at the flat on his way to the office. Tris, he looked at me as if I was crazy. He said we had an agreement. I said certainly we had, and I'd fulfilled my side of it by finishing the book. Now I was ready to go home.

Whereupon he deluged me with a load of gush about how it was much more than a publishing agreement to him. He wouldn't have asked me to write the book if he hadn't believed I was willing to move in with him. I meant more to him than all the money and if I walked out on him now he would drop the typescript in the Thames.

Tris, I'm sure he means it. He knows I need the money and he's going to keep me here like a hostage until the book is in the shops. He could cancel it at any stage up to then. I'll be here for *months.*

There's no way out that I can see. You and I are just going to have to be patient. The day the book is published, I'll be free. And ready to collect my share of the prize. Let's go skiing in February, shall we? And what sort of car shall we buy? We can have that Porsche. One each, if we want. If we both look forward to next year, we can get through. We *must* get through.

Tris, don't try and trace me here, darling. It would be too painful for us both.

I'm thinking of you constantly.

Your soon-to-be-rich, but sorry-to-be-here
Felicity

As Before   1 August.

Tris, my love,
Did you wonder if I was ever going to write again? Are you starting to doubt my existence? Dear God, I hope not. The reason it's been so long is that I get dreadfully depressed. I've written any number of letters and destroyed them when I read them through a second time. It's no good wallowing in self-pity, and it certainly won't do much for you.

So this time, I'll be positive. Another month begins

today. For me, another milestone. I've endured ten weeks now, and I'm still looking at my watch all day long.

I expect you'd like to know how I pass my days. I get up around nine, after he's left for work. Breakfast (half a grapefruit, coffee and toast), then a walk if it's fine. Without giving anything away – and I won't, so don't look for clues – there are some beautiful walks through the woods here. I see squirrels every day and sometimes deer. Often I collect enough mushrooms to have on toast for lunch, or if I'm really energetic I might put them into a quiche. The rest of the morning and most of the afternoon is devoted to my writing. The novel, I mean. It's slow work, but it's good stuff, Tris, a sight better than *Tom the Pom*, which is going to make so much more money. Crazy. (*T the P* was in proof four weeks ago, by the way, and this is the good news: LIBERATION DAY is earlier than I dared to hope – September 30th). Later in the afternoon I might do some reading. The bind is that the only books here are Rosebud Romances, which depress me, even if they're sufficiently well-written to be readable, and boring non-fiction on hunting, shooting and fishing that he only keeps for the leather bindings.

Around six, I get something out of the freezer for the evening meal. He comes home about seven and that's all I'm going to say about my day. I stop living then.

Maybe you wonder why I don't slip away to London during the day to see you. Tris, I've often thought of it. I know I couldn't bear to come back here if I did. He'd stop publication of the book and you and I would have endured all this for nothing. No, I must hold out here.

Less than two months to go!

Love,

Felicity

Tris darling,

I have a horrid feeling Frank suspects something. It's like this. Ever since he moved me here, he's assumed it's for keeps. He constantly goes on about his future as if I'm part of it. Like the two of us (him and me) taking trips to the Bahamas when we've got our hands on the Zenobia Hatt prize. Naturally I play along with this, letting him think I can't imagine anything more blissful than sharing the rest of my life with him and a million bucks.

Up to now, I'm sure he believed me. Up to last night, anyway. Then, out of the blue, he mentioned you, Tris. I don't think either of us has spoken your name since he brought me here. He asked me if I'd been in touch with you, and of course I denied it. Just to sound more convincing, I went a bit further and said I'd dumped you and forgotten all about you.

Frank went on to say he only happened to speak of you because by chance he was driving along Arch Street at lunchtime yesterday and he saw a tall, dark guy in leathers coming out of number 310 with his arm around a strikingly good-looking redhead. I must admit he caught me off guard for a moment. I expect I looked concerned, because he took me up on it at once and asked why I'd gone so pale.

I see now that it was a shabby, underhand trick to test my reactions. I can't fathom how he knows you go in for leathers, because I've never told him, but I'm sure of one thing, and that's that you wouldn't cheat on me while I'm going through hell here.

If Frank wants a battle of wits, he'll find I'm more than a match for him. I'm sure last night was just a try-on, but I'm taking no chances. I'll make certain no one sees me posting this.

I've discovered a way of making my walks more interesting. Among those boring old books on blood sports in the library I found an illustrated guide on the fungi of Great Britain. I take it with me and try and identify the different species along the paths. I'm doing quite well so far, with four different sorts of toadstools as well as the mushrooms I have for lunch.

Six weeks today and we'll be together, Tris. For keeps. I'll write when I can.

Miss you so much.
Felicity

Still Holed Up Here   September 10th

Well, Tris, my darling,

It's a day for celebration. I've actually had a copy of *Tom the Pom* in my hands! The printers delivered on time. But before you uncork the champagne, let me explain that this still isn't publication day. That remains the same, September 30th. They send the books out to the shops and book reviewers ready for the big day, but no one is supposed to sell them before then. In theory, Frank could cancel the publication, call them back and burn them all, and I actually believe he would if he knew I was planning to dump him once I've qualified for the prize.

The book strikes me as pretty abysmal now I've had a chance to read it again. However, they've dressed it up in a shiny laminated cover with cute illustrations by some artist (who won't have any claim on the prize, because it's awarded to the writer) and I expect they'll sell a few hundred.

I'm glad to have something to give me a boost, because

Frank has been driving me mad. He keeps wanting assurances that I'm committed to him for life, and he constantly paws me. I think he senses I find it disagreeable, and that makes him even more persistent. He often mentions you now, and that redhead he is supposed to have seen you with. It's as if he knows what's in my mind and wants me to break down and admit it.

Sometimes I'm so angry I'd like to stop him getting *any* of the prize, like the poms that were put down before they could come into a fortune. You and I would be twice as well off then.

I do my best to divert myself on my walks, which I'm now taking morning and afternoon, in all weathers. I'm becoming quite an expert on fungi. I've found and identified several more species, including *Amanita Phalloides*, known commonly as the Death Cap or the Destroying Angel. Not to be confused with a mushroom, as it is fatal if eaten. There's a small crop of them under an oak only five minutes from here.

Only three weeks now, my love!
Felicity

Here, but not for much longer   One day to Liberation!

Darling Tristram,
By the time you get this, it will be Publication Day and I will have freed myself from Frank for ever. He has become insufferable.

I've come to a momentous decision. It's been forced on

me partly because I'm desperately frightened to tell him I'm leaving him. I don't want the confrontation, and I know if I just walk out, he'll track me down. I don't ever want to see him again. He gives me the creeps. And I feel bitter that he's due to collect such a large share of the prize. It's supposed to go to the writer, Tris, and I was the one who slogged it out for days inventing a story. Frank didn't do a damn thing except hand it to the printer.

I want you to do something for me, Tris. Please, darling, burn every one of the letters I wrote you. I don't want anyone to know I was ever here. *Make sure you do this.*

Trust me, whatever happens, because I love you.
Felicity

6.30

Dear Grizzly,
Quiche in the oven.
Luv
Honeypot

Sydney, Australia   *25th April*

Dear Felicity,
I'm not sure whether you're permitted to receive letters in prison, particularly letters from former boyfriends. Maybe you don't want to hear from me anyway, but I think I owe you some kind of explanation. If it upsets you, well, you've

got twenty years or so to get over it.

I followed your trial in the Aussie papers. They covered it quite fully in the tabloids. Apparently murder by poisoning is still a good paper-seller. They don't have death-cap toadstools here, but there are other kinds of poisonous fungi that I suppose anyone with murder in mind could disguise in a quiche. The reports I read suggested you didn't know it would take up to a week for Frank to die. Books on fungi don't always go into that sort of detail. I wondered why they couldn't save him by washing out his stomach or something, but apparently the toxins are absorbed before the first effects appear. Looking at it from his point of view, poor sod, at least he lived long enough to tell his suspicions to the police.

You'll notice I haven't given an address above. That isn't from secrecy. It's because I'm on a cruise around the world. Some months ago I met this gorgeous redhead called Imogen. To be brutally honest, Immie moved in with me at Earls Court the week after you went to live with Frank. I got lonely, Fel, and I figured you had company, so why shouldn't I?

Imogen is one of those quiet girls who are capable of surprising you. I didn't know she found a bunch of your letters to me and secretly read them. I didn't know she had any talent as a children's writer until last January, when she was announced as the winner of the Zenobia Hatt prize. I don't suppose you had a chance to see the press reports. The trustees received only two entries. Imogen's One Hundred and Two Pomeranians, which she published privately at her own expense in December, was adjudged to be closest to the spirit of the award.

No hard feelings? The cash wouldn't have been much use to you in the slammer, would it?

      Cheers, love.
      Tristram

A GIRL THING

Adrian Magson

"Jill, how do they do that?"

My colleague, Detective Sergeant Steve Bond, was staring up at a small stage, watching a dancer's upper torso ripple in opposite directions like two well-set jellies.

"It's a girl thing," I told him, and went to find George Ackerman, the owner of the Blue Cockatoo nightclub.

A more rounded and upright citizen than Ackerman would have been difficult to find – under a stone. I'd never met him before, but his reputation was formidable. Sadly, so was his nickname of 'Teflon' George. Nothing indictable seemed to stick to him, in spite of his involvement in everything from supplying cheap ecstasy tabs to the sudden disappearance of people he didn't like.

I found him standing by the bar, puffing on a cigar. He saw my reflection in the mirror and turned. Like the stogie, George was fat around the middle and tapered at the ends, with dainty feet and a narrow head. His tailor must have struggled to conceal his strange shape, and was fighting impossible odds.

"Well, well," wheezed George. "A police person of the female... persuasion." He looked past me at Steve, who was still trying to figure out the dynamics of the female body. "And she's got a boy scout in tow. What's up – you afraid we might knock you on the head and take advantage?" He grinned nastily to show it was a joke.

I showed him my card, which wasn't. He ignored it.

"What do you want?" he breathed shortly, stuffing the cigar back in his mouth. Police visits were bad for business

– especially his business.

"I'd like to see your books," I told him. Then, as he was no doubt mentally dialling his lawyer, I added, "Your staff books, I mean – the ones showing the girls you take on." I nodded towards the girl gyrating on stage. "Like her."

"You're joking," he coughed. "Most of them don't stay long enough to get their proper details. What are you after?"

Unfortunately, he was right. There were too many young girls coming through the city hoping to make their fortunes, and a lot of them ended up in slop-buckets like the Cockatoo with their dreams in tatters along with their self-worth. They rarely came with credentials and a birth certificate, and people like Teflon George wouldn't have struggled to get them.

I handed him a photo of a girl. She was blonde, pretty and barely fifteen, although the photo lied convincingly.

"Suzy Welsh," I said. "She's under-age, a ward of court and was last seen two nights ago. In here." Suzy had slipped away from her local council supervisors and headed for the city, hell-bent on having a good time whatever the consequences. We'd been called in too late to catch her.

George assumed an expression of injured innocence. "Come on, love, I can't keep tabs on everyone who walks in here."

"She wasn't walking. She was up there… doing that." I glanced at the stage, where the shimmying queen had ended her rehearsal and was striding off with a flirty backward grin at Steve.

George went a bit tight around the eyes. I guessed he was working out who had given us the information about young Suzy. It wouldn't take him long, and I breathed easily, glad that Sheila Pace, his erstwhile partner, dresser and long-term confidante, had been safely squirreled away before his people could get to her.

Sheila probably knew more about George than anyone on the planet. She'd shared an on-off relationship with him for years until he decided to dump her for a newer model, then she'd suffered further humiliation by finding herself back to dressing the acts. If the girl who'd just raised Steve's blood pressure was any example, she couldn't exactly have been rushed off her feet.

Feeling used and betrayed, Sheila had been mad enough to dish the dirt on George's back-of-house activities. It included much of what we already suspected, along with some fresher allegations about illegal immigrants and smuggling. Like a lot of his contemporaries, George considered himself something of an entrepreneur, and liked to follow the field.

The only problem we had was finding concrete proof. Unfortunately, having been all cosied up with George, Sheila had never bothered recording anything, safe in the belief that she would never need to.

Now George was looking down his nose at me, a sly grin working its way round his mouth. It made my flesh crawl.

"You know, with a figure like yours," he wheezed huskily, "you could make lots of money out there. Know what I mean, doll?"

I wanted to hit him right there and then, he made me feel so unclean. It was the reaction he wanted, of course, because then he'd be able to bring a complaint against me, effectively nullifying my chances of pursuing him further. He'd already neutralised two of my predecessors that way, and the word now was to proceed with utmost caution and leave him alone unless we had cast-iron proof.

Steve arrived just in time to hear him.

"What was that, George?" he asked coolly. "Not an attempt at procurement of a public servant? There are at least three by-laws against that." His face said there was also a good chance George would have more than mere by-laws to worry about.

Just for a second George looked rattled. Then his ego clicked in.

"Dancing, young man," he said quickly. "I was talking about dancing." He blew smoke at us and smiled. "We're always on the lookout for new talent." He smirked at me again. "Especially of the more mature type."

"In your dreams," I snapped, and led the way out of the club.

Back at the station, I ripped off the heavy wig and glasses, and pulled out the rubber cheek pads.

Steve watched with a strange smile on his face. There were times when he did little to hide the fact that he was more than just a bit interested in me, and lately I'd begun to wish the job didn't get in the way so much. "Amazing," he said. "He'd never recognise you if you went back now."

Most people take what they see first without question. I was counting on Teflon George remembering the wig and glasses. That was the theory, anyway.

"I'm going for a shower," I told him. "It's been a long time since anyone made me feel this dirty."

When I came out the chief was waiting, with Steve and two other detectives from the undercover squad. The chief prodded a flip-chart behind him, where someone had pinned an enlarged photo of Suzy Welsh. The grainy print made her look younger and more vulnerable, and her eyes suddenly dominated the room.

"She's been spotted in Tangiers, Morocco," he announced.

"A cop who'd read our international alert saw her being helped into a van yesterday evening at the airport. By the time he woke up the van had gone. But there was a security camera above the entrance, and they sent us a copy. It was definitely her – drugged, of course, to keep her quiet."

"Any idea where she was taken?" Steve asked.

The chief shook his head. "They don't have street cams like we do. But it's probably south towards the Sahara. The only person who might be able to tell us isn't likely to, is he?" He pointed to the two undercover men. "I want you two watching the Cockatoo day and night. Get as close as you can… camp out in the rubbish skips if you have to, but we need to catch the next girl being taken out of that place before they get her out of the country."

He looked angry and flushed with emotion, and I recalled he was the father of two teenage girls. His next words confirmed it. "This man is dealing in young girls. Kids who should still be at school. I don't want to hear slave-trade; if that's not bad enough, that's *not* what he's doing. He's worse than that; he's selling girls into places they'll never come back from. We've got to stop him in his tracks. Anyone disagree?"

For the chief it was an emotional speech, and we all murmured agreement.

"Jill… a word."

I followed him into his office, where he closed the door.

"I want you inside the Cockatoo," he said bluntly. "It's the only way we'll get anything on Ackerman. I want to find young Suzy." He wore the kind of expression I imagined officers in the war had when they sent troops over the top. It was regret and anger and hope all wrapped up in one. "You don't have to, of course." But the words lacked conviction.

"It's OK," I said, and watched his jaw loosen. He hadn't

expected it, since nobody normally volunteered too readily for this kind of assignment. The people Teflon George used were some of the nastiest around, with a scary reputation.

But I was good and mad myself, especially now I knew Suzy had been spirited out of the country. And I kept seeing the arrogant, self-satisfied look on Ackerman's face, and the way he'd looked me over as if I was a piece of cheap meat. I was almost glad I'd experienced it; it was just the motivation I needed.

That evening I pitched up at the Cockatoo on the arm of a bouncer named Charlie Redmond, who worked for a number of local clubs. He had a cousin on the force – a fact not widely publicised – and had agreed to feed me into the club as an acquaintance. It was safer than turning up unannounced, and Charlie's say-so would get me inside. The rest was up to me and Ackerman's own slimy greed.

"I rang earlier," Charlie whispered, as we walked inside. "Said you'd come to the city to make some quick money. From here on, you're on your own." He squeezed my arm and peeled away, leaving me feeling very exposed.

As I approached the bar, I saw George watching me. Steve was somewhere around, although I didn't expect to see him.

I had on a short skirt, showing lots of leg, with blue tights and high heels. Under my denim jacket I'd squeezed myself into a t-shirt two sizes too small. All the clothes were cheap and untraceable, and heavy make-up completed the picture. I felt like Dustin Hoffman in *Tootsie*. Without the glasses and wig, I was hoping nobody would twig I'd been in before.

George shot me a sharp look. "So you want to make some quick cash?" he said. Nearby a couple of his cronies looked me over and smirked. I hoped they didn't expect to do a road-test first.

"Yes," I said. "Charlie said he knew a club where I could get –"

"What've you done before?"

"General stuff," I told him. "Waitressing, coat-check… that sort of thing. But I'm willing to learn."

"One step at a time," he said softly. "One step at a time." He looked at his two companions, who shrugged and pulled faces. It was like I was invisible.

"Can you dance?" he asked.

Given the right circumstances, I can dance my legs off, but I didn't think he was talking church social. "I suppose," I said with what I hoped was the right amount of fresh-from-the-sticks naïveté.

"Any family?" he queried.

"No."

"How old are you?"

"Thirty-three. Charlie said you might be looking for someone older."

"Charlie's a good boy," he said, peeling a flake of tobacco off his wet lower lip. "All right. You can do tables. At 'em, not on 'em. You serve drinks, smokes, whatever, but you don't do nothing else." He smiled nastily round his cigar and puffed some smoke up at the ceiling. "Not till I tell you, anyway…"

I was issued with a minuscule skirt and see-through blouse and told the staff rules. It amounted to keeping my hands off the customers' wallets and out of the till. Nobody bothered asking for any proof of identity.

It took massive restraint to resist smacking the first man who touched me, but I gritted my teeth and kept my fists to myself. After a while, and with advice from the other girls, I developed a way of weaving through the crowds and avoiding most of the gropers. Occasionally I had to fend off the odd drunk, but the floor bouncers were never far away and soon sorted them out. I wonder what they'd have said if they knew I had a black belt in judo.

The first two nights produced nothing. I was too busy learning the ropes and staying out of trouble to do much listening. But on the third night Teflon George stopped me in the corridor and told me to see Gina, one of the lead girls.

"You're on," he said without preamble. "We've got some special clients in, and they like a slightly older woman. Gina'll show you what to do. It ain't exactly rocket science, know what I mean?" He smirked and walked away.

Gina was a slim blonde with a soft, round face. She'd been at the Cockatoo for nearly a month, which was long-term by most standards. She was good, though, and patiently took me through the basic steps and a few tricks which she said the punters liked seeing.

"Nervous?" she asked.

Was I. This was suddenly real; I'd never thought it would come to this. I'd been counting on having it all wrapped up before having to… well, do this.

I noticed Gina putting some of her stuff into a small case.

"You're leaving?" I asked her.

She glanced nervously at the door and nodded. "I'm not supposed to say, but those special clients George said are coming in? They're the ones he's been doing business with lately. Nightclub owners from Dubai, George said." She grinned, a sharp pull of her face muscles. "He said they'll fly me to Boukhalef airport tomorrow, and I'll be working a really posh club by the day after, on top money." She closed the case with a snap. "Goodbye, Cockatoo and hello, hot, sunny Dubai."

I stared at her, wondering how desperate someone had to be to fall for such a line. Saddest of all was that George held Gina in such contempt he hadn't credited her with possibly knowing that Boukhalef airport was nowhere near Dubai.

It was actually in Tangiers, Morocco.

I had to get word to Steve. With the clients in the club, we'd never have a better chance of finding Suzy. And with Gina's statement about where she was headed, it would be enough to give us a trail to follow.

I was by the payphone, scrabbling for change, when a meaty hand descended on my shoulder. It was Teflon George.

"You got work to do," he grated, and pushed me towards the stage.

He knows, I thought.

The lights out front were dazzling, and all I could see was a sea of faces staring up at me. In the front row sat three large men in expensive suits. The clients.

I already felt naked without needing to take anything off, and wondered if I'd make it to the front door before being stopped. A glance at George in the wings and his two henchmen out front soon put paid to that idea.

I gyrated in time to the music, and began to undo the buttons on my blouse. *This wasn't what I joined the police force for!*

Then, in a flash of light from the bar, I saw the most welcome sight ever. It was Steve, staring at me with his mouth open.

I drew my hand across my throat, the signal to stop everything.

For a second, he didn't move, he was so transfixed, so I repeated the signal, this time more urgently. Behind me, I heard George call to his henchmen.

It was enough to bring Steve to his senses. In a flash he drew a radio from his pocket and issued terse instructions. Seconds later the doors burst open and the place was full of uniforms.

As George and his clients were hustled away, already babbling about Suzy, Steve crossed the floor towards me. He held his hand out to help me down, and whipped off his jacket and slung it around my shoulders. The warmth from his body made me shiver.

Then someone switched off the bar lights and the place went quiet. The Blue Cockatoo was closing for business.

"I'm glad you didn't arrive any later," I told him, trying to sound calm. The door slammed shut, making me jump, which spoiled the pretence.

"What – and miss seeing you up there?" He pretended to joke, but I knew he'd been worried. It made me feel rather safe and secure all of a sudden. Wanted, even.

We walked outside and got into his car, and I noticed he shielded me all the way, making sure none of the assembled reporters and onlookers got too close.

"Did that girl ever show you how they do the shimmy?" I asked him as we pulled away from the kerb. I snuggled down in the seat, glad to be out of the club.

He looked sheepish, like a guilty little boy, and I knew why: he was trying not to think about me up on the stage. "No," he admitted. "She didn't."

I thought about the here and now, and how fixated I'd become on the job just recently. More than anything, I thought about how much I needed to break the spell, before it was too late.

"Let's go to my place," I said. I was wondering if I could recall all the moves Gina had shown me.

Well, having learnt such a valuable new skill, it seemed a shame to waste it...

SNEEZE FOR DANGER

Val McDermid

I shifted in my canvas chair, trying to get uncomfortable. The hardest thing about listening to somebody sleeping is staying awake yourself. Mind you, there wasn't much to hear. Greg Thomas was never going to get complaints from his girlfriends about his snoring. I'd come on stake-out duty at midnight, and all I'd heard was the tinny tail-end of some American sports commentary on the TV, the flushing of a toilet and a few grunts that I took to be him getting comfortable in the big bed that dominated his extravagantly stylish studio penthouse.

I knew about the bed and the expensive style because we also had video surveillance inside Thomas's flat. Well, we'd had it till the previous afternoon. According to Jimmy Lister, who shared the day shift, Thomas had stopped in at the florist's on his way back from a meet with one of his dealers and emerged with two big bunches of lilies. Back at the flat, he'd stuffed them into a vase and placed them right in front of the wee fibre optic camera. Almost as if he knew.

But of course, he couldn't have known. If he'd had any inkling that we were watching, it wouldn't have been business as usual in the Greg Thomas drugs empire. He wouldn't have gone near his network of middlemen, and he certainly wouldn't have been calling his partner in crime to discuss her forthcoming trip to Curacao. If he'd known we were watching him, he'd have assumed we were trying to close him down and he'd have been living the blameless life.

He'd have been wrong. I'm not that sort of cop. That's not to say I don't think people like Greg Thomas should be put away for a very long time. They should. They are responsible for a disproportionate amount of human misery, and they don't deserve to be inhabiting the high life. Thomas's cupidity played on others' stupidity, but that didn't make any of it all right.

Nevertheless, my interest was not in making a case against Thomas. What mattered to me was the reason nobody else had been able to do just that. Three times the drugs squad had initiated operations against Greg Thomas's multi-million pound business, and three times they'd come away empty-handed. There was only one possible conclusion. Somebody on the inside was taking Thomas's shilling.

Samuels, who runs the drugs squad, had finally conceded he wasn't going to put Greg Thomas away until he'd put his own house in order. And that's where we came in.

Nobody loves us. Our fellow cops call us the Scaffies. That's Scots for bin men. My brother, who studied Scottish literature at university, says it's probably a corruption of scavengers. Me, I prefer to knock off the first two letters. Avengers, that's what we are. We're there to avenge the punters who pay our wages and get robbed of justice because some cops see get rich quick opportunities where the rest of us see the chance to make a collar.

It's easy to be cynical in my line of work. When your job is to sniff out corruption, it's hard to see past that. It's difficult to hang on to the missionary zeal when you're constantly exposed to the venality of your fellow man. I've seen cops selling their mates down the river for the price of a package holiday. Sometimes I almost believe that some of them do it for the same reason as criminals commit crimes – because they can. And they're the ones who are most affronted when we sit them down and confront them with what they've done.

So. Nobody loves us. But what's worse is that doing this job for any length of time provokes a kind of emotional reversal. It's almost impossible for us Scaffies to love anybody. Mistrust becomes a habit and nothing will poison a relationship faster than that. In the end, all you've got is your team. There's eight of us, and we're closer than most marriages. We're a detective inspector, two sergeants and five constables. But rank matters less here than anywhere else in the force. We need to believe in each other, and that's the bottom line.

Movement in the street below caught my attention. A shambling figure, staggering slightly, making his way down the pavement opposite our vantage point. I nudged my partner Dennis, who rolled his shoulders as he leaned forward, focused the camera and snapped off a couple of shots. Not that they'd be any use. The three a m drunk was dressed for the weather, the collar of his puffa jacket close round his neck and his baseball cap pulled down low. He stopped outside Thomas's building and keyed the entry code into the door. There were sixteen flats in the block and we knew most of the residents by sight. I didn't recognise this guy, though.

Through the glass frontage of the building opposite, we could see him weaving his way to the lift. He hit the call button and practically fell inside when the doors opened. I was fully alert now. Not because I thought anything untoward was going down, but because anything that gets the adrenalin going in the middle of night surveillance is welcome. The lift stopped on the second floor, and the drunk lurched out into the lobby, turning to his left and heading for one of the flats at the rear of the building.

We relaxed and settled back into our chairs. Dennis, my partner, snorted. "I wouldn't like to be inside his head in the morning," he said.

I reached down and pulled a thermos of coffee out of my bag. "You want some?"

Dennis shook his head. "I'll stick to the Diet Coke," he said.

It was about fifteen minutes later that we heard it. Our headphones exploded into life with a volley of sneezing. I nearly fell out of my chair. The volume was deafening. It seemed to go on forever. A choking, spluttering, gasping fit that I thought would never end. Then, as suddenly as it had started, it ended. I looked at Dennis. "What the hell was that?"

He shrugged. "Guy's coming down with a cold?"

"Out of the blue? Just like that?"

"Maybe he decided to have a wee taste of his own product."

"Oh aye, right. You wake up in the night, you can't get back to sleep, so you do a line of coke?"

Dennis laughed. "Right enough," he said.

We left it at that. After all, there's nothing inherently suspicious about somebody having a sneezing fit in the middle of the night. Unless, of course, they never wake up.

I was spark out myself when Greg Thomas made his presence felt again. Groggy with tiredness, I reached for the phone, registering the time on my bedside clock. Just after one o'clock. I'd been in bed for less than four hours. I'd barely grunted a greeting when a familiar voice battered my eardrum.

"What the hell were you doing last night?" Detective Inspector Phil Barclay demanded.

"Listening in, boss," I said. "With Dennis. Like I was supposed to be. Why?"

"Because while you were listening in, somebody cut Greg Thomas's throat."

On my way to the scene, I called Jimmy Lister and tried to piece together what had happened. When the dayshift hadn't heard a peep out of Thomas by noon, they'd grown suspicious. They began to wonder if he'd somehow done a runner. So they'd got the management company to let them into Thomas's flat and they'd found him sprawled across his bed, throat gaping like some monstrous grin.

By the time I got to the flat, there was a huddle of people on the landing. Drugs Squad, Serious Crime guys, and of course the Scaffies. Phil Barclay was at the centre of the group. "There you are, Chrissie," he said. "So how the hell did you miss a murder while you were staking out the victim?"

For Phil to turn on one of his own in front of other cops was unheard of. I knew I was in for a very rough ride.

Before I could answer, Dennis emerged from the stairwell. "Listen to the tapes, boss," he said. "Then you'll hear everything *we* did. Which is nothing."

"Except for the sneezing," I said slowly.

All the eyes were on me now. "About twenty past three. Somebody had a sneezing fit. It must have lasted a couple of minutes at least." I looked at Dennis, who nodded in confirmation.

"We assumed it was Thomas," he said.

"That would fit," one of the other cops said. I didn't know his name, but I knew he was Serious Crime. "The pathologist estimates time of death between two and five am."

Samuels from the Drugs Squad stuck his head out of the flat. "Phil, do you want to take a look inside, see if anything's out of place from when you had the video running?"

Barclay looked momentarily uncomfortable. "Chrissie, you and Dennis take a look. I didn't really pay much attention to the video footage."

"Talk about distancing yourself," Dennis muttered as we entered the flat, sidestepping a SOCO who was examining the lock on the door through a jeweller's loupe.

I paused and said, "Key or picks?"

The SOCO looked up. "Picks, I'd say. Fresh scratches on the tumblers."

"He must have been bloody good," I said. "We never heard a thing."

Greg Thomas wasn't a pretty sight. I was supposed to be looking round the flat, but my eyes were constantly drawn back to the bed. "How come we never heard it? You'd think he'd have made some sort of noise."

One of the technicians looked up from the surface he was dusting for prints. "The doc said it must have been an incredibly sharp blade. Went through right to the spine, knife through butter. He maybe would have made a wee gurgle, but that's all."

At first glance, nothing in the flat looked different. I stepped round the bed towards the alcove where Thomas had his workstation. "His laptop's gone," I said, pointing to the cable lying disconnected on the desk.

"Great. So now we know we're looking for a killer with a laptop," Dennis said. "That'll narrow it down."

Back on the landing, Phil told us abruptly to head back to base. "We'll have a debrief in an hour," he said. "The Drugs Squad guys can run us through Thomas's known associates and enemies. Maybe they'll recognise somebody from our surveillance."

I walked back to my car, turning everything over in my head. The timing stuck in my throat. It felt like an uncomfortable coincidence that Greg Thomas had been killed the very night we'd lost our video cover. I knew Phil Barclay and Samuels were tight from way back and wondered whether my boss had mentioned the problem to Samuels. If the mole knew we were watching, he might have decided the best way to avoid detection was to silence his paymaster for good. That would also explain the quiet. None of Thomas's rivals could have known about the need to keep the noise levels down.

Slowly, an idea began to form in my head. We might have lost the direct route to the drugs squad's bad apple, but maybe there was still an indirect passage to the truth. I made a wee detour on the way back to the office, wondering at my own temerity for even daring to think the way I was.

The debrief was the usual mixture of knowledge and speculation, but because there were three separate teams involved, the atmosphere was edgy. The DI from the Crime Squad told us to assume our unidentified drunk was the killer. He hadn't been heading for a flat, he'd been making for the back stairs. Apparently the lock on the door leading to the penthouse floor showed signs of having been forced. He'd probably left by the same route, using the fire door at the rear of the building. He showed our pix on the big screen but not even the guy's mother could have identified him from that. "And that is all we know so far," he said.

The silhouette I'd been expecting finally showed up outside the frosted glass door of the briefing room. I put up my hand. "Not quite all, sir," I said. "We also know he's allergic to lily pollen."

As I spoke, the door opened and the desk officer walked in, looking sheepish behind a big bouquet of stargazer lilies. The fragrance spread out in an arc before him as he walked towards Samuels. "I was told these were urgent," he said apologetically.

I held my breath, my eyes nailed to the astonished faces of Samuels and his cohort of Drugs Squad detectives.

And that's when Phil Barclay shattered the stunned silence with a fusillade of sneezes.

POOR OLD FRANKIE

Barbara Nadel

Father forgive me for I have sinned…

For a time, Frankie made shifts at the Runfold Psychiatric Hospital worthwhile, and I let him down. When you work for a nursing agency you don't usually get close to the patients. But Frankie Driscoll was different. He was still in there. He hadn't turned into a shuddering vegetable like so many of them do on the long-term chronic wards. Frankie Driscoll was a far greater person than just his diagnosis or even the medication that coshes most of his kind to the ground.

I met Frankie one morning in December. Loping past the dead tangle of bushes that were allowed to straggle unkempt outside the chronic ward, the first words he ever said to me were, "Can I trust you, girl?"

Suspicious as ever with unknown patients about what might be about to follow, I nevertheless replied, "Yes."

"Come here." He beckoned me over with one thin, sharp-nailed finger. He was old, at least seventy I reckoned at the time, and his hair was as white as the sheets on the patients' beds should have been.

"What's your name?" I asked.

"What's yours?" he countered.

I watched him shift what remained of his roll-up from the left to the right hand side of his toothless mouth. "You a nurse, a new nurse," he said. "I seen you."

"I'm with the agency," I said.

"I know that!" he responded as if to an idiot. "Why you

219

think I want to talk to you?"

It isn't easy to do a good job as a temporary or agency nurse working with people who are physically ill. You don't know the patients or the other staff, and getting information out of stressed or overworked people isn't easy. In a psychiatric setting it's even harder. Psychiatric patients need to be listened to, understood and not just dismissed as 'delusional'. Not all the tales they tell exist only in their heads. Before I started working for the agency, I was on the permanent staff of the Wicklow Psychiatric Hospital twenty miles back towards London. I got to know patients on what had been my own chronic ward well. Only sometimes did my patients' stories live only in their minds.

"I'm Frankie," the old man in front of me said.

"Julia," I said.

He nodded. "Well, Julia," he said, "it's about what happens in the evenings. Them horrors on that ward, they trying to poison poor old Frankie."

Handover to the night staff was at five-thirty in the afternoon. It was now five, but because it was winter it was already dark. The six of us who had covered the day shift had to sit crammed into the tiny ward office which was lit, for some reason, by a light bulb struggling to push out forty watts of power. Pat, the ward manager, liked to have a chat with 'her' staff before the ward was given over to the night nurses.

"Any other bits of business?" she said after the various medication and therapy regimes that patients were on had been discussed. "Problems?"

Pat McCauley wasn't the easiest woman to work for. Like me she was in her mid-forties with the full Monty of husband, kids and mortgage back home. Unlike me she was both enormously overweight and very, very sociable. Pat didn't 'do' criticism and neither did her two deputies, Tracey and Janice. The three of them were a team. On my first day at Runfold, which had only been the previous week, I had witnessed – sort of – what had happened when the only other permanent member of staff, Geoff, had questioned something Pat had done. The three of them had taken him into the office, Pat had pulled the blinds down and half an hour later Geoff had emerged, quiet and seemingly thoughtful. It was at that point that I made a promise to myself not to tangle with Pat or any of her acolytes. After what had happened at the Wicklow I knew I didn't need it. Against all my natural instincts I swallowed back what Frankie had told me and said nothing. At the end of the meeting Pat and the other two waved the rest of us on our way home with cheery smiles.

"See you tomorrow," Pat said thickly as we left, "unless any of us wins the lottery!"

Sarah, the other agency nurse, muttered words to the effect that after a lottery win we couldn't expect to see her for dust. Pat shut the door behind us and I heard her, Tracey and Janice sit back down again.

I was walking from the ward to the car park when Frankie loomed up at me again.

"You never said nothing about me to that great fat dollop and her pals did you?" he said as he nervously rolled his cigarette around the edges of his mouth.

"No." I sighed. The story Frankie had told me that morning, embellished with various paranoid details like the one about the KGB parachuting into the hospital grounds, had basically revolved around a belief he had that he was being injected with something – he didn't know

221

what – against his will. This was happening just before handover every afternoon and Frankie named Pat McCauley as his assailant. Her acolytes apparently helped by holding him down. Much as the three of them gave me the creeps, I couldn't believe that they would do such a thing.

"But why would Pat and the others want to do that?" I said. "You're no trouble, Frankie."

I'd read his file. Frankie was diabetic but not badly so, and was given his intravenous insulin along with his psychiatric medication every morning.

Frankie leaned in towards me, his rank cigarette-scented breath blasting into my face. "She want my money, that fat lazy dollop!" he said.

"Yes, but…"

"They keep giving me medicine, see," he said. "That make me not know what I'm doing. I could sign anything they want me to like that."

"Yes, but…"

"Then they'll kill me!" he gabbled. "I need help, girl! Don't know what I have done and what I ent! You're new here, you look as like you can be trusted. I hope to Christ that you can! Get a letter to my friend, will you, girly?"

Frankie – Francis – Driscoll had been, so his file had told me, a merchant seaman in his youth. He'd been very far from his native Cornwall, all over the world in fact, before he'd started hearing voices in his early forties. Diagnosed with schizophrenia decades ago, he'd been at Runfold ever since. There was no mention on his file of any money, property or family. The only hint of anything vaguely connected to wealth was the name of his home town, Padstow, which now, over ten years later, had been made fashionable by the celebrity chef, Rick Stein.

"Frankie, I don't know about all this," I said, looking down at the car keys now in my hands.

"Think I'm just a raving nutter, do you?" Frankie said, his lank white hair shaking with anger. "Just like the rest of them! Thought you was different, I did! Thought I saw summat there in your eyes, some human feeling, so I did! You's with the agency!"

Quite what Frankie thought my being an agency nurse meant, I didn't know. But I suspected he imagined I was maybe, in reality, with a friendly security force of some sort. A lot of patient delusions revolve around war, politics and espionage.

However, real or not, Frankie was frightened of something and I knew from my own experiences of fear in the past, just how awful that was. His eyes were full of tears, he was shaking, I felt for him. Whether or not I believed the stuff about Pat McCauley and her friends at this point I do not know. I looked into Frankie's face and smiled. "Who's this friend of yours, then?" I said.

"King Fahd of Saudi Arabia," Frankie replied.

Of course anything is possible. Ordinary people do meet up with kings and celebrities and strike up friendships with them from time to time. Frankie had been all over the world and so it was just possible he had met up with a Saudi prince at some point in his travels. My oldest who wants to study politics at college told me King Fahd was about Frankie's age. He had also, apparently, travelled a lot when he was young.

Because it was her ward, I had to tell Pat what I was doing. Frankie hadn't seen King Fahd, so he said, since they were both youngsters and so we'd agreed just to send a letter to say that Mr Driscoll wasn't well. Pat said, "I don't see the harm. It's a load of eyewash of course, and you'll never hear back, but if it keeps Frankie happy…"

She smiled across at him. I took my pen and writing paper over to Frankie's bed and sat down beside him. "So Frankie," I said, "what…"

"Vicious bitch!" Frankie said. I saw that his eyes were still firmly fixed on Pat. "Rotten cow!"

"Frank…"

"Don't wanna write no letter today!" Frankie said. He looked down at me and I could see the heaviness of the drugs in his eyes. "Feel too rough. Big fat cow make me feel too rough."

"Yes, well maybe another…"

I was interrupted by Frankie's noisy unconscious breathing. I put my pad and pen back in my handbag.

The occupant of the bed next to Frankie's, an elderly man called Stephen said, "Ashes. From the crematorium. Everywhere."

Tracey, who was as thin and wasted as Pat was fat and blooming came over and looked at Frankie with a smile on her face.

"He sleeping again?" she asked me.

"Yes," I said. "We were going to write a letter but…"

"Oh, bless!" Tracey said and then she walked back towards the ward office, went in and pulled the door shut behind her.

We eventually got the letter written three days later. Frankie was, as had become usual for him that week, in his bed when he dictated it to me. But he was hopeful of an answer from his 'old friend' who he had addressed informally as 'Fahd'. I asked him where I should send the letter and he looked at me struck and said, "Well, to the Royal Palace,

and he stood still, e[...]
a press of faces. Fire[...]
inviting and irresistib[...]
bench near the blaze. [...]
he ordered ale and ste[...]
own voice surprising h[...]

Tomorrow it woul[...]
leave Leeds and really [...]

The warmth of the f[...]
left him weary. He nee[...]
that would pose no pro[...]
woman.

The last time had bee[...]
gift the master had pre[...]
one night. She lay, brow[...]
forced himself on her. [...]
alone, and only the hea[...]
assured him it hadn't be[...]

Outside, the sky had [...]
breath clouded the air an[...]
few flakes of snow flutter[...]

She stood half on Brigg[...]
name he didn't rememb[...]
pathetic, patched shawl dr[...]
light picking out the pale [...]

He moved closer, aston[...]
fast.

"Looking to warm your[...]
to sound cheery, but her v[...]

He nodded.

"Down here then, luv."

He followed her down th[...]
in sight of the main stree[...]

the skills of his old life still sharp. He ignored the port whores, all pox-ridden, rowdy and consumptive, and bought a hot meal and bed for a night instead. In the mirror he caught a glimpse of himself, his shoulders stooped, face burned dark and lined, hair matted and hanging to his shoulders, thin and grey though he wasn't yet thirty. He pulled the worn blanket over his body. There were fleas in the sheets but at least the bed didn't rock and shiver in the waves. The next morning, without a second thought, he turned his back on the coast and began walking east.

By the time he reached Winnat's Pass the pain of cold had seared to his bones and his old boots were ribbons of leather, feet flayed and bloody from the stones and ice on the roadway. But he was lucky, finding a stranger for company whose corpse at least provided new shoes even if it added nothing to his small supply of coins; when the snows melted in the spring they'd find the body and never know what happened.

From Sheffield he made his way north, face set tight and grim against the snow and the weather, the ragged coat held tight around his body by a cord as the gusts tore at his cheeks more brutally than any overseer's whip.

He passed Wakefield in the early dusk. His money was running precious thin and he was looking at a hungry, freezing night burrowed in a copse when he saw the farmer, a florid man with ugly, fat thighs jiggling in his breeches as he walked briskly home through the field.

It took little to slice him, pull the body into the trees and take the rich, warm coat. There were coins in the pocket too, enough to see him back to Leeds.

Back to his home.

Back to Richard Nottingham.

Back to kill.

He crossed Leeds
with the market
their wares up on
walls and houses
treacherous in the
Swine Gate and th
on Dyers' Garth. F
up at the bulk of tl
Soon he was at the
people lurched and

He'd been standin
as if he was still sh
wind's frigid tongue
he followed, unnotic
the Moot Hall with i
the ground floor, up
the window as Nott
House, hailed some n
his view through the

He'd seen what he r
creased his lips. The n

He could do it tonig
the blood stained the
live again.

His fingers twitched
No, not tonight.

He wanted the act to
the memories could tu
ahead.

Slowly, almost carele
passed the Ship, once
Talbot.

Inside the door the n

a sense of relief in her smile, her hands already hoisting her skirts, he rested his blade lightly against her throat so that a faint line of tiny red drops bloomed on her skin.

He didn't need words; she understood. He pushed her back against the wall, tore at her skirt and entered her. Her eyes opened wide, their blank, hopeless stare a muted echo of the girl in Jamaica. It was only seconds later that his backhanded blow sent her to the floor, still mute, and he dashed back into Briggate, still tying his breeches.

It was God's joke, he decided, that he'd end up in a rooming house in the same yard where he'd been a boy, before his parents had died of the vomiting sickness and he'd made his way on the streets. He glanced at the old door as he passed, but any memories were held like secrets behind the wood. It was just one night here. By this time tomorrow he'd be finished here and on his way to York or London, to anywhere he could disappear, to where life could begin. There was only one tie here, and he'd loose it soon enough.

The dank room already held two men with ale on their breath, their sleeping farts sweetening the air. He lay on the straw pallet fully clothed, the wretched rag of a blanket over him, and drifted away.

Something cold and metallic was pushing against his mouth. Confused, still sleep-drunk, he thought it was a dream and struggled to open his eyes, pawing at his face with one hand.

"Sit up."

The words came as a command, colder than the bitter air. Without even thinking, he sat up. Thin early light came though a small window covered by years of grime.

The man towered over him, seeming to fill the space, his presence full of menace. He was tall, older, with unkempt hair, but his back was straight and his chest wide under dirty clothes. One large fist held a silver-topped walking stick lightly.

He knew who this was; it was impossible to have lived on the edge of the law in Leeds and not know. Amos Worthy.

"I hear you were with one of my girls last night." The man's eyes were dark, his voice slow, as deep and resonant as any preacher. "You didn't pay her. I can't allow that."

He paused, letting the words hang ominously in the air.

"But then you had to cut her, didn't you? So now I have to make an example of you."

Nick started to reach for the knife in his pocket. The man simply shook his head once and gestured over his shoulder. A pair of thickset youths, faces hard and scarred, arms folded, stood inside the door. The two other beds were empty.

"I know who you are," the man, speaking softly and conversationally. "Oh aye, you've got the Indies burned on your face, Nick Andrews. Seven years is a long time away from home."

All he could do was nod. Whatever words he'd once possessed had deserted him. Worthy was offhand, almost casual in his certainty and Nick felt the piss burn hot down his leg as his bladder emptied. He was going to die here, in this room, in this bed, before he could finish his work. And all for a few short seconds with a cheap whore.

"All that time doesn't seem to have made you any wiser. Just back, are you?"

Nick nodded again.

"A short homecoming, then." He raised his thick eyebrows. "You crossed me. You can't do that here."

He brought the stick down on Nick's face. He saw it fall, quick, effortless, but it burst his nose, the shock of pain hard and sudden, blood gushing chokingly into his mouth.

"You can kill him now, lads. You know what to do with the body."

HUNGRY EYES

Sheila Quigley

The archaeologist, a tall, very thin man with a heavy grey moustache, smiled at his audience.

The hall was full of people eager to learn about the recent dig at St Michael and All Angels church in Houghton le Spring. A new floor was being laid, so the archaeologists had moved in.

His lecture was finished, and he summed up, "So what have we learned? That this was once a prehistoric ritual site? Perhaps... A Roman temple? Possibly; it was after all standard practice for Romans to take over earlier religious sites. There is definite evidence of Normans and Saxons, and during the last excavation in the churchyard in the late nineties an erratic line of whinstone boulders, probably from the Hadrian's Wall area, do suggest a prehistoric use of the site. Several other such boulders have now been found inside the church, so there is a suggestion – not proof, mind you – that perhaps there was a stone circle on the site."

PC Steven Carter gasped in awe. He couldn't wait to get back to the station and tell his boss, DI Lorraine Hunt. She was always so interested in the history of Houghton le Spring, he thought, applauding along with everyone else.

As Carter made his way outside, he was followed by three men. They were locals from the Seahills estate in Houghton le Spring; Carter hadn't noticed them because they had been sitting at the back.

"So what do yer reckon?" Danny Jorden asked his two friends. Danny was a chancer, had been all his life, skirting

245

the boundary between legal and illegal, nothing big, nothing bad, just enough to keep his kids in shoe leather and food on the table.

"Hmm, don't really know." His cousin Len Jorden scratched his chin, looking sideways at the other member of the trio. Like Danny, Len was dark-haired with green eyes. The resemblance ended there though; Danny was tall and thickset, and frequently wore a smile, while Len was as tall as the archaeologist but even thinner, and had the look of a professional pall bearer.

"You're a bloody old woman, Len." Adam Glazier, at twenty-six the youngest by nine years, grinned at Len.

"And your jokes stink," Len retorted.

"Knock knock," Adam laughed.

"Piss off."

"Shut up, the pair of you. What we gonna do? I reckon there's a fortune in coins lying in this old church. We need to get to them before those archaeologist blokes do, and it has to be tonight. Tomorrow they start filling the floor in."

"It's a damn shame they couldn't go deeper – God knows what they might have found. I mean, all those old bones." Len shivered.

Danny shook his head. "That's the point, Len, they can't dig any further. But we can."

"I don't know, the church in the middle of the night… Kinda spooky if yer ask me."

"Old woman," Adam hissed.

"All right, for God's sake," Danny snapped, the pressure of new shoes for his oldest making him edgy. "Are youse in or not?"

Adam shrugged. "Yeah, fine by me."

"Len?" Danny looked at his cousin.

Len thought about it for a moment, sighed then answered,

"I suppose so. But the first sign of a ghost…"

Adam burst out laughing. "Bloody ghosts, no such thing, yer soft shite… We gonna cut Jacko in?"

"Jacko." Danny thought for a minute. Jacko was a good mate and probably would have been here if he wasn't ill. "Depends what we find, I suppose."

They continued arguing all the way to Danny's van. When they got there Danny kissed his fingers and patted the wing mirror. Len tutted but Danny ignored him. The van, which he called Elizabeth after his dream woman Elizabeth Taylor, was his pride and joy. At the moment his girlfriend wasn't speaking to him because three nights ago he'd called out, "Oh more, Elizabeth, more," at totally the wrong moment, and not for the first time either.

As they drove away, another man came out of the church, tall and dark-skinned with a heavy beard. He was talking on his mobile phone in an east European accent, and he was angry. "You get to him and you get to him now. You have two hours, or it's your skin I'll be stretching over my lampshade." He snapped his phone shut and strode over to the waiting Mercedes.

DI Lorraine Hunt glared at her partner Detective Luke Daniels. "I swear I will kill him," she mouthed. "Any minute now."

Luke, tall, handsome and black, with a presence about him that turned heads, tried not to laugh out loud. Unaware that his boss was reaching meltdown, Carter was droning on and on about the history of St Michael and All Angels church.

Two minutes later Lorraine had had enough. She stood up. "Yeah, OK, Carter, that's all very interesting, but old bones and stones that may or may not be four thousand years old can't very well help us with today's problems, can they?"

Luke smiled. Carter actually got away with more than anyone in the station. Luke knew that Lorraine genuinely liked the young, naïve officer, who had somehow got it into his head that Lorraine shared his love of the area's history. But at the moment Luke was as concerned as Lorraine about the news that had come over the wires less than an hour ago.

"So what's up?" Carter asked.

"Fill him in, Luke. I'm in need of some liquid refreshment; back in a mo." She left them, her long blonde ponytail swishing from side to side as she strode out of the office.

Five minutes later she was back, a can of diet Coke in her hand. From the look of horror on Carter's face she guessed Luke had told him most of what there was to know about Kirill Tarasov.

"So." She sat down at her desk, eyebrows raised.

Carter swallowed hard, then felt sick. "A… a cannibal?"

"Yes. A cannibal who collects antiques."

"There's no accounting for tastes, is there?" Luke said, shaking his head.

Carter and Lorraine groaned in unison, and Lorraine went on, "He's been wanted all over the world for years, nearly caught twice. Believe me this guy makes Dracula look like a pussy cat. He skins his victims, eats them, then decorates his house with their skin."

"Oh, gross," Carter shivered. "But why haven't I heard about him before now?"

"Classified information. There's enough fear in the world today without adding to it. Besides, why give him glory? There's plenty weirdoes out there that would worship him… Actually Kirill, if that's even his real name, if he's even really Russian, is a variant of an old Greek word which means lord."

"Yeah, in his case lord of darkness," Luke put in. "No one's safe when this guy's around."

"Please don't tell me he's in Houghton, please." Carter was thinking of his mother, all alone until he got in from work, and it was getting dark out there already. The hairs stood out on the back of his neck when he thought of the gruesome things Luke had told him.

"Get a grip, Carter," Lorraine said. "He was followed from Germany to France, where they lost him for the second time this year. But then luck struck and he was recognised getting off a plane in Newcastle. He was followed, but the agent's car died on him. Tarasov was last seen heading for Durham."

As Carter opened his mouth to ask more questions the phone rang. Lorraine quickly snatched it up.

The two officers watched her face go from dismay to outright disbelief. She muttered a few words, put the phone down and stared at Luke and Carter.

"Well?" Luke urged.

Lorraine slowly shook her head, blew air out of her cheeks before saying, "There's been a prison break at Durham, one man dead, two escaped… Both escapees were doing life for murder… Vicious murder." She stood up. "Come on, guys, we're all out on patrol."

It was a dark night, no stars and hardly any moon. Danny, Len and Adam met up outside the church. They had each taken a different route up from the Seahills; some of the gossips on the estate hardly slept, and if the three of them were seen together after midnight, they'd have put two and

249

two together and come out with an odd number.

"So where we gonna dig first?" Len whispered.

"I reckon up the front, near the altar." Danny replied.

Adam nodded. "Sounds good to me."

They made their way quietly to the door. Danny pulled out a crowbar and set to work on the heavy locks. "Once upon a time churches used to be open all the time," he grunted as he struggled with the lock.

"Aye, but that was before thieving bastards started to rob them," Adam said with conviction.

Len looked at him, "So what the hell are we, then?"

Adam shrugged. "That's different. We're not robbing the church. I reckon coins and ancient stuff belong to the people, it's our… our birthright." He nodded at Len then at Danny.

"Will the pair of yers shut the fuck up and give me a hand, for Christ's sake?"

"OK, OK, keep yer hair on." Adam lent his weight to Danny's and the lock snapped with a sudden crack like a gunshot.

"Shit." Len ducked and quickly looked around.

They all held their breath as Danny slowly pushed the door, expecting it to start creaking at any moment. But the hinges were well oiled and it opened silently. "Remember," he hissed, "keep the torches pointed at the ground; we don't want any lights showing through the windows."

They crept quietly along to the altar. They were three feet away from their target when Len squealed.

"What the..?" Danny glared at him.

"Yer nearly frightened the life outta me, yer great prat." Adam gave Len a push.

"Something ran over me foot," Len muttered.

"I'll run over yer fucking foot in a minute." Danny thrust

a spade at Len. "Here, this is as good a place as any."

"It was probably a rat," Adam whispered. "Or maybes a ghost." He grinned.

Len glared at him, and started digging. Danny pulled a lantern and another spade out of the holdall. He handed the spade to Adam and lit the lantern. The light spread over a six-foot radius, enough for them to see what they were doing. All three of them started digging in a yard-wide square.

Twenty minutes later Len's spade hit something solid.

"Oh my God." He dropped to his knees, quickly followed by the others. Adam held the torches as Len and Danny began to scrape away at the soil. In moments they uncovered a large metal box.

"That doesn't look really old," Len observed, though he had to keep his feet solid on the ground to stop himself dancing with excitement. He gave a deep sigh; the others knew how he felt. Rich at last, was the one thought running through their heads.

"It's bloody heavy though." Danny lifted the box and carried it to the altar.

Practically slavering, Adam rubbed his hands together in excitement. "Bet it's full of gold coins. We should have had Jacko here."

"He's got the flu. He could hardly get out of bed this morning." Len stared at the box as Danny stepped back. "But we'll see he's all right, won't we, Danny?"

Kirill Tarasov watched as the two he'd been waiting for ran from behind the trees to the car. One of them was limping badly. He frowned; a weakling. When they had climbed into the back of the Mercedes he turned to face them.

"Everything went to plan, then?" He eyed them up and

251

instantly dismissed the smaller man who had limped and was less than skin and bone. To register on Tarasov's radar you needed some meat on your bones.

"Yeah," Simon Dupri, alias the Slasher, a nickname he'd been given by the press, answered quickly. " He definitely buried the box in the church, in front of the altar. He swore to it as he begged for his life."

The smaller man sniggered. He was Vinnie Grey, doing life for murdering his whole family then starting on his neighbours one dark winter night. He was cut short by a look from Tarasov.

"OK." Tarasov pulled into the road, "We go to the church now, and you tell me all about how he died on the way."

And you, skinny man, he thought, will not be coming out of the church. Fatso, though, I will keep close, in case rations are hard to come by some day soon.

"Open it, open it," Adam practically shouted.

"Shh," Danny and Len hissed.

For a moment there was silence. Adam took a deep breath and controlled himself, then nodded at the other two. Danny slowly pried the lid off the box. A sound behind him made him gasp, and the three of them spun round.

There was nothing but the pitch darkness with a lighter patch right it the back where the stained glass window reigned supreme. Len wiped the sweat off his brow, and Adam placed a shaking hand over his heart.

"Just the fucking rats again," Danny snapped.

The lid was off the box now, and all three peered inside, holding their breath in anticipation.

Tarasov, followed by Dupri and Grey, quietly made his way past the old gravestones to the church. When they reached the door, Tarasov held his hand up and stared in dismay at the broken lock.

He clenched his fists and gritted his teeth. He had searched for years for the box, and wasn't going to be outdone now. He put his finger to his lips to quell any outbursts from the others, and cocked his head like an inquisitive dog listening, stretching his senses.

At first he heard nothing. He stepped through the door and paused, listening again, concentrating hard, then looked towards the altar. As his eyes adjusted to the darkness he saw the light beneath the altar, beckoning like a beacon.

Bastards!

"Hurry up, hurry up." Adam was unable to control himself any longer. "What is it… Is it gold coins? Fucking tell us, man."

Len squashed up to his cousin on the other side, every bit as excited. "Are we rich? I can't stand this any more – how much?"

Danny pulled a large piece of carefully folded canvas out of the box and held it up. The other two shone their torches on it. "For God's sake, it's just a bloody painting." Unable to hide his disappointment, he shook his head. "It's a painting of a woman, who believe me is no Elizabeth Taylor."

"Yer can say that again." Adam stared at the painting. "I've seen that ugly mug somewhere before though."

Len tutted. "Oh you bloody pair of idiots, for God's sake, it's the Mona Lisa."

Danny and Adam stared at Len. After a moment Danny said, "Do yer think it's the real I am?"

Len looked in awe at the signature. Slowly he nodded.

"Is it worth anything?" Adam beat Danny to the question.

The answer came from behind them. "Yes, gentlemen… millions."

For a moment they froze, then slowly, as if trained by a choreographer, they turned together. Danny swallowed hard, feeling Adam and Len tremble beside him – and who could blame them, faced with a huge man holding a large knife in each hand?

Tarasov moved closer. "For years I have followed this painting, then seven years ago the trail went cold. The fools in the museum think they have the real one. Ha."

"What, er, what yer gonna do, like?" Danny didn't quite succeed in keeping the tremble out of his voice. Judging by the man's face, he could guess exactly what he was going to do.

He smiled at them, and Len trembled even more. Adam found his voice. "Who are you like? Standing there like some crazy fuck out of a horror movie. Think we're frightened, like?"

"You should be, cocky twat." Grey stepped out from behind Tarasov.

"Oh God," Len moaned. "We're well and truly up shit creek without a paddle this time, guys." A second later he screamed as he was grabbed from behind.

The scream forced Adam into action. Without thinking he threw himself at Grey, leaving Danny to deal with Tarasov and his knives. Len bent over then quickly threw his head back, snapping his assailant's nose. More by luck than anything else, Adam kicked Grey in exactly the right spot on his injured leg; when he yelled in pain and reached down, Adam launched a left hook and knocked him out flat.

As Len peeled himself away from the dead weight still clinging to him, Adam quickly moved to Danny's side.

Tarasov laughed. "You think you can take me? Ha, I don't think so. Not even two or three of you." He jumped forward and the knife in his right hand slashed down, taking a piece of Adam's ear off and slicing the side of his neck. Blood spurted, and Adam collapsed to his knees in shock.

Advancing on Danny, Tarasov laughed again.

"Fuck off," Danny yelled, wondering if this would be a good time to run, but knowing he couldn't leave Adam at the mercy of this grinning freak.

Then he had a brainwave. He snatched the painting up and shook the canvas. Tarasov stopped, a look of pure horror on his face.

"No, no… Do not damage it." His eyes burned into Danny's. "I will give you anything."

"Do yer honestly think for one minute that I'd trust you, yer creepy bastard?" Danny shook the painting again, as Len, finally untangled from Dupri, bent down to help Adam.

Tarasov curled his lip. "Enough of this," he shouted, his arms held high. Each long blade caught the light as he prepared to leap forward again.

"Oh yes, well said, definitely enough of this." DI Lorraine Hunt hurried into the church with Luke Daniels and Carter close behind.

They had been cruising round the Seahills estate visiting a couple of known criminals recently released from Durham prison when Lorraine had suddenly remembered something Carter had said about the church. On a hunch they had quickly sped up to Houghton.

"Kirill Tarasov, I am arresting you on… Well, just about any crime known to man."

"Fucking hell." Danny wiped sweat from his brow. "Talk about saved by the bell." He bent down to see to Adam, but

Len stared at him and shook his head.

"NO!" Danny yelled.

Using the sudden distraction Tarasov ran at Lorraine, but she was ready for him. Using a karate sidestep, she swiftly moved to one side, and as Tarasov ran past her she kicked his leg from under him. He fell to the floor, and Carter and Luke were on top of him in seconds.

Luke cuffed him. Tarasov looked at Lorraine; mixed with the contempt was a smattering of admiration. "Brought down by a woman."

"Save it, creep." Lorraine moved to check on Adam. It took her a few moments to find a pulse, but find it she did: erratic, but still a pulse. She took Len's hand and pressed it over the wound in Adam's neck. "Keep it there…" She looked over her shoulder. "Carter? Ambulance."

"On its way, boss."

Danny and Len breathed twin sighs of relief. Lorraine looked at them, shook her head and said, "Please tell me why I am not at all surprised to find you bloody lot here."

THE MASQUERADE

Sarah Rayne

I seldom attend parties unless I think they might be of use in my career, so it was all the more remarkable to find myself attending this one. This is not due to shyness, you understand, nor to a lack of self-confidence – I value myself and my attainments rather highly. But I have always shunned larger gatherings – the chattering, lovely-to-see-you, how-are-you-my-dear, type of event. Loud music, brittle conversation, ladies air-kissing one another and then shredding each other's reputations in corners. Not for me. My wife, however, has always enjoyed all and any parties with shrieking glee, telling people I am an old sobersides, and saying with a laugh that she makes up for my quietness.

But here I was, approaching the door of this house whose owners I did not know, and whose reasons for giving this party I could not, for the moment, recall.

It was rather a grand-looking house – there was an air of quiet elegance about it which pleased me. One is not a snob, but there are certain standards. I admit that my own house, bought a few years ago, is – well – modest, but I named it Lodge House, which I always felt conveyed an air of subdued grandeur. The edge of a former baronial estate, perhaps? That kind of thing, anyway. My wife, of course, never saw the point, and insisted on telling people that it was Number 78, halfway down the street, with a tube station just round the corner. I promise you, many are the times I have *winced* at hearing her say that.

This house did not appear to have a name or a number,

or to need one. There was even a doorman who beckoned me in; he seemed so delighted to see me I felt it would be discourteous to retreat.

"Dear me," I said, pausing on the threshold. I do not swear, and I do not approve of the modern habit of swearing, with teenagers effing and blinding as if it were a nervous tic, and even television programme-makers not deeming it always necessary to use the censoring bleep. So I said, "Dear me, I hadn't realised this was a fancy-dress party. I am not really dressed for it –" You might think, you who read this, that someone could have mentioned that aspect to me, but no one had.

"Oh, the costume isn't important," said the doorman at once. "People come as they are. You'll do very nicely."

He was right, of course. Dressed as I was, I should have done very nicely anywhere. I am fastidious about my appearance although my wife says I am pernickety. Downright vain, she says: everyone laughs at you for your old-fashioned finicking. I was wearing evening clothes – one of the modern dress shirts the young men affect, with one of those narrow bow ties that give a rather 1920s look, and I was pleased with my appearance. Even the slightly thin patch on the top of my head would not be noticeable in this light.

Once inside, the house was far bigger than I had realised; huge rooms opened one out of another and the concept put me in mind of something, although I could not quite pin down the memory. Some literary allusion, perhaps? It would be nice to think I had some arcane poet or philosopher in mind, but actually I believe I was thinking of Dr Who's *Tardis*. (Pretentious, that's what you are, my wife always says. We all have a good laugh at your pretensions behind your back.)

There were drinks and a buffet, all excellent, and the service – Well! You have perhaps been to those exclusive, expensive restaurants in your time? Or to one of the palatial gentlemen's clubs that can still be found in London if one knows where to look? Then you will have encountered that discreet deference. Food seemed almost to materialise at one's hand. I was given a glass of wine and a plate of smoked salmon sandwiches straight away and I retired with them to a corner, in order to observe the guests, hoping to see someone I knew.

The term *fancy-dress* was not quite accurate after all, although a more bizarre collection of outfits would be hard to find anywhere. There was every imaginable garb, and every creed, colour, race, ethnic mix – every walk of society, every profession and calling. Try as I might I could see no familiar faces, and this may have been why, at that stage, I was diffident about approaching anyone. It was not due to my inherent reticence, you understand: in the right surroundings I can be as convivial as the next man. This was more a feeling of exclusion. In the end, I moved to a bay window to observe, and to drink my wine – it was a vintage I should not have minded having in my own cellars. Well, I say *cellars*, but actually it's an under-stairs cupboard containing several wine-racks bought at our local DIY centre. It is not necessary to tell people this, however, and I always remonstrated with my wife when she did.

By an odd coincidence, the wine seemed to be the one I had poured for my wife quite recently, although I have to say good wine was always a bit of a waste on her because she never had any discrimination; she enjoys sugary pink concoctions with paper umbrellas and frosted rims to the glass. Actually, she once even attended some sort of all-female party dressed as a Piña Colada: the memory of that still makes me shudder and I shall refrain from describing the outfit. (But I found out afterwards that Piña Colada translates, near enough, as strained pineapple, which seems to me very appropriate.)

But on that evening we had been preparing to depart for my office Christmas dinner, so I was hoping there would be no jazzily-coloured skirts or ridiculous head-dresses. It's a black tie affair, the office Christmas dinner, but when my wife came downstairs I was sorry to see that although she was more or less conventionally dressed, her outfit was cut extremely low and showed up the extra pounds she had accumulated. To be truthful, I would have preferred to go to the dinner without her, because she would drink too much and then *flaunt* herself at my colleagues all evening; they would leer and nudge one another and I should be curdled with anger and embarrassment. Those of you who have never actually walked through a big office and heard people whispering, "He's the one with the slutty wife," can have no idea of the humiliation I have suffered. I remember attending a small cocktail party for the celebration of a colleague's retirement. Forty-three years he had been with the firm, and I had been asked to make the presentation. A silver serving dish had been bought for him – I had chosen it myself and it was really a very nice thing indeed and a change from the usual clock. I had written a few words, touching on the man's long and honourable service, drawing subtle attention to my own involvement in his department.

You will perhaps understand my feelings when, on reaching the hotel, my wife removed her coat to display a scarlet dress that made her look – this is no exaggeration – like a Piccadilly tart. I was mortified, but there was nothing to be done other than make the best of things.

After my speech, I lost sight of her for a couple of hours, and when I next saw her, she was fawning (there is no other word for it), on the Chairman, her eyes glazed, her conversation gin-slurred. When she thanked him for the hospitality she had to make three attempts to pronounce the word, and by way of finale she recounted to four of the directors a joke in which the words *cock* and *tail* figured as part of the punch line.

The really infuriating thing is that until that night I had known – absolutely and surely *known*! – that I was in line to step up into the shoes of my retiring colleague. I had been passed over quite a number of times in the past (I make this statement without the least shred of resentment, but people in offices can be very manipulative and the place was as full of intrigue as a Tudor court), but this time the word had definitely gone out that I was in line for his job. Departmental head, no less!

And what happened? After my wife's shameless display at the retirement party they announced the vacancy was to be given to a jumped-up young upstart, a pipsqueak of a boy barely out of his twenties! I think I am entitled to have been upset about it. I think anyone would have been upset. *Upset*, did I say? Dammit, I was wracked with fury and a black and bitter bile scalded through my entire body. I thought – you lost that promotion for me, you bitch, but one day, my fine madam, one day…

Nevertheless, I still looked forward to that year's Christmas party. I had always counted the evening as something of a special event, so before we left, I poured two glasses of the claret I kept for our modest festivities, setting hers down on the low table by her chair. She did not drink it at once – that was unusual in itself and it should have alerted me, but it did not. I remember she got up to find my woollen scarf at my request, and then, having brought it for me, asked me to go upstairs for her evening bag. She knows I hate entering her over-scented, pink-flounced bedroom, but she sometimes tries to tempt me into it. I have learned to foil her over the years: the room makes my skin crawl and her physical importunities on those occasions make me feel positively ill. It was not always so, you understand. I fancy I have been as gallant as any man in my time.

So, the evening bag collected as hastily as possible, I sat down with my wine although it was not as good as it should be. There was a slight bitter taste – it reminded me of the almond icing on the Christmas cake in its tin – and I remember thinking I must certainly complain to the wine shop. I set down the glass, and then there was confusion – a dreadful wrenching pain and the feeling of plummeting down in a fast-moving lift… Bright lights and a long tunnel…

And then, you see, I found myself here, outside the big elegant mansion with the doorman inviting me in…

It was instantly obvious what had happened. The sly bitch had switched the glasses while I was getting her evening bag. She realised what I was doing – perhaps she saw me stir the prussic acid into her glass while she pretended to find my scarf, or perhaps she had simply decided to be rid of me anyway. But whichever it was, I drank from her glass and I died instead. The cheating, double-faced vixen actually killed me!

It seems this house is some sort of judgement place, for the doorman came back into the room a few moments ago and said, "Murderers' judgements," very loudly, exactly as if he was the lift-man at a department store saying, "Ladies' underwear."

Are these oddly-assorted people all murderers, then? That saintly-looking old gentleman in the good suit, that kitten-faced girl who might have posed for a pre-Raphaelite painting? That middle-aged female who looks as if she would not have an interest beyond baking and knitting patterns…?

Having listened to fragments of their talk, I fear they are.

"… and, do you know, if it had not been for the wretched office junior coming in at just that moment, I would have got away with it… But the stupid girl must go screaming off to Mr Bunstable in Accounts, and I ended in being convicted on the evidence of a seventeen-year-old child and the bought-ledger clerk… Twenty years I was given…"

"Twenty years is nothing, old chap. I got Life – and that was in the days when Life meant Life…"

"… *entirely* the auditor's own fault to my way of thinking – if he hadn't pried into that *very* small discrepancy in the clients' account, I shouldn't have needed to put the rat poison in his afternoon tea to shut him up…"

"…I always made it a rule to use good old-fashioned Lysol or Jeyes' Fluid to get all the blood off the knitting needle and they never got me, never even suspected… But that man over there by the door, he very stupidly cut costs: a cheap, supermarket-brand cleaner was what he used, and of course it simply wasn't thorough enough and he ended his days in Wandsworth…"

"…my dear, you should *never* have used your own kitchen knife, they were bound to trace it back to you… An axe, that's what I always used, on the premise that you can put the killing down to a passing homicidal maniac – what? Oh, nonsense, there's always a homicidal maniac some-where – I've counted six of them here tonight as it happens

– matter of fact I've just had a glass of wine with a couple of them… Charming fellows…"

Well, whatever they may be, these people, charming or not, *I'm* not one of them. *I'm* not a murderer. This is all a colossal mistake, and I have absolutely no business being here because I did *not* kill my wife. I suppose a purist might argue that I had the *intention* to kill her, but as far as I know, no one has yet been punished for that, although I believe the Roman Catholic Church regards the intention as almost tantamount to the actual deed —

And that's another grievance! I may not actually have attended church service absolutely every Sunday, but I never missed Easter or Christmas. As a matter of fact, I rather enjoy the music one gets in a church. (Once I said this to my wife – hoping it might promote an interesting discussion, you know – but she only shrieked with laughter, asked if I was taking to religion, and recounted a coarse story about a vicar.)

But I have been a lifelong member of the Church of England and I should have thought as such I would have been taken to a more select division. However, there may be chance to point this out later. Presumably there will be some kind of overseer here.

It's unfortunate that for the moment I seem to be shut up with these people – with whom I have absolutely nothing in common. And all the while that bitch is alive in the world, flaunting her body, drinking sickly pink rubbish from champagne flutes. Taking lovers by the dozen, I shouldn't wonder, and living high on the hog from the insurance policies… Yes, that last one's a very painful thorn in the flesh, although I hadn't better use that expression when they come to talk to me, since any mention of thorns in the flesh may be considered something of a *bêtise* here.

They'll have long memories, I daresay.

But I shall explain it all presently, of course. There's bound to be some kind of procedure for mistakes. I shall stand no nonsense from anyone, either. I did not kill my wife, and I'm damned if I'm going to be branded as a murderer.

I'm *damned* if I am...

NO BABY

Linda Regan

I always knew I would kill her. I had watched her over the months. I had followed her on many occasions, but that was all after the trial. Before the trial was just a blur; I wasn't thinking of anything then. I even found standing up hard. I used to lie in the dark. It had to be the dark, I had become afraid of light. In the dark I could hear her voice. Everyone said it was the effect of the drugs, but I knew it wasn't.

It was nine months before the trial started, and by then I could stand up and walk. I walked from the car unaided, along the road, until the flashing of cameras stopped me in my tracks, bringing it all back; then someone blocked my way, asking me questions, pushing a microphone in my face, and I couldn't walk on. I needed someone either side of me to get me up the stairs.

I divided my time in the court between him and her. First I watched him, and then when the vomit rose in the back of my throat and threatened to erupt, I turned to her. She looked – nothing really. She looked as if… as if all this was an annoyance, taking up too much of her time, when she could be doing other things, like tending one of her other nine children! That's when I decided to kill her.

But I would bide my time. I'd watch her, and learn her movements, and plan my course. It wasn't that I cared about being caught; I cared nothing about what happened to me afterwards, but I couldn't afford to fail – for Jennifer's sake.

I wanted her to suffer, and feel a lot of pain. That's why I decided on a knife. It was easy to get hold of too, without drawing attention to myself. I could conceal it about my person and when the time came I could make sure it hit the right spot, causing maximum pain. I would strike into her chest, between her lungs, and watch her face as her heart split open and bled from the wound; I'd watch her as she writhed around in agony. Then I would ask her how it felt, and I wouldn't allow her to die until she told me that it hurt, really hurt, and begged me to make the pain go away, choking on her sobs as she implored me to drive the knife into her again, because the pain was too much for her to bear.

And so I watched her.

I remember coming home from watching her so late one night that Dion was waiting for me. He had been out of his mind with worry, asked where I had been. Why I didn't tell him that I had just gone walking? I cried then, and when I started, I found I couldn't stop. He was gentle and loving, and held me; but I didn't want his arms around me, I wanted Jennifer's, and I wanted them so badly that I started screaming. He rocked me like a child, held me tenderly, told me it would be all right, but I knew it wouldn't, not ever again.

And that's all I remember until I woke up the next morning and he told me the doctor had been back and there were more pills if I needed them. But I didn't. I needed revenge! I needed it so badly now it was eating me away. I needed to know why *he* had only got a few years in youth offenders, and why *she* had another nine children and I had none. I wanted to know why my beautiful thirteen-year-old princess who dreamed of being a hairdresser and making other people happy was dead, a bullet lodged in her brain from a drug-crazed sixteen-year-old who had been allowed to roam the streets and buy a Mac-10 sub-machine gun on the proceeds of the crack that he melted down with the aid of a microwave and a few bits of tinfoil, and then sold to kids too young to know any better.

I had to make her feel the pain I was feeling, so my little princess could rest in peace.

And so the day came. I followed her. I knew her routine now; she was going to playschool to fetch her youngest daughter, and the child would stay with the neighbour while she went off to work her shift at the hamburger bar. The other children would make their own way home and the second oldest would get their tea until she got back.

I had the knife tucked safely inside my coat; it was just a matter of choosing the precise moment now. I watched as the tiny, ringletted child ran to her mother and hugged her, holding her tightly around her knees, and I swallowed down the lump in my throat as she called her Mummy and told her she loved her. Tears streamed down my cheeks as I watched, remembering that feeling when my Jennifer hugged my knees and told me she loved me, all those years ago when she was four. This little girl, too, was beautiful, pretty, innocent and needy.

That was the moment I knew I couldn't do it. I turned and walked, feeling the sharp knife pressing against my chest, and knowing it wouldn't do its worst. That little girl needed her mother, as my Jennifer had needed me. My Jennifer who lay wax-white, cold and still as I begged her to wake up. I hadn't even been there to hold her as she slipped away in excruciating pain on the urine-and-bleach-smelling, graffiti-clad concrete stairway, her life's blood leaving her inch by agonising inch, trying and failing to crawl home to her mother.

How must she have felt, dying alone, at thirteen years old, in agony: No; I wouldn't be responsible for causing another little girl any pain. The smiling face of that ringletted child

I saw today was inside my head, her voice resonating around my brain. "I love you, Mummy," she said as she clung to her mother's knees.

I now had another plan.

Because planning my kill had consumed every waking hour, I had avoided taking the sleeping pills the doctors prescribed for fear of being too fuzzy to follow it through. Now was the time to put them to good use. Tonight was the night. Dion worked at night.

I knew my Jennifer would be there waiting for me.

I wanted to walk around the estate that night before I finally came in. I wanted to visit the steps, and I wanted to see what was happening on my own doorstep for the last time.

And so I walked. I looked at the run-down playground, the rusty roundabout and the unused swings where the dealers now sold their wares, but they didn't bother me any more. I no longer had to worry about keeping my princess away from them, so I walked through it and watched them.

They spoke to me, asked me how I was. I shook my head, but I couldn't take my eyes off one of them. He was no more than seven or eight, and he was earning money as a look-out for the dealers.

I asked him his name. He made something up; I could tell he made it up because he looked at the older boys before he spoke. He called himself No Baby. I asked him where his mum was; he said he didn't know, so I enquired about his dad. He didn't seem to know if he had one of those. He said lived with an aunt on the estate, when she was around. I gathered from the look on the other boys' faces that it wasn't often. They told me it was cool, and that they looked out for him.

Then No Baby asked me how I was doing. I stared at him. He was very grown up for his seven or so years. He told me he'd heard about Jennifer. The older dealers nodded and asked me there was anything they could do... a terrible, terrible accident, they said.

I shook my head, and said if they couldn't turn back the hands of time there was nothing they could do.

I felt a strange mixture of emotion as I spoke to them. I was on my way home to kill myself, and watching them changed my life.

One of them, his face scarred from drug dealing or living on the streets or living in fear of being shot or stabbed, all the things that were becoming everyday occurrences around this estate, shook his head at me.

"You could take No Baby home for tea," he said to me.

I shook my head. "His auntie should be doing that," I said.

"His auntie is too out of it to know he exists, innit?"

"Do Social Services know?" I found myself asking.

He furrowed his forehead and lifted his eyebrows as if I had dropped from the moon. I took his point. No one came around this estate; it lived by its own rules. I should know; I lived there myself.

I walked away.

No Baby knocked on my door an hour later, and asked me if I had anything to eat. I didn't; Dion was out working, and the only thing I was planning for supper was a packet and a half of pills and an early night. I was about to close the door, when he pulled a takeaway pizza menu from behind his back and presented it to me. "Got a phone?" he asked.

He had front, that much I knew. As I stood deciding whether to close the door or do my last good deed ever, he added, "And some money."

I relented. I brought him in, bought him the pizza and a drink, and while we waited for it to arrive I asked him how old he was. He told me he was seven. I told him if he carried on the way he was then he would end up on a bad road. He asked me how I thought he could eat if he didn't. I asked if he ever went to school. He said sometimes, he quite liked it, but he had to look out for his auntie, make sure she woke up, and that no punters were still there. I asked if she ever cooked him some tea, he said no, she never had any money. He referred to the street crack sellers as the crew; they looked after him, gave him money for food, and in return he worked for them as a lookout.

I found myself making a deal with him. Every day, for the rest of term, if I knew he had been to school, I would cook his tea and help him learn to read and write.

He agreed.

And so it all began.

Dion left me for a woman with three children, a year later. He said he needed a new start.

And No Baby's aunt died the year after that, of an overdose. Of course I didn't want him to go into care. He wasn't yet nine, and I selfishly looked forward to his visits.

So I have taken over foster duties for him. Adoption might be difficult, they say, as I am single, over a certain age, and a different colour and race; and I still take medication. But, they say that the courts would take into consideration the circumstances surrounding the loss of my beautiful princess, and that getting adopted at nine isn't easy. So I am giving it a try, I have just filled in the forms and No Baby is writing a letter saying he loves me and wants to stay here.

I am so glad I taught him to write.

OFF DUTY

Zoë Sharp

The guy who'd just tried to kill me didn't look like much. From the fleeting glimpse I'd caught of him behind the wheel of his brand new soft-top Cadillac, he was short, with less hair than he'd like on his head and more than anyone could possibly want on his chest and forearms.

That was as much as I could tell before I was throwing myself sideways. The front wheel of the Buell skittered on the loose gravel shoulder of the road, sending a vicious shimmy up through the headstock into my arms. I nearly dropped the damn bike there and then, and that was what pissed me off the most.

The Buell was less than a month old at that point, a Firebolt still with the shiny feel to it, and I'd been hoping it would take longer to acquire its first battle scar. The first cut is always the one you remember.

Although I was wearing full leathers, officially I was still signed off sick from the Kerse job and undergoing the tortures of regular physiotherapy. Adding motorcycle accident injuries, however minor, was not going to look good to anyone, least of all me.

But the bike didn't tuck under and spit me into the weeds, as I half-expected. Instead it righted itself, almost stately, and allowed me to slither to a messy stop maybe seventy metres further on. I put my feet down and tipped up my visor, aware of my heart punching behind my ribs, the adrenalin shake in my hands, the burst of anger that follows on closely after having had the shit scared out of you.

I turned, to find the guy in the Cadillac had completed

his half-arsed manoeuvre, pulling out of a side road and turning left across my path. He'd slowed, though, twisting round to stare back at me with his neck extended like a meerkat. Even at this distance I could see the petulant scowl. Hell, perhaps I'd made him drop the cell phone he'd been yabbering into instead of paying attention to his driving...

Just for a second our eyes met, and I considered making an issue out of it. The guy must have sensed that. He plunked back down in his seat and rammed the car into drive, gunning it away with enough gusto to chirrup the tyres on the bone dry surface.

I rolled my shoulders, thought that was the last I'd ever see of him.

I was wrong.

Spending a few days away in the Catskill Mountains was a spur-of-the-moment decision, taken in a mood of self-pity.

Sean was in LA, heading up a high-profile protection detail for some East Coast actress who'd hit it big and was getting windy about her latest stalker. He'd just come back from the Middle East, tired but focused, buzzing, loving every minute of it and doing his best not to rub it in.

After he'd left for California the apartment seemed too quiet without him. Feeling the sudden urge to escape New York and my enforced sabbatical, I'd looked at the maps and headed for the hills, ending up at a small resort and health spa, just north of the prettily-named Sundown in Ulster county. The last time I'd been in Ulster the local accent had been Northern Irish, and it had not ended well.

The hotel was set back in thick trees, the accommodation provided in a series of chalets overlooking a small lake. My physio had recommended the range of massage services they offered, and I'd booked a whole raft of treatments. By the time I brought the bike to a halt, nose-in outside my designated chalet, I was about ready for my daily pummelling.

It was with no more than mild annoyance, therefore, that I recognised the soft-top Cadillac two spaces down. For a moment my hand stilled, then I shrugged, hit the engine kill switch, and went stiffly inside to change out of my leathers.

Fifteen minutes later, fresh from the shower, I was sitting alone in the waiting area of the spa, listening to the self-consciously soothing music. The resort was quiet, not yet in season. Another reason I'd chosen it.

"Tanya will be with you directly," the woman on the desk told me, gracious in white, depositing a jug of iced water by my elbow before melting away again.

The only other person in the waiting area was a big blond guy who worked maintenance. He was making too much out of replacing a faulty door catch, but unless you have the practice it's hard to loiter unobtrusively. From habit, I watched his hands, his eyes, wondered idly what he was about.

The sound of raised voices from one of the treatment rooms produced a sudden, jarring note. From my current position I could see along the line of doors, watched one burst open and the masseuse, Tanya, come storming out. Her face was scarlet with anger and embarrassment. She whirled.

"You slimy little bastard!"

I wasn't overly surprised to see Cadillac man hurry out after her, shrugging into his robe. I'd been right about the extent of that body hair.

"Aw, come on, honey!" he protested. "I thought it was all, y'know, *part of the service*."

The blond maintenance man dropped his tools and lunged for the corridor, meaty hands outstretched. The woman behind the reception desk jumped to her feet, rapped out, "Dwayne!" in a thunderous voice that made him falter in conditioned response.

I swung my legs off my lounger but didn't rise. The woman on the desk looked like she could handle it, and she did, sending Dwayne skulking off, placating Tanya, giving Cadillac man an excruciatingly polite dressing down that flayed the skin off him nevertheless. He left a tip that must have doubled the cost of the massage he'd so nearly had.

"Ms Fox?" Tanya said a few moments later, flustered but trying for calm. "I'm real sorry about that. Would you follow me, please?"

"Are you OK, or do you need a minute?" I asked, wary of letting someone dig in with ill-tempered fingers, however skilled.

"I'm good, thanks." She led me into the dimly lit treatment room, flashed a quick smile over her shoulder as she laid out fresh hot towels.

"Matey-boy tried it on, did he?"

She shook her head, rueful, slicked her hands with warmed oil. "Some guys hear the word *masseuse* but by the time it's gotten down to their brain, it's turned into *hooker*," she said, her back to me while I slipped out of my robe and levered myself, face-down, flat on to the table. Easier than it had been, not as easy as it used to be.

"So, what's Dwayne's story?" I asked, feeling the first long glide of her palms up either side of my spine, the slight reactive tremor when I mentioned his name.

"He and I stepped out for a while," she said, casual yet

prim. "It wasn't working, so we broke it off."

I thought of his pretended busyness, his lingering gaze, his rage.

No, I thought. *You* broke it off.

Later that evening, unwilling to suit up again to ride into the nearest town, I ate in the hotel restaurant at a table laid for one. Other diners were scarce. Cadillac man was alone on the far side of the dining room, just visible round the edges of the silent grand piano. I could almost see the miasma of his aftershave.

He called the waitress 'honey', too, stared blatantly down her cleavage when she brought his food. Anticipating the summer crowds, the management packed the tables in close, so she had to lean across to refill his coffee cup. I heard her surprised, hurt squeak as he took advantage, and waited to see if she'd 'accidentally' tip the contents of the pot into his lap, just to dampen his ardour. To my disappointment, she did not.

He chuckled as she scurried away, caught me watching and mistook my glance for admiration. He raised his cup in my direction with a meaningful little wiggle of his eyebrows. I stared him out for a moment, then looked away.

Just another oxygen thief.

As soon as I'd finished eating I took my own coffee through to the bar. The flatscreen TV above the mirrored back wall was tuned to one of the sports channels, showing highlights of the latest AMA Superbikes Championship. The only other occupant was the blond maintenance man, Dwayne, sitting hunched at the far end, pouring himself into his beer.

I took a stool where I had a good view, not just of the

screen but the rest of the room as well, and shook my head when the barman asked what he could get me.

"I'll stick to coffee," I said, indicating my cup. The painkillers I was taking made my approach to alcohol still cautious.

In the mirror, I saw Cadillac man saunter in and take up station further along the bar. As he passed, he glanced at my back a couple of times as if sizing me up, with all the finesse of a hard-bitten hill farmer checking out a promising young ewe. I kept my attention firmly on the motorcycle racing.

After a minute or so of waiting for me to look over so he could launch into seductive dialogue, he signalled the barman. I ignored their muttered conversation until a snifter of brandy was put down in front of me with a solemn flourish.

I did look over then, received a smug salute from Cadillac man's own glass. I smiled – at the barman. "I'm sorry," I said to him. "But I'm teetotal at the moment."

"Yes, ma'am," the barman said with a twinkle, and whisked the offending glass away again.

"Hey, that's my kind of girl," Cadillac man called over, when the barman relayed the message. Surprise made me glance at him and he took that as invitation to slide three stools closer, so only one separated us. His hot little piggy eyes fingered their way over my body. "Beautiful *and* cheap to keep, huh?"

"Good coffee's thirty bucks a pound," I said, voice as neutral as I could manage.

His gaze cast about for another subject. "You not bored with this?" he asked, jerking his head at the TV. "I could get him to switch channels."

I allowed a tight smile that didn't reach my eyes. "Neil Hodgson's just lapped Daytona in under one minute thirty-eight," I said. "How could I be bored?"

Out of the corner of my eye, I saw Dwayne's head lift and turn as the sound of Cadillac man's voice finally penetrated. It was like watching a slow-waking bear.

"So, honey, if I can't buy you a drink," Cadillac man said with his most sophisticated leer, "can I buy you breakfast?"

I flicked my eyes towards the barman in the universal distress signal. From the promptness of his arrival, he'd been expecting my call.

"Is this guy bothering you?" he asked, flexing his muscles.

"Yes," I said cheerfully. "He is."

"Sir, I'm afraid I'm gonna have to ask you to leave."

Cadillac man gaped between us for a moment, then flounced out, muttering what sounded like 'frigid bitch' under his breath.

After very little delay, Dwayne staggered to his feet and went determinedly after him.

Without haste, I finished my coffee. The racing reached an ad break. I checked my watch, left a tip, and headed back out into the mild evening air towards my chalet. My left leg ached equally from the day's activity and the evening's rest.

I heard the raised voices before I saw them in the gathering gloom, caught the familiar echoing smack of bone on muscle.

Dwayne had run his quarry to ground in the space between the soft-top Cadillac and my Buell, and was venting his alcohol-fuelled anger in traditional style, with his fists. Judging by the state of him, Cadillac man was only lethal behind the wheel of a car.

On his knees, one eye already closing, he caught sight of me and yelled, "Help, for Chrissake!"

I unlocked the door to my chalet, crossed to the phone by the bed.

"Your maintenance man is beating seven bells out of one of your guests down here," I said sedately, when front desk answered. "You might want to send someone."

Outside again, Cadillac man was going down for the third time, nose streaming blood. I noted with alarm that he'd dropped seriously close to my sparkling new Buell.

I started forward, just as Dwayne loosed a mighty round-house that glanced off Cadillac man's cheekbone and deflected into the Buell's left-hand mirror. The bike swayed perilously on its stand and I heard the musical note of splintered glass dropping.

"Hey!" I shouted.

Dwayne glanced up and instantly dismissed me as a threat, moved in for the kill.

OK. Now I'm pissed off.

Heedless of my bad leg, I reached them in three fast strides and stamped down on to the outside of Dwayne's right knee, hearing the cartilage and the anterior cruciate ligament pop as the joint dislocated. Regardless of how much muscle you're carrying, the knee is always vulnerable.

Dwayne crashed, bellowing, but was too drunk or too stupid to know it was all over. He swung for me. I reached under my jacket and took the SIG 9mm off my hip and pointed it at him, so the muzzle loomed large near the bridge of his nose.

"Don't," I murmured.

And that was how, a few moments later, we were found by Tanya, and the woman from reception, and the barman. "You a cop?" Cadillac man asked, voice thick because of the stuffed nose.

"No," I said. "I work in close protection. I'm a bodyguard."

He absorbed that in puzzled silence. We were back in the bar until the police arrived. Out in the lobby I could hear

Dwayne still shouting at the pain, and Tanya shouting what she thought of his stupid jealous temper. He was having a thoroughly bad night.

"A bodyguard," Cadillac man mumbled blankly. "So why the fuck did you let him beat the crap out of me back there?"

"Because you deserved it," I said, rubbing my leg and wishing I'd gone for my Vicodin before I'd broken up the fight. "I thought it would be a valuable life lesson – thou shalt not be a total dickhead."

"Jesus, honey! And all the time, you had a gun? I can't believe you just let him –"

I sighed. "What do you do?"

"Do?"

"Yeah. For a living."

He shrugged gingerly, as much as the cracked ribs would let him. "I sell Cadillacs," he said. "The finest motorcar money can buy."

"Spare me," I said. "So, if you saw a guy broken down by the side of the road, you'd just stop and give him a car, would you?"

"Well," Cadillac man said, frowning, "I guess, if he was a pal –"

"What if he was a complete stranger who'd behaved like a prat from the moment you set eyes on him?" I queried. He didn't answer. I stood, flipped my jacket to make sure it covered the gun. "I don't expect you to work for free. Don't expect me to, either."

His glance was sickly cynical. "Some bodyguard, huh?"

"Yeah, well," I tossed back, thinking of the Buell with its smashed mirror and wondering who was in for seven years of bad luck. "I'm off duty."

DOES IT ALWAYS RAIN IN MANCHESTER?

Caroline Shiach

I wasn't there when my mother was mugged. I wasn't standing at the bus stop in the rain when a man shoved her hard from behind, causing her to twist and crumple in a dizzying heap. He slipped a bag off her outstretched arm as she lay moaning; I stared at a computer screen in another part of the city. Nor did I hear the delicate snap as her femur fractured into irregular bony shards which would need three operations to repair. The sullen thump as her face hit the pavement, breaking her nose, blackening her eye, loosening three teeth, was not part of my morning. But then, it didn't seem to be part of anybody's morning. In a queue of fifteen people, no one saw anything. The police struggled to show any interest and thought it unlikely that they would catch the criminal.

The last time I had seen her had been at breakfast. Rushing out of the door, I had pulled out a muesli bar from the cupboard.

"Raheela, that's not a proper breakfast." My father had drifted in from the shop and was eating a chapatti. "How much time would it take to eat a decent meal? Mummy, have we got some leftover curry?"

Mummy, as innocent as milk, was sitting in the corner eating cornflakes. I knew that this was the point of my father's remarks. He didn't much care what I was eating, but that his wife should veer away from her own traditional cooking to something out of a cardboard box was a confusing betrayal. My mother had shrugged.

"What does it matter what she eats in the morning, Anwar? She isn't fading away."

A flush of anger had crept over my father's face and I thought it was a good time to leave.

Four hours later I was sitting in Casualty next to an old man. He seemed to be having difficulty breathing, sucking in air in short gasps. Sometimes I thought he wasn't going to breathe out. His fingers were rubbing together making a dry, papery, old man's sound. He kept fiddling with his buttonholes, then dropping his hands to his side. On top of this he was chewing his lips, releasing an occasional disgusting, slapping noise. It was intolerable. I reached into my bag and pulled out a small mirror.

"Look," I said. "You look like Grandfather, the day after he died."

I thought my father was going to hit me, but the anger did it. Colour returned to his cheeks and his breathing settled.

"What have I done to deserve all this? I have a disrespectful daughter and a wife who gets mugged when she goes on mysterious errands. She won't tell me what she was doing in Oxford Road. How can that be? A wife should tell her husband everything."

He sighed deeply. "We should never have come to this country."

This was my father's closing remark for everything problematic. I used to be terrified that we were suddenly going to pack up and return to my grandfather's remote village in Pakistan, seven hours from the nearest city. I have come to realise that it is more in the way of an incantation. My father looks back to a way of life he never had, in the way that people of a certain age in this country get nostalgic about the Second World War.

Finally we were allowed through to see my mother, who was pale and detached, as though not mentioning pain keeps it at bay. She shook her head when I tried to ask for more information, but as we left she grabbed my hand.

"Ask me tomorrow."

On the way out we were handed a sad bundle of rags. My mother's torn salwar kameez, scarf and a bright pink umbrella, decorated with peony roses, now snapped neatly in two.

My mother told me nothing the next day. I was uneasy. My aunt Faiza had had a similar experience a few months earlier, although her bones didn't break. They wouldn't dare. Auntie would have spoken to them very firmly. Was this just about race? Hadn't we served our time yet?

Lee Huckley was in my class at school, a weedy kid who sat at the back of the class, always sniffing, terrified of his mum, who had the size and destructive properties of a wrecking ball.

He now worked in the Parks Department. I met up with him, standing in a tatty donkey jacket, planting dahlias. His hair was reduced to near absence by a number one cut. The crude tattoos on his hand and neck sent unequivocal messages of hate and revenge. As I approached, he wiped his nose on a dirt-streaked sleeve, glancing all around.

"Lee, have your lot been targeting my lot?"

"Dunno."

"What do you mean, dunno? I thought you were the main man."

"Yeah, well… there's always a bit of freelance stuff." He sniffed and repeated the nose to sleeve action.

I leaned forward and grabbed both his lapels. "Somebody put my mother in hospital. I want to know who."

"Stop it, Raheela, you're hurting me."

"Why should I care?"

"I wouldn't… no, not your mum… I don't think it's us. We've been… well, we haven't been in this area. No, it's not us. Let go of me."

Lee might be chairman of the local BNP, but he frightened easily when it was one to one. Despite that, I was sure that he knew what went on among his unpleasant comrades, in the name of freedom. I would have to try elsewhere.

I had a heavy black thought hovering just at the edge of my consciousness. It had been sending muted signals since my visit to Casualty. That evening I was sitting in my room, listening to music, when the thought slipped. It gradually squeezed its way along until it was right in the centre of my mind and I could no longer ignore it. What if this was Asians attacking Asian women? I knew that a group of young lads had set up a group called Manchester Muslim Men, which seemed to involve hours of reading the Qu'ran and discussing how wicked everyone was. They disapproved of Muslim women with attitude, which, in my experience, was all of them. Would they be twisted enough to injure elderly women in the way that my mother had been hurt. I wasn't certain that the answer was no.

"Rafiq, we need to talk."

"I can't, Raheela. I have my class."

"That's why we need to talk."

My cousin Rafiq, son of Auntie Faiza, was born to have a tendency. He could have been a computer geek or a sci-fi nut. Instead he was a Muslim Fundamentalist. Would he condone an attack on his own mother?

"Raheela, are you mad?"

"In a way. My mother has been really sick. Somebody

did it. I need to know."

"And you think you can solve it."

"Who else will?"

"Raheela…" He touched my arm, but quickly pulled his hand away. "The Movement believes in peace, not violence." He paused. "And definitely, definitely not on our own people."

I think that Rafiq believed what he said.

"I've gotta go," he muttered. "Maybe you need to give up this detective stuff. Just let it go. It's not the first time Asians have been targeted."

I tried to leave it. I was tired of asking questions that no one seemed to want answered. I struggled to embrace my old way of life, my way of life of seventy-two hours ago. It no longer fitted me. I was itchy, uncomfortable, unable to sleep.

Two days later, after work, I was struggling through autumn gloom on Stockport Road. Thick coils of Manchester rain slapped against the car. The wipers, at their fastest setting, were offering me limited visibility. I was looking at the city through the ends of milk bottles. As far as I could make out the street was lined with handsome, solid, Victorian, brick buildings with large bay windows, suggesting prosperity, but the shops on the ground floor gave them away; they offered house clearances or everything for a pound. This was no longer a smart neighbourhood. Years ago, when Moss Side and Hulme were being tarted up after decades of poor housing and high crime, I asked my father where criminals would go if there was no place for them in the smartened district.

"Longsight and Levenshulme," he had grunted, hauling a pile of newspapers.

And this was where I was: Levenshulme. The haven for

Moss Side's rejected low life. I shivered, although the car's heater was blasting out hot air, and scanned the street for house numbers. Finally I parked.

I climbed stairs to the second floor of a red brick building next door to a reclamation centre. The door had frosted glass with letters picked out in dull gold; Philip Marlowe, Private Investigator. It had been the nerve, or the wit, of this fellow that made me select him. Now I wondered if I was being stupid.

The door opened and I was looking at a tall, handsome man with no fedora, no raincoat, no cigarette, no quart of hooch. The colour of his skin placed his roots in Southern India, maybe Sri Lanka, so this Chandler stuff was just an angle. I could relate to that. I knew all about needing an angle.

"Come in, Miss Ashraf." He ushered me in to a small, clean office. "Perhaps I should explain the name on the door, but you tell me your problem first. Let's see if I can help you."

I ran through the details as best I could.

"Have I got this straight? Your mother left the NatWest Bank with a thousand pounds in cash in her bag, which the police know nothing about."

I nodded.

"And she won't tell you why."

A further nod.

"And your dad has no idea of the existence of this account."

"That's right."

"And I can't speak to your mother because she doesn't know that you've hired me."

"Exactly."

"Well, sister, you've given me a tall order."

I couldn't work out if the faint American drawl was part of the Marlowe act or part of him.

"What's your real name?"

"Mike, Mike Thompson, but I find that Philip Marlowe pulls in the punters." He grinned broadly. "I'll bet that's why you picked me out."

I smiled back, wondering how many layers of deception there were. "So will you take my case, Mike?"

"Let me check out some contacts. Come back in a week and we'll see if this will run."

A week later I met Mike in a coffee bar in the city centre. He was late, but it wasn't difficult to make out his distinctive build and long loping stride as he pushed his way through the crowd. It was raining again and he was having to defend himself from umbrella spokes. We'd had a sodden summer and the rain wasn't letting up as autumn fell.

I sat at a covered pavement table, surrounded by students and office workers marking the end of their working day. Mike wasn't smiling. For a few moments he said nothing.

"There's something going on, Raheela." He lit a cigarette and sighed.

"There have been fifteen bag snatches in a quarter-mile stretch of Oxford Road in the last six months. They have all been Asian women. They all claim they had nothing in their bag." He swallowed some coffee. "And none of them have pressed charges. Does that not strike you as odd?"

I thought for a minute. "Doesn't it strike the police as odd?"

Mike shrugged his broad shoulders. "Apparently not."

"There's one other thing." He paused. "According to a source who's nothing to do with the police, they've all been mugged leaving a bank, but mostly they haven't said that. Now, does that not strike you as odd?"

I studied his handsome features, his large brown eyes, his smile that lit up his face, and hoped that everyone in the café thought we were a couple.

"Absolutely," I breathed.

Mike hesitated and looked at me closely. "Unless we can get one of the women to talk, I'm not sure how much further I can take this."

He stopped. I realised that I needed to respond.

"My mum won't. Have you got any other names?"

He slid a piece of paper over to me, grinning, "Data Protection at your service."

I scanned the list. "That's my next door neighbour."

Mike looked at me expectantly.

"No, no go. They haven't spoken to us for years. Some sort of dispute about the back garden." I looked further down the list. "There's Auntie Faiza, my mother's sister, and the woman who lives across the road from her. What is going on?"

"Would your aunt talk?"

"Try stopping Auntie Faiza talking."

"We should speak to her on her own, soon." Mike was serious again. "Let's get this thing sorted before someone is killed."

"No problem. My uncle is a mini-cab driver. He works evenings. My cousins have all left home. I'll give her a call."

Auntie Faiza seemed relieved that we'd come.

"I think we know that the party is over," she said, settling her round body deep into the sofa cushions. "But it has been fun."

I'll skip the details of Auntie Faiza fussing round with tea and cakes, of her making up to Mike as though we were engaged. Finally we got the story. A group of Asian women met up once a week. Well, I knew that. It had started with

English classes years ago and they never stopped. As my own generation became more independent, they began to think that they should have their own security. Their husbands had small businesses. They had nothing of their own.

"How did you get money? Where did it come from?"

"You young people think you know everything." Auntie was smug. "Who does the books? Not our men. They have no attention to detail. They can't be bothered."

"And..."

"I think it's called creative accountancy."

Faiza rested back on the sofa, waiting for it to sink in.

"So, in a nutshell, Auntie, you've all been stealing from your husbands."

She squirmed a little, but only a little.

"Well, not really, Raheela. It was more a case of spreading investments. These men put all their money in banks which follow Sharia rules. There is no interest paid. We just wanted to look after a little of the money."

"You are unbelievable," I said. "And my mother?"

"She had the most. You know what your father is like. So chaotic."

I thought of my father sitting at the dining room table puzzling over his accounts, shaking his head and blaming one of my cousins who worked in the shop, but always with a helpless, desperate look in his eye. A pulse of anger was quickly tempered with powerlessness. What could I do?

"If any of you ever do this again, I will personally go to the police."

On the way back with Mike I laughed a tight, mirthless laugh. "Tell the police. As if they would care."

It took Mike another two weeks or so to work out the details. I met him one evening for a curry in a new restaurant with contemporary, simple décor. I was tired of the fake, mock-traditional stuff.

"So, what's the story?"

Mike put down his glass. "Well, Raheela, in its way it was quite clever. It was all to do with rain. And let's face it, they picked the right city." He made a face. "A young man in the bank took it upon himself to fuss over some of the older women customers. When it was raining he would accompany them out with a big bank umbrella. So far, so courteous." Mike looked up. "However, the umbrella was the clue for his accomplice hanging about outside, letting them know that this woman had a fat wad in her bag."

"How did you find out all this stuff?"

"Trust me Raheela, you really don't want to know."

"What happens now?"

"Not much as far as I can see. Nobody's reported a crime. Problem? What problem?"

The conversation turned to other matters, but I was still turning things around. As we were waiting for the bill I made a decision.

"It's time for me to move out and look for my own place. Mum and Dad have to sort themselves out."

Mike smiled. "Freedom," he said. But there was a question behind it.

I waited for the question.

None came.

As we were leaving he looked at me. "That was my last case, Raheela. I'm... I'm quitting Manchester, week after next."

I felt deflated. "Was it that bad?" I whispered.

"It was good, Raheela. It's just the timing that was bad."

He stopped at the half-landing, turning round slowly.

"If I was really Philip Marlowe I would pull you to me,

pull off the glasses you're not wearing, tell you you were kind of cute, and kiss you hard."

Do it, I said inside my head. I'll even buy the specs. Just do it.

"Do it."

He put his hand on my right cheek. It was warm and smooth. It was the hand of a man who could lead me into temptation.

"My leaving has nothing to do with you, Raheela. The decision was made months ago."

I waited.

"I just can't stand this goddamn weather."

"That doesn't mean that you can't kiss me."

So he did.

SINGER OF LOST SONGS

Roz Southey

Newcastle upon Tyne 1736

I had hardly stepped on to the Tyne Bridge when I realised there was a furore ahead of me. It was probably only a drunken beggar, but I had spent a long day in Gateshead trying to teach a half-hearted pupil to play the harpsichord, and I was in the mood for entertainment.

Dodging farmers' wives on their way home from market and carters whipping up their horses, I worked my way between the houses and shops to the very centre of the bridge where the townships of Gateshead and Newcastle meet. Over the heads of jeering onlookers, I glimpsed a sober figure dressed in black. Not a beggar. A Quaker.

He was preaching with his feet on either side of the blue stones that mark the boundary between the two towns, hoping, I fancied, to confuse the local constables about jurisdiction. I had to admire him; it takes a great deal of courage to tell respectable men and women that they are miserable sinners destined for hell. And in such a loud voice too. I have always been bemused by Quakers; publicly they thunder but privately they worship in silence. Not a situation I could be happy with – to me, music is as spiritual an act as praying. But then it is both my profession and my passion.

I stood on a step to get a better view. The crowd were giving as good as they got, debating the Quaker's points with gusto. But the fellow was effortlessly making himself heard above the clamour, answering their jibes with an even temper.

A yard or two away on the other side of the bridge, the door to Fleming's stationers opened and a young girl hesitated on the doorstep. I recognised her at once: Catherine Forster, sixteen years old, dark curls blowing about her face, a book clasped to her breast. She was staring at the Quaker with that earnest fierceness she brings to her music, which is the whole of her life. When she was six, Catherine decided she wanted to play the harpsichord and pestered her parents until they gave in for the sake of peace. Being canny tradespeople, they sought out the cheapest teacher; I was fifteen and Catherine was my first pupil. And still my best. She is a far better singer than I will ever be and bids fair to be as good a harpsichordist. I have a fondness for her that I do not have for other pupils; we have, in a way, grown up together, like brother and sister.

I wondered why Catherine was interested in the Quaker. He was a personable enough man, about forty years old; his mousy brown hair was tied back, revealing an open honest face. But he was too old a man to appeal to Catherine on a personal level, and Quaker views on music – that it is a trivial worldly distraction – would be anathema to a girl whose whole existence revolved around the art. But Catherine, I realised, was looking not at the Quaker but at me, steadfastly, with an odd patience, as if wanting to be certain I was watching her. Then, still clasping the book to her chest, she turned and walked composedly off the bridge towards Newcastle.

A moment later, James Fleming erupted from his shop, huge old-fashioned wig flapping about his ears. Waving his hands, pushing through the bystanders, yelling after Catherine.

"Stop that thief! Stop her!"

The Forsters sent for me in the early evening; it was cold for late April and I shivered all the way from All Hallows church into the narrow but respectable street where the Forsters lived. Their message said that Fleming had been, and the constable had been, and the chaplain had been, and Catherine still sat in silence. Would I see what I could do?

I am a musician, but in the last half year I have also gained a reputation as a solver of mysteries. I don't know if I like this much but it augments my income; Catherine's father promised me a guinea if I could unravel this matter to his satisfaction.

By the time I got there, Catherine's mother had done what the constable and the chaplain could not. She met me at the door, a severe woman of fifty or more, with lips tight closed.

"She's making sense now, Mr Patterson," she said briskly. "She'll tell you what happened and then you can go to Fleming and get him to drop this ridiculous charge."

Not much of a mystery left, I reflected, but still, a guinea is worth running a few errands for.

"Which book was involved?" I asked, out of curiosity.

Mrs Forster gave a bitter laugh. "*Paradise Lost*! What would a child want with a book like that!"

The Forsters' drawing room was genteel, austere and without fripperies; a branch of candles on a table cast a pool of flickering light over Catherine, sitting on an upright chair. Her hands were folded in her lap, her head bowed, her simple white gown making her look even younger than she was.

"I knew they would send for you," she said in a low voice. I didn't know whether she was glad or sorry.

"Now, Catherine." Her mother sat down beside her in a flurry of skirts. "Tell Mr Patterson what happened."

Catherine bit her lip.

"Do as I tell you," Mrs Forster said sharply.

Catherine hesitated, but she was after all only sixteen, and well-brought-up young girls do not disobey their parents. Her hands trembled in her lap. No wonder, considering the situation she was in. I wondered if she had realised the full extent of it yet.

She told me the story, in tones so low as to be at times almost inaudible. Or rather, she told me the story her mama had carefully taught her. She'd gone into Fleming's shop to look at the latest books, she said; she was alone, as she'd sent her maid on to the cheesemonger's. Mr Fleming was serving another customer, so she'd browsed along the shelves and found *Paradise Lost*.

"Why that particular book?" I asked. Something nagged me about it.

She darted a quick look at her mother and mumbled: "I heard Papa talking about it."

To pass the time, she'd looked at the engraving opposite the title page. As she told me this, she held my gaze as if she expected me to find this detail significant. I did not.

Then she'd heard a commotion outside. "I went to the door to see what was happening," she said. "It was a Quaker." She hesitated. "He was very interesting."

"Catherine!" her mama said sharply.

She persisted. "He was talking of the necessity of giving up the things of this world in order to gain the greater benefits of the next."

"Like money, I suppose," Mrs Forster said, sarcastically. "I don't suppose *he* earns a penny – lives off other people's charity, I daresay." She gave me a frosty smile. "You know what young girls are like, Mr Patterson, always hankering after excitement. Catherine went to see what was happening and forgot she was holding the book." She glowered at her daughter. "That is correct, is it not, Catherine?"

Catherine opened her mouth to say something then subsided. Her fingers gripped tightly together. "Yes, Mama."

"Pure forgetfulness," Mrs Forster reiterated. "Now, if you please." She stood up. "Go and tell Mr Fleming Catherine is sorry and then we can forget this silliness."

Catherine glanced up at me as I pushed back my chair. "Is it true?" she asked in a trembling voice. "If I'm found guilty of theft, could I be transported?"

So she did understand the worst of it; I'd hoped the thought would not occur to her. What a prospect for a young girl – to travel in a stinking ship unprotected, forced to survive on her own wits, surrounded by men of the lowest and worst kind. And once in the Colonies, in America, what would happen to her there?

"It won't come to that," her mother said briskly. "Fleming will see sense."

"But if he doesn't?" Catherine insisted.

I would not lie to her; I said: "It is possible, yes."

Catherine took a deep breath. "Mr Patterson – "

Her mother swept me out of the room.

I went out into the street grasping at hints. The story Catherine had spun had been of her mother's devising – no doubt of that. Who could blame her? She wanted to save her daughter.

But that look Catherine had given me when she'd asked if she could be transported – a steadfast look, not shrinking away from the worst but facing it. The way she'd plainly waited until I was watching her before she walked off with the book. And she expected me to find significance in the fact that the book was *Paradise Lost*. I could not understand the girl. And I'd thought I knew her so well.

The last light of the day was turning the sky a translucent blue. As I pulled my coat around me against the chill, I heard my name called from above. I glanced up; a faint, greenish light gleamed on a lamp bracket. A spirit, and one who had died a long time ago, I suspected, lingering the last of its eighty- or hundred-year sojourn in the place of its death.

"Are you the music fellow? Charles Patterson?" The spirit slid lower. It had been a man in life, one who'd died old and querulous. "You're supposed to get Miss out of trouble, aren't you? Can't be done. She took the book deliberately."

"How do you know?" I asked, suddenly interested.

"Heard 'em arguing over it. Heavens, you should have heard the shouting. *You've been a trial to me all your life! Always want your own way!* And *we've always been a respectable family!*"

The spirit hung off the end of the bracket. "*Dull*, that's what *respectable* means. I was her great-uncle, you know, and God knows *I* led a dull life. Ever been a linen-draper? Take my advice, don't try it. I blame it all on him."

"Her father?"

"The Quaker!"

I'd learnt the fellow's name since the encounter on the bridge: George Rutherford. "You've seen them together?"

"Any number of times."

It didn't amount to a great deal once he'd told me the story. Spirits cannot move from the place of their death and he had a limited view along the street, but he'd glimpsed Catherine with the Quaker four or five times in the last month. Just talking, he said. What the devil was going on? I couldn't imagine it was a romantic affair; Catherine was not a foolish girl nor Rutherford the sort of rascal who might try to take advantage of her. And they certainly did not have a common interest in music!

There was something else, something I was missing…

When I climbed the slope on to the bridge, most of the shops were closed. But lights still gleamed in Fleming's shop; I pushed open the door.

He looked up from unpacking a parcel of books and scowled. Under the big old-fashioned wig, he looked old and tired.

"It's no use, Patterson," he said brusquely. "I'll not change my mind. I've had a great number of thieves recently and I've acted the same way by all of them. The law's the law."

I've known Fleming many years and respect him greatly. "I suppose she did steal it?" I asked. "You don't think it could have been mere forgetfulness?"

"It was a deliberate act," he said firmly.

"What happened?"

He sighed and put down the book he'd unpacked. "I was talking to a gentleman from Durham," he said, "and Miss came in to look through the latest volumes. She was alone," he added disapprovingly. "No maid."

Catherine had moved idly around the shop. "I saw her pick up a book and thought nothing of it," Fleming said. "Then, out of the corner of my eye, I saw her walk out of the door with it. Bold as brass!"

"She says she was distracted by the commotion outside."

"She knew what she was doing," he said. And from that position, he would not be budged.

Rutherford's lodgings were in a shabby tenement in the shadow of the castle's Black Gate, among some of the poorest, and worst, inhabitants of the town. The house door was wide open to a dark room with a few rickety chairs in it. At the back of the room, candlelight flickering down from above showed a steep flight of wooden stairs; I heard a woman's voice, conversationally talking of God's will for the world.

I went up, and found myself in a room full of people.

Startled, I stopped dead. Twenty or more people sat on benches round the walls, hands in their laps, staring into the flickering candlelight in silence. A woman by the door shifted to make room for me and courteously indicated I should sit down. In my green coat, I felt ostentatiously out of place among these black-clad crows.

George Rutherford stared long and hard at me from across the room.

There was nothing I could do but wait until the meeting was ended. I'd heard of this Meeting for Worship but never anticipated taking part in it, and it was one of the oddest experiences of my life; we sat in total silence except for one moment when an elderly man lurched to his feet and said in humble tones, "God bids Friends to offer a welcome to all seekers after truth, no matter who they are." This, I am told, is *ministering* – speaking under the irresistible urging of the Holy Spirit. Since the comment was plainly aimed at me, I felt horribly embarrassed. Yet the meeting was some-how soothing, and made me feel more reverent than half a dozen sermons. Though I would have liked a good hymn or two.

After the meeting, we filed downstairs. I was wondering what to do when Rutherford brought me tea; we took our dishes out into the street to sit on the bench outside the house, shivering in the cold night air.

"I've heard of you, Charles Patterson," Rutherford said. He looked both tired and faintly amused. "You have a nose for a mystery."

I contemplated him; he seemed an honest man, not given to deception. The idea of him engaging in an illicit romance with Catherine was preposterous.

"The Forsters have asked me to help their daughter," I said. "Fleming the stationer is intent on prosecuting her at the Assizes and if she's found guilty she will almost certainly be transported."

He contemplated his tea-dish. "I would not wish that on anyone – I have seen the ships they travel in. But what can *I* do?"

This was the most difficult moment, and after the kind welcome and the hospitality I'd received, I felt churlish to suggest it. But Catherine needed to be rescued.

"The only chance I see of saving her," I said, carefully, "is if Fleming can be convinced she was acting under the influence of some third party, that she was in some way led astray."

"By our Society of Friends, you mean?" Rutherford said forthrightly. He shook his head. "I cannot say anything of the sort – it would be a lie."

"But you know the girl?"

He nodded. "She joins us to worship – she finds solace here, and the word of God, the *true* word, unlike all the fancy nothings you hear in the churches." He sipped the tea, to gain a moment's respite, I thought. "She is a God-fearing woman. The Bible says *thou shalt not steal*, and she would obey that injunction."

"Yet she did take the book," I pointed out.

"Does she not say she forgot she had it?"

"That's what her mother told her to say."

He smiled wryly.

"Catherine came here to worship," I pursued. "Does she

want to become a Quaker?"

A long pause. "It is a very difficult situation," Rutherford said at last. "It is not right to turn away someone so eager to serve God. Yet her parents forbid it, and I cannot sanction her defying their wishes – that would also be contrary to God's commandments. So I told her to have patience. I told her that if joining our Society was right for her, God would make all things possible."

"I don't think patience was ever one of Catherine's virtues," I said, dryly. "She sets her mind on something and must have it as soon as she can." I finished my tea and rose to my feet. "Thank you for your honesty."

Rutherford took the dish from my hand. "You won't join our Society, then?" he asked with a teasing smile.

"Alas," I said, "to tell a musician to keep quiet in church is an impossibility."

"Silence is better. Did you not feel that tonight?"

I shook my head. "Music is the best part of me. In truth, it is all I have to offer to man or God."

A night's sleep brought no counsel, and on Sunday morning I went off to play the organ in All Hallows in some depression. I missed Catherine in church; I was used to hearing her voice raised in the psalms, leading the more timid members of the congregation with her clear tones and inspiring them all with her evident enjoyment. I thought of her at home, fearful for what might happen, and thought of her too in that silent meeting for worship. How could she have contemplated joining the Quakers? She was a musician to the depths of her heart, as I was. We had spent so many hours together, talking about music, performing it. She was not one of those girls who practises merely for the sake of attracting a husband with graceful movements; she wanted the music for its own sake. As I did.

I found myself angry with Rutherford and his Friends. They *must* have influenced her unduly; why else would she contemplate giving up everything she held dear?

When I went out of church, Rutherford was waiting among the graves, the churchwardens gathered in a suspicious group as if they suspected he was about to preach to the dispersing congregation. I glared at him.

"I thought I must do what I could," he said. "I have spoken to James Fleming."

"And?" I said, brusquely.

"He asked if I had told her to steal the book."

"And you said?"

"That I had not. I cannot lie," Rutherford said. "Not even in a good cause." He contemplated my face. "She speaks highly of you."

"Does she?"

"She says that playing music with you has given her a great deal of joy."

"Yet if she joins your Society, she must give it all up," I said bitterly. "It cannot mean very much to her after all."

"You are offended."

I stared at the over-long grass of the churchyard, wanting to avoid the question but forced by Rutherford's own honesty to confront it.

"Yes," I admitted. "She is my best pupil, and if she tells me that music is trivial, a distraction from the important things of life, then it is a kind of rebuke. Music is my whole existence."

Rutherford gave a wry laugh. "Charles Patterson, you tempt me to preach at you! *God* should be your whole existence. But for the time being, I will be silent. I wanted you to know that I have written to Friends in Philadelphia. If Catherine is indeed transported, they will meet her off the boat and look after her."

"She'll be dead or ruined before she gets to Philadelphia!"

Rutherford said nothing for a moment, then: "Perhaps that is God's will."

"His will that she's raped or even murdered?" I said furiously. "His will that she is thrown on her own devices in a ship full of criminals of the roughest sort?"

He took a deep breath. "My greatest fear is that it is not his will." He gave me a steady look and said: "I fear that it is Catherine's will."

I found her in the small garden at the back of the Forsters' house, sitting among the roses; she had a book of sermons in her hands but was meditatively fingering the silken petals of a blossom that hung by her shoulder. She glanced round as she heard my footsteps, with a scared wariness that touched my heart.

I was in no mood for sympathy. I said directly: "Did you steal *Paradise Lost*?"

Her hands were trembling; she straightened, met my gaze. "Yes."

"Deliberately?" I pressed. "Knowing the probable consequences?"

She clasped her hands together more tightly and nodded.

"In heaven's name, why?"

"Because that is what God wants me to do," she said simply. "He wants me to spread the Truth."

"You *want* to be transported?"

"No," she admitted. "But it's the only way. When I asked my parents if I could go to America, my father laughed and my mother said I had been reading too much."

"They're right," I said forcibly. "You have no idea what

the voyage will be like."

She said nothing. In her demure white gown, with her hair down around her shoulders, she looked absurdly young. And obstinate.

"It's what I want to do," she said.

"Damn it!" I walked about for a moment, trying to contain my anger. She waited, composedly.

"Why did you deny stealing the book when I saw you yesterday?"

She bit her lip. "My mother insisted. I was weak, I gave in. But I will not do that again."

I suspected her mother had bullied her but I said gently, "She's frightened for you."

Her voice trembled. "*I'm* frightened."

That's when I knew I could not influence her further. She had grown beyond me, beyond any of us. Whatever the obstacles, whatever the danger, she was determined to carry her plan through. Something had changed her; Rutherford was right to describe her as a woman, not a girl. And with such inward strength, I was tempted to think she might succeed.

There was nothing more I could do. At the appropriate time and place, the judge listened to Fleming's evidence and decided he was a man of sense and integrity, and that he told the truth. His Lordship strongly condemned the degeneracy of the young and said it was particularly distressing to see in one brought up in so caring a home.

Catherine's mother wept; her father raged. George Rutherford promised succour at journey's end, if she promised to sin no more.

The judge sentenced her to seven years' transportation.

On the evening of the trial, I went to James Fleming's shop. He was standing on his doorstep, staring out at the sun setting red over the bridge.

"It gives me no pleasure," he said without preamble. "Quite the opposite." He stared into the darkening sky. "And all for a book. The girl gave up a loving family, her friends and neighbours, the prospect of a husband and children, all for a book. A great book, mind, but still a book."

"She liked the engraving at the front," I said, trying to make light of it because I wasn't sure I didn't want to weep.

"Opposite the title page," Fleming said. "A nice piece of work."

I was reminded of that look Catherine had given me when she first mentioned the picture. I wondered now if she had been trying to make me look at it. It suddenly seemed important. "Can I see it?"

He nodded, went back into the shop. I waited, pondering on Catherine, in a stinking cell, waiting for transportation. On the ship even now moored in the Tyne, waiting to take her to the Colonies. On the silence that awaited her there in the company of Quakers; no more singing, no more quick fingers on the harpsichord, not even psalms raised to the glory of God. How could she contemplate that? Rutherford was right; I did regard it as a betrayal.

Fleming brought the book out. An anonymous-looking book that still smelt new. He opened it to the title page, held it out to me.

Opposite the title was a picture of Lucifer being thrown out of Paradise. The unknown artist had been more interested in Heaven than in Lucifer's downfall, for the fallen angel was a small figure and all his safe friends in Heaven loomed much larger. Behind the angels with swords and shields, cherubs grasped harps and viols, all lovingly drawn, hands gripping bows or fingering strings as if they were about to play. I could almost hear the music.

I stood in the reddening light, staring at the engraving. Here was Paradise about to be lost. I thought of Catherine's voice raised in the psalms, her fingers dancing across the harpsichord, her all-embracing love of music; and the Quakers' insistence on silent worship.

I knew why she had stolen that particular book above all others.

It was a message for me: an apology. A plea for forgiveness.

WAITING FOR MR RIGHT

Andrew Taylor

I live in a city of the dead surrounded by a city of the living. The great cemetery of Kensal Vale is a privately-owned metropolis of grass and stone, of trees and rusting iron. At night, the security men scour away the drug addicts and the drunks; they expel the lost, the lonely and the lovers; and at last they leave us with the dark dead in our urban Eden.

Eden? Oh yes – because the dead are truly innocent. They no longer know the meaning of sin. They can never lose their illusions.

Other forms of life remain overnight – cats, for example, a fox or two, grey squirrels, even a badger and a host of lesser mammals, as well as some of our feathered friends. At regular intervals, those splendid security men patrol the paths and shine their torches in dark places, keeping the cemetery safe for its rightful inhabitants. Finally, one should not forget to include, perhaps in a special sub-human category of their own somewhere between life and death, Dave and the woman Tracy.

In a place like this, there is little to do in the long summer evenings once one's basic animal appetites have been satisfied. Fortunately I am not without inner resources. I am never bored. In my own small way I am a seeker after truth. Perhaps it was my diet, with its high protein content, which helped give me such an appetite for learning. In my youth, I taught myself to read. Not for me the sunlit semi-detached pleasures of *Janet and John*. My primers were the fruity orotundities of funereal inscriptions, blurred and sooty from decades of pollution. Once I had mastered my letters, though, I did not find it hard to find more varied reading material.

We live, I am glad to say, in a throwaway society.

It is quite extraordinary what people discard in this place, either by accident or design. The young prefer to roam through the older parts of the cemetery, the elderly are drawn to the newer. Wherever they go, whatever their age, visitors leave their possessions behind. Litter bins have provided me with a range of periodicals from *The Spectator* to *Marxism Today*. The solar-powered palm-top personal organiser on which I am typing this modest memoir was carelessly left behind among the debris of an adulterous picnic on top of Amelia Osbaston (died 1863).

I have also been fortunate enough to stumble upon a number of works of literature, including *Jane Eyre* and *Men Are From Mars, Women Are From Venus*. Charlotte Brontë is, without doubt, my favourite author. How could she peer so penetratingly into the hidden chambers of the heart? Jane Eyre and I might be twin souls.

On one occasion, after an unexpected shower, I came across a damp but handsomely illustrated copy of *Grave Conditions*, a scholarly survey of Victorian funerary practices. This enabled me to identify the Bateson's Belfry of Kensal Vale.

Perhaps the term is as unfamiliar to you as it was to me. Bateson's Belfry was a Victorian invention designed to profit from the widespread human fear of being interred alive. In essentials it consisted of a simple bell pull, conveniently situated in the coffin at the right hand of the corpse, which would enable one, should one find oneself alive and six feet under, to summon help by ringing a bell mounted above the grave.

Usually, and for obvious reasons, Bateson's Belfries were designed as temporary structures. But there were circumstances in which a longer-lasting variant was appropriate. Thanks to *Grave Conditions*, I learned to look with fresh eyes at what I had previously assumed was a purely decorative feature of the family mausoleum of the Makepeace family.

The mausoleum, which is illustrated in full colour on page 98 of *Grave Conditions,* was situated in a relatively remote corner of the cemetery, an area where the dead lie beneath a coarsely-woven shroud of long grass, thistles and clumps of bramble. A flight of steps led down to a stout, padlocked door leading below the monument into the chamber itself, which measured perhaps eight feet square. Two banks of four shelves faced each other across the narrow gangway. Only three of the shelves were occupied – with the remains of the Reverend Simon Makepeace, the first incumbent of St George's, Kensal Vale, his wife, Charlotte, and their son Albert Victor, both of whom had predeceased him. The rest of the family had apparently preferred to make other arrangements. On ground level there was a rather vulgar monument consisting of four weeping angels clustered round the base of a miniature campanile, at the top of which hung the bell.

Having studied *Grave Conditions*, I was not surprised to find that a fine brass chain passed from the top of the bell through a pipe which penetrated the roof of the chamber. It emerged at the end of the gangway, opposite the door, within easy reach of the upper ends of the coffins. I imagine Mr Makepeace stipulated that the lids should not be screwed down.

During the day, especially around lunchtime and in the

early evening, the cemetery can become almost crowded. But the gates are locked half an hour before sunset, and once the security men have done their sweep (and they are commendably efficient at this) the only people left are – or rather were – Dave and Tracy in their cottage by the gates in the majestic shadow of the cemetery chimney. Dave and Tracy did not get on – and as Dave was very deaf, owing to a passion for the music of Aerosmith, Black Sabbath and Led Zeppelin, one sometimes heard his wife's trenchantly expressed opinions about his sexual inadequacy and his low income. Tracy was tall, and big-breasted, with dyed blonde hair, sturdy legs and a taste for very short skirts. She and Dave rarely had visitors and never indulged in nocturnal rambles through the cemetery. Often Tracy would go off by herself for days at a time. I sometimes surprised myself by entertaining a certain sisterly regard for her.

So, given their habits and the secluded nature of a cemetery at night, you will understand my surprise when I saw Tracy arm in arm with a tall, well-built man, guiding him through the gravestones by the light of a small torch. At the time I was sitting on a table monument, and eating a light snack of Parma ham and wholemeal bread. I was interested enough to discard my sandwich and follow the couple. Tracy led the man to the Makepeace vault. Her companion was carrying a briefcase. They went down the steps together, and I heard a rattle as she unlocked the padlock.

"Christ," I heard the man say in a hoarse whisper. "You can't leave me here. They're coffins, aren't they?"

"There's nothing here could harm a fly," Tracy told him. "Not now. Anyway, beggars can't be choosers, so you might as well get used to it."

"You're a hard woman."

For an instant she shone the torch on him as they stood at the foot of the steps. He was broad as well as tall, with a stern, dark face. I noticed in particular his big eyebrows jutting out above his eyes like a pair of shelves. I am not a sentimental creature, but I must confess a jolt went through me when I saw those eyebrows.

"Stay here, Jack," Tracy said. "I'll get you a sleeping bag and some fags and stuff."

"What about Dave?"

"He wouldn't hear a thing if you dropped a bomb on him. Anyway, he's drunk a bottle of vodka since teatime."

She left Jack with the torch. I slipped under the lowest shelf on the right-hand side and watched him. When he thought he was alone, he squatted down and opened the briefcase. I was interested to see that it contained an automatic pistol and piles and piles of banknotes. He rummaged underneath the money, took out a mobile telephone and shut the case.

He stared at the telephone but did not use it. He lit a cigarette and paced up and down the gangway of the vault. Despite his agitation, he was a fine figure of a man.

My hearing is good, and I heard Tracy's returning footsteps before he did. She dropped a backpack on to the floor of the vault. It contained a sleeping bag, several cans of Tennents Super Lager, a plastic bucket, some crisps and a packet of Marlboro cigarettes. Jack watched as she unrolled the sleeping bag on one of the lowest shelves and arranged the other items on the shelf above.

"Listen," he said when she had finished. "Get some passport photos done and go and see Frank." He snapped open the case, took out a wad of notes and slapped it down on the shelf. "That'll cover it." He took out another wad and added it to the first. "Buy a motor. Nothing flashy, maybe two or three years old. There's a place in Walthamstow – Frank'll give you the name."

Tracy stared down at the open briefcase. "And where do we go then, Jack? Shangri fucking la?"

"What about Shangri fucking Amsterdam for starters? We take the ferry from Harwich, then move on from there."

"I got nothing to wear. I need some clothes."

He scowled. Nevertheless he gave her another bundle of notes. "Don't go crazy."

"I love it when you're masterful." Tracy dropped the money into the backpack. "Careful with the torch. You can see a glow round the edge of the door. And I'm going to have to lock you in."

"What the fuck are you talking about?"

"The security guys check the door at least twice a night. We had a bit of trouble with kids down here earlier in the summer. Orgies and what not. Pathetic little bastards."

"You can't just leave me here," Jack said.

"You got a better idea?"

"I can't even text you. There's no signal. So what do I do if I need you?"

"I can't bloody wait," she said. "Big boy."

"For Christ's sake, Trace. If it's an emergency."

She laughed. "Ring my bell." She leant over and touched the handle that hung between the shelves. "You pull that, and the bell rings up top."

"Sure?"

"We had this weirdo from the local history society the other month who tried it. Built to last, he said. But for God's sake, Jack, don't use it because if anyone hears it but me, you're totally fucked."

Tracy put her hand on his shoulder and kissed his cheek. "See you tomorrow night, all right? Got to get my beauty sleep."

She slipped out of the vault and locked the door. Jack swore, a long monotonous stream hardly above a whisper. His torch beam criss-crossed the vault and raked to and fro along the dusty shelves. Finally he reached floor level and for an instant the beam dazzled me. He let out a screech. I dived into the crack between two blocks of masonry that was my usual way in and out of the vault. A moment later, as I emerged into the cool night air, I heard the frantic clanging of the bell.

Tracy came pounding through the graves. She ran down the steps and unlocked the door.

"Jesus, Jack, what the hell are you up to?"

He clung to her, nuzzling her hair. He muttered something I couldn't hear.

"Oh, for God's sake!" she snapped, drawing away from him. "I bet it's a damn sight more scared than you are. Give me the torch." A moment later, she went on, "There you are – it's buggered off."

"Can't you do something? Can't you put poison down?"

"It won't be back," she said as though soothing a child. "Anyway, they seem to like poison. I'm sure there's more of them than there used to be."

"I can't stay here."

"Then where the hell else are you going to go? It's not for long."

"How am I supposed to sleep? They'll crawl all over me."

"Jesus," said Tracy. "And I thought women were the weaker sex. It won't be back."

"How do you know?"

"You probably scared the shit out of it. Listen, I tell you

317

what I'll do: you can have some of Dave's pills. A few of those and you'll be out like a light."

Off she went again, and returned with a handful of capsules, which Jack washed down with a can of lager. He insisted she stay with him, holding his hand, while he went to sleep. Yet despite this display of weakness, or perhaps even because of it, there was something very appealing about him. I came back down to the vault and listened to them billing and cooing. Such a lovely deep voice he had, like grumbling thunder. It made something deep within me vibrate like a tuning fork. Gradually his words grew thicker, and slower. At last the voice fell silent.

There was a click and a flare of flame as Tracy lit a cigarette. Time passed. Jack began to snore. Edging out of my crack into the lesser shelter of the space beneath the lowest shelf I had an extensive though low-level view of the vault. I saw Tracy's legs and feet, wearing jeans and trainers. The cigarette fell to the floor. She ground it out beneath her heel.

I saw the briefcase, and Tracy's left hand with its blood-red nails and big flashy rings. I watched in the torchlight as her fingers made a claw and hooked themselves through the handle of the case. The trainers moved across the vault. The door opened and softly closed. The padlock grated in its hasp.

After a while I scaled the rough stone wall to the shelf where Jack lay. I jumped lightly on to his chest and settled down where I could feel the beating of his heart. I stared at his face. Through my breast surged a torrent of emotions I had never known before.

Was this, I wondered, what humans felt? Was this love?

So it began, this strange relationship, and so it continued. I do not intend to chart its every twist and turn. There are secrets locked within my bosom which I shall never share with another soul.

Late in the afternoon of the day after Jack's arrival, I happened to glance through a copy of the *Evening Standard* which I had found in a litter bin on the other side of the cemetery. His face loomed up at me from one of the inside pages. The police, it seemed, were anxious to interview John Rochester in connection with a murder at the weekend in Peckham. The dead man was said to have been a prominent member of a south London gang.

On the second day, the police arrived. They interviewed Dave in the lodge cottage. They did not search the cemetery. Halfway through the morning, Jack finished his lager, his crisps and his cigarettes, in that order. Early in the evening, the bucket overflowed. He tried to ration his use of the torch, but inevitably the battery died. Then he was alone with me in the darkness.

Is it not strange that a grown man should be so scared of the dark? "If only I could see," he would mutter, "Christ, if only I could see." I have no idea why he thought the faculty of sight would improve his plight, but then I have found little evidence to suggest that humans are rational animals.

Just before dawn on the third day, it occurred to Jack – bless him, he was not a fast thinker – that Tracy might not be coming back, and that he would be able to escape from this prison and move into one of Her Majesty's if he rang the bell in Bateson's Belfry long enough and loud enough.

Alas for him, I had anticipated just such an eventuality.

The bell wire was sound for most of its length, I believe, but at the end it met a metal flange which was in turn attached to the spindle from which the bell depended. Where the wire had been inserted, bent and twisted into a hole in the flange, rust and metal fatigue had already caused many of its constituent strands to snap apart. All one needed to deal with the remaining strands was a certain physical agility, perseverance and a set of sharp teeth. So it was that when Jack gave the bell wire a sharp tug all that happened was that he pulled the wire down on top of him. He clenched his fists and pounded them against the oak and iron of the door. That was one of the occasions when he wept.

Later, after he had sunk into an exhausted slumber, I licked the salty tears from his cheeks, my tongue rasping deliciously on the abrasive masculinity of his stubble. It was one of those small but intimate services which seem to be peculiarly satisfying to the females of so many species.

The days passed, and so did the nights, and they passed agreeably enough for me. When he was awake, Jack was increasingly distraught, and was still terrified of me. Are we always scared of those who love us? When he was asleep, though, and defenceless, he became mine. I spent as much time as possible with him – indeed, whenever I could, on top of him or curled into some crevice of his person.

Can one ever be close enough to the man one loves? Oh, that oft-imagined bliss of perfect union! One soul, one flesh!

Sometimes he screamed, and banged on the door, and yelled, and wept; but no one except myself heard him. On one occasion, Dave was only twenty yards away from the vault when Jack began to wail, but of course Dave was too deaf to hear.

There remained a possibility that a passer-by might hear his cries, even in this remote and overgrown quarter of the cemetery. Here, however, the British climate played its part. Rain fell with unlovely determination for most of three days. As a result, Kensal Vale attracted far fewer visitors than usual.

Among those who braved the weather was a brace of middle-aged ladies from Market Harborough searching without success for the last resting place of an ancestor. They left me the remains of a very acceptable chicken mayonnaise salad, and even more to the point, they discarded their newspaper. For hard news and sound principles one cannot do better than the *Daily Telegraph*.

My eye fell on a short but intriguing item to the effect that Jack Rochester and an unnamed lady friend were believed to be in Rio de Janeiro. Knowing Tracy as I did – a special sort of knowledge unites two females with a man in common – I had little doubt that this was a false trail designed to throw the authorities off the scent.

I come now to the final act in my story, to a resolution which is both melancholy and edifying. All passion spent, blind in his own darkness, my poor Jack sank slowly into a coma. I grieved and rejoiced in equal measure. I sat on his chest and felt the beat of his heart growing slower and feebler. My night vision is good, and I gazed for long hours at his manly features. A lover is like a beloved city. I explored Jack's public squares and great thoroughfares. I strolled through tree-lined suburbs and splendid municipal parks. I wandered through twisting side streets and lost myself in the labyrinth of his bazaar.

In his final hours, as he drifted inexorably towards another city, to the dark heart of this metropolis of the dead, Jack rested his hands on my warm fur. Then, to my inexpressible joy, he stroked me.

Soon afterwards, the life left him altogether – or very nearly so. And then?

Reader, I ate him.

COMING IN 2009 FROM
CRÈME DE LA CRIME

SECRET LAMENT
Roz Southey

Italian actors…
French spies…
At least the thugs are English…

Charles Patterson is not happy. It's the hottest June for years; he's stuck in musical rehearsals with a family of Italians; some local ruffians are after his blood; and someone is trying to break into the house of Esther Jerdoun, the woman he loves.

When a murder is discovered he fears Esther may be next. It's time to ask some tough questions.

Who is the strange man masquerading under a patently false name? Are there really spies abroad in Newcastle? Why is a psalm-teacher keeping vigil over a house in the town?

And can Patterson find the murderer before he strikes again?

Praise for Roz Southey's previous Charles Patterson mysteries:
… an elegantly-written and atmospheric mystery which continues to surprise and satisfy to the very last page.
– R S Downie, author of the Ruso historical mystery series
Southey has a real feel for the eighteenth century…
– Booklist (USA)

ISBN: 978-0-9557078-6-5   £7.99

DEAD LIKE HER
Linda Regan

Sex, drugs – and Marilyn Monroe…
A potentially lethal combination.

It seems like a straightforward case for newly promoted DCI Paul
Banham and DI Alison Grainger: the murdered women all bore an
uncanny resemblance to Marilyn Monroe and worked for a lookalike
agency.

But the enquiry soon unearths connections with a covert
investigation into drug-running and people-trafficking. A new member
of the team, uniquely qualified but inexperienced, is placed in a
dangerous situation – made more difficult when love rears its
complicated head!

Can Banham and Grainger save her from the villains – and from
herself?

Praise for Linda Regan's previous Banham/Grainger mysteries:
*Regan exhibits enviable control over her characters in this skilful and
fascinating whodunit.*
- Colin Dexter OBE
I loved it. Don't miss it.
– Richard Briers CBE
Regan is a writer well worth keeping an eye on.
– Martin Edwards, author of the acclaimed Harry Devlin mysteries
… one of the best up-and coming writers
– Peter Guttridge, the Observer

ISBN: 978-0-9557078-8-9   £7.99

BLOOD MONEY
Maureen Carter

When family loyalties are at stake
can a woman can be as hard as a man?
Detective Sergeant Bev Morriss is in a very dark place.

Personal tragedy has pushed her close to self-destruct mode; both colleagues and friends have started to give her a wide berth.

But Bev is still a cop, and there are villains to battle as well as demons. Enter the Sandman, a vicious serial burglar who wears a clown mask and plays mind-games with his victims.

When the violence spirals into abduction, blackmail and murder, the bad guys soon discover Bev is in no mood to play…

Praise for Maureen Carter's earlier Bev Morriss titles:
If there was any justice in this world, she'd be as famous as Ian Rankin!
– Sharon Wheeler, Reviewing the Evidence
British hardboiled crime fiction at its best…
– George Easter, Deadly Pleasures
I liked [it] so much that I have ordered the first 3 books in this series.
– Maddy Van Hertbruggen, I Love a Mystery Newsletter

ISBN: 978-0-9557078-7-2   £7.99

THE FALL GIRL
Kaye C Hill

It begins with a mysterious death in a lonely cottage…
but where will it end?

Mystery piles on top of mystery for Lexy Lomax, still masquerading as a private investigator in Clopwolde-on-Sea.

Did Aunt Elizabeth fall out of the cottage window – or was she pushed?

What makes Kinky the chihuahua run a mile from the cottage when everyone else wants to get their hands on it?

Is there really a Black Dog, or is it Lexy's imagination playing tricks?

And why on earth has Gerard, her obnoxious ex, turned up in the village?

Dark forces are not only at work – they're positively running amok…

Praise for Kaye C Hill's first Lexy Lomax mystery:
Into the prevailing noir of contemporary crime fiction Kaye C Hill brings a welcome splash of colour and humour.
– Simon Brett
I just love Lexy - and Kinky. I hope I'm going to meet [them] again.
– Jean Currie, The New Writer
Crisp prose and a plot laced with animal tomfoolery will keep readers… eager for a sequel.
– Publishers Weekly (USA)

ISBN: 978-0-9557078-9-6   £7.99

LOVE NOT POISON
Mary Andrea Clarke

A husband dead in a fire – but was it an accident?

A wife hysterical – but is it with grief?

The Crimson Cavalier is in search of the truth...

In the 1780s young ladies are expected to apply themselves to the social round and the business of finding a husband – but Miss Georgiana Grey is no ordinary young lady.

The death of ill-natured Lord Wickerston in a fire leads her to ask questions, to the chagrin of her strait-laced brother Edward, and the alarm of her friend Mr Max Lakesby.

Who would want Lord Wickerston dead? Does Edward know more than he is willing to say?

And how is the notorious highwayman known as the Crimson Cavalier involved?

Praise for Mary Andrea Clarke's first Crimson Cavalier adventure:

... sparkling period crime fiction with a lively touch
– Andrew Taylor, award-winning author of The American Boy
... a delightful and entertaining novel with an engrossing plot.
– Historical Novels Review
Clarke captures the flavor of the period...
– Publishers Weekly (USA)
... fans of Georgette Heyer... will snap this title up. Another winning tale from Crème de la Crime.
– US Library Journal

ISBN: 978-0-9560566-0-3   £7.99

MORE GRIPPING TITLES FROM CRÈME DE LA CRIME

by Maureen Carter:

WORKING GIRLS	ISBN: 978-0-9547634-0-4	£7.99
DEAD OLD	ISBN: 978-0-9547634-6-6	£7.99
BABY LOVE	ISBN: 978-0-9551589-0-2	£7.99
*HARD TIME	ISBN: 978-0-9551589-6-4	£7.99
BAD PRESS	ISBN: 978-0-9557078-3-4	£7.99

a series which just gets better and better
– Sharon Wheeler, Reviewing the Evidence

by Adrian Magson:

NO PEACE FOR THE WICKED	ISBN: 978-0-9547634-2-8	£7.99
NO HELP FOR THE DYING	ISBN: 978-0-9547634-7-3	£7.99
*NO SLEEP FOR THE DEAD	ISBN: 978-0-9551589-1-9	£7.99
*NO TEARS FOR THE LOST	ISBN: 978-0-9551589-7-1	£7.99
*NO KISS FOR THE DEVIL	ISBN: 978-0-9557078-1-0	£7.99

Gritty, fast-paced detecting of the traditional kind
– Maxim Jakubowski, The Guardian

by Penny Deacon:

A KIND OF PURITAN	ISBN: 978-0-9547634-1-1	£7.99
A THANKLESS CHILD	ISBN: 978-0-9547634-8-0	£7.99

a fascinating new author with a hip, noir voice
– Mystery Lovers

by Linda Regan:

*BEHIND YOU!	ISBN: 978-0-9551589-2-6	£7.99
PASSION KILLERS	ISBN: 978-0-9551589-8-8	£7.99

… readable and believable… extremely well written…
– Jim Kennedy, Encore

PUTTING THE MYSTERY IN HISTORY
Crème de la Crime Period Pieces

by Roz Southey
BROKEN HARMONY   ISBN: 978-0-9551589-3-3   £7.99
CHORDS AND DISCORDS   ISBN: 978-0-9551589-2-7   £7.99

Southey has a real feel for the eighteenth century…
– Booklist (USA)

by Gordon Ferris
*TRUTH DARE KILL   ISBN: 978-0-9551589-4-0   £7.99
*THE UNQUIET HEART   ISBN: 978-0-9557078-0-3   £7.99

… a hero that will appeal to readers as much as Richard Sharpe
– Historical Novels Review

by Mary Andrea Clarke
*THE CRIMSON CAVALIER   ISBN: 978-0-9551589-5-7   £7.99

… Clarke captures the flavor of the period…
– Publishers' Weekly

SPARKLING CONTEMPORARY CRIME
TO THRILL AND CHILL YOU

IF IT BLEEDS   Bernie Crosthwaite
ISBN: 978-0-9547634-3-5   £7.99

A CERTAIN MALICE   Felicity Young
ISBN: 978-0-9547634-4-2   £7.99

PERSONAL PROTECTION   Tracey Shellito
ISBN: 978-0-9547634-5-9   £7.99

SINS OF THE FATHER   David Harrison
ISBN: 978-0-9547634-9-7   £7.99

DEAD WOMAN'S SHOES   Kaye C Hill
ISBN: 978-0-9551589-9-5   £7.99

Titles marked * are also available in unabridged audio.

INNOVATIVE INDEPENDENT PUBLISHERS CRÈME DE LA CRIME WOULD LIKE TO OFFER **YOU** A CHANCE TO **SOLVE A MURDER MYSTERY**

Everyone loves a puzzle, and ours present a real tangled web. Teams of crime fiction fans can test their powers of investigation on a choice of three scenarios.

Fatal Exit
Crème de la Crime's best investigative minds are agreed about one thing: Luke Weller the sleazy theatre odd-job man had it coming. But days into the investigation they're baffled.

Fit to Drop
Murder at the health club! Gym instructor Rob Harkness is found dead in his own exercise studio – and everyone has a motive!

Dance of Death
The Hon Hector Bonham-Ware is discovered with an ornamental dagger in his neck during a ball at his in-laws' country house. The question is, who disliked him most?

PIECE together the clues and discover who took a hammer to Luke's skull, attacked Rob with an exercise weight, or stuck Hector with the paper-knife.
EARN points for every element of the mystery you solve – and points mean prizes…

For further details e-mail us at info@cremedelacrime.com